THE WRONG TWIN

LORNA DOUNAEVA

PROLOGUE

The ghost of a smile played on her blue-tinged lips. Her eyes were frozen in a startled expression, staring yet unseeing, pupils dilated. Her body was heavier than anticipated, even before the weights were attached. Her arms were bound neatly with cable ties, a steal at £2.50. Couldn't do much about her neck though. It lolled about as her body bumped along. Blood trickled down her ears and seeped into the ribbons of hair that still smelled faintly like peaches, and left dark, bloody marks across the deck.

A sound like breaking glass shattered the silence as the body hit the cold water. Long blonde hair billowed above the surface, swirling in bloody bubbles. Fingers drummed impatiently on the side of the boat, watching, waiting as the body plunged down into the Atlantic. The weights did the trick, pulling her under, and all became eerily still as she disappeared from view, gathering seaweed as she made her descent, down towards the ocean floor. Above the water, it was as if nothing had happened. Waves splashed against the hull, and the engine jolted back to life, humming as the boat sped away.

A lone suitcase squeaked along the conveyor belt as Mel wheeled by with her overstuffed trolley. She'd had to bring as much as possible since she had no intention of ever going back. Not that she *could* go back. She was pretty certain she'd burnt her bridges in Australia.

She turned her head from one side to the other, waiting for her ears to pop. She hated navigating through the packed airport. She pushed through the door that led out to the arrivals hall, scanning the room for her twin sister, Abbie. She rubbed her bleary eyes and did a second sweep of the room. *Where is she?*

There were people everywhere, chubby babies in buggies, bespectacled students trailing heavy suitcases, tourists clutching their duty-free. A few stood like islands in the sea of chaos, casually sipping their disposable cups of coffee and staring up at the arrivals screen. They seemed not to notice as their fellow travellers navigated around them. Mel felt her shoulders tighten. She hated the sensation of people breathing down her back.

It felt like there were people everywhere, bumping against her, intruding on her space.

One small child was having a meltdown in the middle of it all. Mel could empathise, but the high pitch of his cries was like a series of explosions going off inside her head.

"Excuse me!" She tried to cut through the crowd, but there were too many people, all lost in their own private worlds. She couldn't see round the large man who had planted himself directly in front of her. She stood on her tiptoes and tried to get a glimpse of her sister's blonde ponytail.

"Excuse me!" she said a bit louder.

When he still didn't budge, she was forced to wheel around him, her bags wobbling precariously. She saw a few people holding up signs with passengers' names on. She wouldn't put it past Abbie to make one of those with something silly on it, like: "Welcome home, Mel. Sorry to hear about the syphilis!"

She glanced down and checked she still had the presents she'd picked up for Abbie in duty-free: two litres of Baileys and a small bottle of her favourite perfume. She hoped they'd make up for her descending on her out of the blue like this.

Eventually, the crowd thinned out as people departed from her flight. She could see right across the room now, and Abbie was not there. What was she doing? Getting coffee? Impatiently, she brought out her phone and dialled her sister's number. No answer. She must still be on her way. "Pete's sake."

A minute later, Abbie rang back. "Hello?"

"Where the hell are you?"

"What, are you there already?" She sounded like she was chewing gum.

"Yes! Where are you?"

"At home. I thought you weren't going to get in till two this afternoon?"

"Twelve! I said twelve!"

"Oh, bugger!"

"Yeah." She could hear something in the background. "Have you got someone there with you?"

"No, it's just the TV. You still want me to come and get you?"

Mel's shoulders slumped. "No. No, it will take you bloody forever. I'll get a taxi."

"Okay, then. See you soon."

"Not that soon."

"No, I suppose not."

She waited for Abbie to apologise, but she just continued to chew her gum. "See you later, then."

Mel hung up without another word.

She let out a puff of exasperation. The airport was at least an hour from home, and that was assuming she didn't hit traffic. This was really going to cost her. A lump welled up inside her throat as she shunted her trolley towards the exit. She'd held it together through the horrendously long flight because she'd thought Abbie would be there waiting for her at the end of it. She'd thought Abbie would take her home.

She struggled forward, careful not to catch anyone's eye. An unexpected tear slid down her cheek, and she wiped it angrily away. Abbie had always been a little self-centred; still, it was hard to picture how she'd screwed this up. How did twelve sound anything like two?

The automatic doors slid open. The cool air was like a sharp slap in the face.

Brr.

She definitely wasn't in Sydney anymore. She glanced down at her cut-off shorts and thin black tank top. At least she'd thought to change from her usual sandals into a pair of trainers, but damn, she was cold. She needed to get her winter coat out of her suitcase. As she tugged at the zip, her duty-free bag slipped from her grasp and fell to the ground with a loud crack. Pale brown sludge spilled all over the tarmac. There went the two-litre bottle of Baileys and the fancy perfume. There were jagged glass fragments all over the pavement. She cast her eyes around. Why was there never a bloody bin? As she swept the worst of the shattered glass to one side with her shoe, her phone pinged. She grabbed it out of her pocket, hoping Abbie would tell her that it was all a joke and she was in fact waiting for her with the car. But no, the text was from Peter, wanting to know when she was coming back. Why couldn't he get it through his thick skull? She was never going back.

AN IMAGE FLASHED through her mind of the last time she'd seen him. The silent accusations that had hung in the air. Giving up on finding her coat, she pulled a shirt out of her suitcase and wriggled into it, but the thin fabric didn't provide much warmth. She struggled on towards the taxi rank, but a large family group surged past her, almost knocking her off her feet. She gripped tightly to her trolley.

"Hey!" she yelled as the group overtook her and piled into the last taxi waiting at the rank. They were talking excitedly amongst themselves, and no one took the slightest notice of her as the car doors slammed and the taxi sped off. Mel bit the inside of her cheek. She searched through her case again, but she still couldn't find her coat, and the bitter wind blew down her back. Why the hell hadn't she thought to dress in layers? She'd been in too much of a hurry, that was why. There had been no time to think or plan things out. She'd just shoved all her stuff into bags and headed for the airport.

She leaned against the railing, all the energy drained out of her as she waited for another taxi to appear. At that moment, she'd have given anything to curl up in bed with a hot drink. She pictured her childhood home, so warm and familiar. Perhaps Abbie would have a fire going, and they could toast marshmallows on it while they caught up on each other's news. She perked up a little as she imagined the warmth of the flames. Then she felt something drip down her forehead. More droplets hit her bare shoulders. The rain came out of nowhere, pelting her without mercy. She put one arm up to cover her head, the other still firmly on her trolley. She still needed her coat, but she didn't want to miss the next taxi. It rained so hard she could barely see. Her teeth chattered, and she was ugly crying now, tears and raindrops mixed with mascara as they dripped down her cheeks. A random car pulled into the taxi rank, and she was annoyed, thinking it was taking up a taxi's space. Then she noticed the thin aerial poking out of the roof. The driver rolled down his window.

"Where to, love?"

She swallowed back her tears. "Weymouth. I want to go to Weymouth."

"Lovely day for it!"

He chuckled to himself and hopped out, quickly filling the boot with her bags. The rest would have to go in the back with her. Not that she cared. There was something comforting about sitting in the back of the warm cab with her possessions piled around her. The taxi ride was going to cost her an arm and a leg, but at least she was on her way home.

She looked out the window as they pulled out onto the road. It had been springtime in Australia, but it was autumn here. Some of the trees were dying, shrivelling back into the ground, while others looked like they'd caught fire, their red and yellow leaves fluttering in the wind.

"Been on your holidays?" the taxi driver asked.

Why did everyone always want to talk?

"Er, yeah."

"Where you been?"

"Sydney."

"Very niiice!" He seemed to purr like a cat. "How long you been away for?"

"Twenty years, give or take."

He shot her a look in the rear-view mirror. "Come again?"

"I married an Aussie," she elaborated. "Been back a few times, but…"

"So now you're on your holidays?"

"No. I've left him."

"Have you now?" He didn't seem fazed. Probably heard all sorts. "Banging someone else, was he?"

"No!"

"So you just got bored of him?"

"Not exactly."

He waited, but she refused to spill any details.

"Let me guess. You're a…" He looked at her far longer than she was comfortable with, taking in her small, pointed chin and uneven eyebrows, one a little higher, the other a little lower. There was a small dent in her nose from a piercing she no longer wanted, and her only jewellery was a studded black bracelet that she liked to rub when she was feeling anxious, which had been rather a lot lately.

"I'm in IT," she told him.

"Oh, you fix computers?"

"Not quite. I'm a developer."

He looked blank.

"I make computer games."

"Well, bugger me if that ain't my dream job."

For the first time that day, she smiled. It had been her dream as well once. Now it had all gone to shit.

The sun was out by the time they arrived in Weymouth, and a watery rainbow stretched like a bridge across the coast. Mel strained against her seatbelt, eager to take in the familiar sights and sounds of her home town. The ugly clock still took pride of place in the town centre, its gaudy red, gold and blue paint unchanged by time. And there were the stony walls of her primary school, and the ramshackle hut where she and Abbie had gone to youth club. She couldn't believe that thing was still standing. She remembered her mortification when Abbie, aged thirteen, had climbed up onto the roof during a game of hide-and-seek. The youth club leader had practically had kittens, threatening to call the police if she didn't get down. She'd thought Abbie would get kicked out of the club for sure, but she'd got away with it. Abbie always landed on her feet.

"When were you last here?" the taxi driver asked, taking her past the Georgian pier.

Mel ran her tongue over her chapped lips. "About four years ago."

She remembered how Abbie had called her at work. Her voice had sounded strained, as though she'd been crying, and she'd told Mel she had something to tell her.

"I want you to leave your desk first. Go somewhere private; go home."

"I can't just leave work," Mel had protested before the penny had dropped. She didn't know if it was because of the way Abbie sounded, or whether it was some kind of twin telepathy, but she'd known right then what was up.

"It's Mum and Dad, isn't it? Just tell me how bad."

Abbie had been hysterical, totally incoherent. It had taken a while for Mel to get the full story out of her. A drunk driver had come out of nowhere and smashed into the back of their parents' Mercedes, causing them to crash into the van in front. They hadn't stood a chance, the way they'd been sandwiched between two bigger vehicles. Dad had died instantly, crumpling at the wheel, but Mum had held on for a few days, giving them a false sense of hope. Mel had taken the first plane home, but she'd had to accept a layover in Singapore, and then she was delayed due to adverse weather conditions. That delay had cost her the chance to say goodbye. It had hurt so much that she hadn't been there to hold her mum's hand as Abbie had. It had all been over by the time she'd landed. She'd helped make all the funeral arrangements, but Abbie had been all over the place, and Mel had found it hard to talk to her. It had felt too fresh, too raw. Things were never quite the same between them after that, even though they had still messaged each other from time to time and spoke on special occasions, such as their birthday and Christmas. But nothing would make up for the fact that she hadn't been there when Abbie had needed her most.

"Take the next turning on the left," she told the taxi driver, spotting her road coming up. It was tucked away in a quiet suburban area, in a neat row of detached houses and well-maintained lawns. She'd thought it dull and boring when she was a teenager, but in recent years, she'd come to appreciate the calm, scenic location for what it was. No wonder Abbie had never left.

The taxi pulled up outside number fifteen, and she rummaged in her wallet, pulling out several Australian dollars before she found her pounds. She paid the driver an eye-watering sum and thanked him as he helped haul out her bags.

"Nice garden," he commented.

"Thanks."

The garden did look nice, come to think of it. The red-hot pokers were in full bloom, and the rose bush was as bright and fragrant as ever. Abbie had clearly been mowing the grass and pruning back the weeds, although there was an odd little hole in the middle of the lawn, as if she'd recently taken down a bird feeder.

The old crab-shaped door knocker was gone, replaced with a shiny new one that was more in keeping with the neighbourhood. She rang the bell and waited impatiently for Abbie to answer. The curtains in the living room were drawn, so she couldn't see in. She rang again, and rapped on the door for good measure.

"For heaven's sake, Abbie. Will you bloody let me in?"

Abbie came to the door, looking hacked off and dishevelled. She wore ill-fitting blue jeans and a jumper with frayed sleeves. Her blonde hair was shorter than the last time she'd seen her, and her eyes looked hollow and tired, with dark shadows underneath. Instinctively, Mel went in for a hug, but found her uncharacteristically stiff. Abbie patted her on the back, then pulled away. She looked Mel up and down. "You look like a drowned rat."

"Cheers." Mel reached up and touched her hair. It was still a bit damp from the rain, and no doubt she still had mascara smudged down her cheeks.

Abbie stepped past her and hauled a couple of her bags into the house. Mel grabbed a few more, and between them, they lugged all of Mel's worldly goods inside.

"Thanks," Mel said as she set the last case down at the foot of the stairs.

Abbie took a step towards the door. "Welcome back, sis. Sorry, gotta run."

Mel stared at her. "Why? Where are you going?"

"The boat. I've got clients waiting."

"What, now?"

"Yeah, special charter. I'd have cancelled it if I'd known you were coming, but you didn't give me much notice, did you?"

Mel shook her head bleakly. She supposed she deserved that.

2

Mel watched as Abbie slammed the car door behind her and reversed at speed down the driveway. She took the corner sharply, almost taking out a wall in the process. She couldn't stop staring as the car screeched away.

"Well!" That was a nice welcome! She spun on her heel and headed back inside, shutting the door behind her. She was immediately confronted by her mountain of belongings. Her bags and suitcases filled the hallway. One had split open, and her jumpers and T-shirts had spilled out onto the beige carpet. She'd take them up to her room later. Not now – she was too tired, weary to her bones. She leaned against the cool, familiar wall, taking a moment to appreciate the stillness. She'd square things with Abbie later too. The main thing was that she was here now.

She looked around her childhood home, breathing it in. The house smelt of…what was that? A heady combination of freshly baked bread, cut flowers, and a subtle hint of lemon. She took a few steps into the living room and stopped. Were all the carpets new, or had Abbie cleaned them to such a degree that they'd changed hue? The walls had definitely been repainted. She remembered there had been a splash of red wine on the wall by the door from when one of Abbie's parties had got a bit out of hand. The stain was totally erased now; she couldn't even tell where it had been.

She smiled when she saw the vase of fragrant begonias on the mantelpiece. Was this a present from an admirer, or had Abbie simply treated herself? She turned and strode into the kitchen to find the kettle warm, an unopened packet of shortbread out on the counter. She tore into it with her teeth. She hadn't eaten on the plane. Couldn't face the thought of it, but a good old shortbread biscuit, that was another matter. She munched while she opened the tea cupboard and took down the caddy. Then her eye fell on the wine rack, and she shoved the caddy back in.

Sod tea. Her homecoming called for something a little stronger. Heaven knew she needed it after the couple of days she'd just had. She selected a cheap and cheerful red wine. To her annoyance, the bottle required a corkscrew. She opened a couple of drawers but couldn't see one. Then she tried the cutlery drawer, and her eye fell on a rather nifty Swiss army knife.

She picked it up, enjoying the weight of it in her hand. Flicking it open, she admired a small blade, large blade, tin opener, scissors, fish scaler and, yes, a corkscrew. *Score.*

She brandished it triumphantly, plunging the corkscrew through the centre of the cork, then pulling it out with a satisfying pop. She set the knife down on the table and poured herself a large glass. Then she picked the knife up again and examined it. It was a great knife, but she couldn't imagine Abbie buying such a thing. Perhaps it had been a present, or more likely purloined from some bloke she'd been seeing. She wouldn't mind a knife like this herself. It was a nice toy.

She finished the first glass while scrolling through her phone, then poured another, not really knowing what to do with herself. She was tired, but it was too early to sleep. The house was too quiet, too still without Abbie.

She took her wine and settled in the living room, wondering how long it would be until Abbie returned. Better not be too long if she wanted a taste of the wine. Besides, it would be dark in a couple of hours; she'd have to come back. Unless these clients of hers had wanted a sunset cruise. She remembered Peter taking her on one of those years ago, when they were both little more than teenagers. Ah, young love. How little she'd known then.

She settled back against the sofa and let her eye wander around the room. The house seemed different. It felt…unlived in. It was too empty, devoid of character. Everything was either white or beige. There was no real colour to it. Clearly Abbie had been on a massive decluttering spree. She shouldn't be completely surprised – after all, she'd been doing a social media 'detox' for several months. Mel was impressed how long she'd kept it up. She'd thought she'd be back on Facebook and Instagram within a day of announcing it, but no, there hadn't been a peep out of her since.

Her eye fell on a cutesy little wooden boat on the windowsill. There was another on the speakers, and she'd noticed one in the kitchen too. They were about the only ornaments Abbie had left out.

She put on the TV, but there was nothing she wanted to watch, so she ended up hopping from channel to channel. Then she noticed the big empty space beside the fireplace. Where was Dad's harp? It had always been here. She pictured her father strumming his way through 'Scarborough Fair', and a feeling of dread crept over her.

Please tell me she hasn't thrown it out.

She yanked her phone out of its charger, ignoring the missed calls from Peter.

- Where's Dad's harp?

She pinged the message to Abbie, and she waited impatiently for a reply. Abbie didn't respond. Of course, she'd probably be out of range. She took a deep breath to calm down, but it didn't help. Dad had loved his harp. Abbie couldn't have got rid of it, surely not?

The phone beeped, and she grabbed it. *Abbie!*

- I gave it to someone in need. Sorry, Mel, I didn't think you'd mind.

Not mind? Was she off her head?

Angrily, Mel returned to the kitchen and grabbed a different bottle from the rack. Let Abbie finish the cheap red. She was going to drink the oak-aged Rioja.

Her phone rang, and she grabbed it, hoping Abbie would tell her the harp was safe, but it was her boss, Derick, calling. Mel stared at the phone, picturing his puffy, irate face, and watched it ring. She couldn't deal with him now. She couldn't deal with any of it. Derick left her a message, no doubt wanting to know where the hell she was. She took a long swig of her wine and set the phone down on the table. She was about to reach for the remote again when she heard a strange noise.

What was that?

It was a low, whining sound, rather like a young child. Or a dog. Abbie had got a dog, hadn't she? She jumped to her feet and dashed into the kitchen. There it was again. Where was it coming from? Was it in the garden? She looked out, but she couldn't see anything. She pressed her face against the glass and finally saw a black Labrador looking up at her with big mournful eyes.

"Hey, you must be Otto!"

Abbie had told her so much about him. He looked cold out there, his eyes wide and watery, his body quivering slightly. Mel's brow furrowed. It would be dark soon; she had to get him in. She turned the key in the door, and Otto bolted into the house, his muddy paws skidding on the kitchen tiles. He dived under the table and huddled there, growling softly.

"Hey, it's all right, boy. I'm Mel."

What was she doing? The mutt could hardly be expected to understand.

How do you gain a dog's trust?

"You hungry?"

She looked over at his food bowl, which was empty.

"Where does she keep your food, then?"

She opened the cupboard under the sink. There were some spare bowls there, but that was it. She tried the cupboard next to it and the one behind her, but all she found was a sack of dried dog biscuits. They would have to do.

"Here you go, mutt."

She poured some biscuits into a clean bowl, and Otto sprang to his feet. In his excitement, he overshot the bowl and had to right himself. Once he did, he wasted no time sticking his face in the food.

"Steady, you'll get indigestion," Mel said. *Did dogs get indigestion?* She really didn't know. She'd always been more of a cat person. She liked their intelligence and found them independent and undemanding.

Otto licked the bowl clean, then looked at her again. His eyes were hypnotic, large and soulful. Impossible to ignore.

"No, don't do that," she said, finding it hard to look

away.

She didn't know what food regime he was on, but she was sure Abbie would feed him when she got in. *She had left him out in the cold though.* Otto looked down at his empty bowl again and inspected it to see if any more food had magically appeared.

"Oh, all right." Mel went to the cupboard and gave him another handful from the sack. Otto let out a little whine and gobbled it down like he hadn't been fed, but Mel was wise to him. She wasn't going to fill it a third time.

She returned to the living room and her wine. A gust of wind blew through the room. She checked the windows, but they were all closed. New windows had not been a part of Abbie's recent home improvements, then. Pity, because while all the windows at the front of the house were double glazed, the ones at the back were not, which led to a cold drafty house that was expensive to heat.

After a few minutes, Otto came in and snuggled up next to her in front of the TV. He raised his eyebrows, as if to say: "What we watching?"

What was she watching? Somehow, she'd managed to stumble upon *Houses Down Under*. She switched over abruptly, not wanting to be reminded of what she'd left behind. She pulled out her laptop and took a look at *Artful Assassin*, the game she'd spent the last few years working on. It was about an ingenious assassin who could disguise himself as anything. He could be a schoolgirl, a greengrocer, or a nun. There was no way of knowing until he struck. In order to win, you had to kill him before he (or she) could assassinate you, but if you killed an innocent by mistake, then it was game over.

Artful Assassin had been long anticipated, and there had been a lot of media hype. The original concept was hers, and she'd been proud when she'd been given the go-ahead. She was good at her job. She'd thought she'd be able to handle the pressure, but weeks into starting the project, her parents had died, and everything had come crashing down around her. How could she concentrate on the game when her life had imploded?

Even with a team to help, she'd fallen way behind. It had got to the point where she was taking sleeping pills to help her sleep. She was an intelligent woman, but somehow she'd got locked into a vicious cycle. The pills had made her drowsy in the mornings, so she'd counteracted them by taking stimulants. Then Peter found out, and he'd totally overreacted. He'd dragged her to the doctors and got her signed off work. That was when she had truly fallen apart. Without her work to focus on, she'd been forced to face up to her parents' death. So she'd stayed in bed and wept and lost interest in doing anything but lying around and watching TV. Peter had referred to it as her little 'wobble'. The way people talked about it, you'd think she'd had a nervous breakdown. Even her doctor had skirted around that idea, but for Mel, the truth was simpler. She'd simply been grieving.

Peter had driven her crazy at home, so she'd gone back to work too soon, and she'd never really got back into the flow. The game went over budget, and Derick went from understanding to downright annoying. He was constantly on her back. In the end, he had insisted they just release the damn thing, but it hadn't been properly tested, and the users soon reported bugs, some minor, others more significant. Mel had felt humiliated by this, horrified that she had let it happen.

Her phone was vibrating again. She watched it hop across the table with rage. It was Derick calling again. She supposed she'd better face the music.

"Mel? What the fuck was that garbled message you left me? Where the hell are you?"

"I'm in England."

"You're supposed to be here, fixing that bloody mess you created!"

"I can work here just as easily," she told him coolly. "I'm sorry I didn't give you much notice. I...I had a family situation to take care of. It couldn't be helped."

Derick neatly sidestepped her 'family situation'. He didn't care what was up. He just wanted to know how it was going to impact him. "Well, are you going to be able to fix the bugs or not?"

"I am," she said firmly. "Just give me a few more weeks."

"Weeks!"

"Okay, days."

It would be weeks, but he clearly needed her to sugar-coat it.

"Don't think you're getting a sniff of your bonus money until this thing is fixed," he warned her.

And once I do, you can stick your job where the sun doesn't shine.

"Mel?"

"Sorry, I've got a bad connection my end."

"Right, well, you get on it pronto. I expect an update by Friday at the latest."

"Will do."

He hung up without another word, and Mel scowled at the screen. He needed her more than she needed him. It would do him well to remember that. She could do her job with her eyes closed. Or at least, that used to be the case. She swallowed the rest of her wine and lay back against the soft cushions, wishing the room would swim back into focus.

3

Mel heard the front door slam around midnight, but she was too far gone to even open one eye. She turned over in bed and sucked on the corner of her pillow. The bed smelled like apple blossom. Must be a new detergent.

She drifted back to sleep. A film was playing in her mind. She saw herself running after the assassin from her game, ducking, weaving, hiding behind corners. Sometimes he had Peter's face. Sometimes it was Derrick. She was safe as long as she could keep him in her sights, because the minute she lost him, that was it, she was toast.

She woke face down on the bed, one arm thrown over the side, the sheets twisted around her waist. She yawned and stretched, hitting her head against the wall she hadn't expected to be there.

"Ow!"

Her brain still expected Sydney. Instead, she was in her childhood bedroom, the light spilling in through the blinds. This was new. As a child, she had never, ever left a blind open. She'd been too paranoid that a passer-by would peer in at her in all her teenage angst. Only now could she see how unlikely it was that anyone would look up at her, from the quiet sheltered street.

According to her laptop, it was half past nine in the morning. She'd slept through the night for the first time in ages. It had helped that she hadn't had Peter snoring and huffing beside her, asking what time it was every time she moved, nor had she missed the jerk with the car alarm that inevitably went off at four in the morning.

She looked around the room, at the familiar walls she'd grown up with. It wasn't the biggest bedroom in the house, and she could just as easily have chosen one of the others – they had five, after all, but there was nowhere Mel would rather sleep than here, even with the bare walls.

Her room had clearly had the declutter treatment, same as the rest of the house. The bed linen was brand new, a tasteful floral design, as opposed to the old Spiderman duvet her mum had always put out for her. Her teenage posters had been taken down too. Mum had kept them up for years. She'd said she liked seeing them there after Mel left for Australia. They reminded her of the bad old days when Mel was a moody teenager who lived in her room and only spoke in grunts. Mum had loved pulling her leg about what a terror she'd been, but she knew her mother had only been kidding. Mel had been a bit antisocial, she supposed, spending hours gaming, but she hadn't been that bad. Not by a long shot.

She stuck one foot out of bed, then the other. She'd forgotten how the floorboards creaked. She took a step towards the window. The sky was as grey as the gutter, and the air was heavy and damp, somewhere between fog and rain. There wasn't a lot to see aside from the house across the street. The old bloke still had the same blue Renault, and the neighbours still kept their lawns neat and their hedges trimmed. She sat on the windowsill as she used to, her feet up on the desk. She caught the faint whiff of new paint mingled with the citrus smell of a plug-in air freshener. It was her room, but it wasn't. Still, she couldn't blame Abbie for making changes. She wasn't to know she was coming back. She hadn't even known herself.

She thought about the mess she'd left at the bottom of the stairs. Perhaps she had better bring her stuff up to her room. She went down and grabbed as many bags as she could carry and heaved them upstairs, then made a return trip. There, she'd earned her coffee.

Abbie was sitting in the kitchen, drinking coffee from Dad's mug, a pint-sized one with a picture of a wolf on it. She didn't remember when or where he had come by that mug, possibly at a car boot sale or something, but it had always been his favourite.

"Sleep all right?" Abbie asked. Her voice sounded a little hoarse, Mel thought. As if she'd been shouting to make herself heard.

"Not bad."

She made a beeline for the coffee machine. She wanted to ask again about the harp, but Abbie looked half dead, so she thought it might be wise to wait until later. Abbie slung back the last of her coffee and wiped her mouth with her hand.

"Got to run."

"Oh?"

"Got another boat tour this morning."

"Really?"

Mel was surprised. The boat business was usually

winding down by this time of year. The autumn weather wasn't particularly amenable to pleasure cruises or fishing trips, and besides, most of the summer tourists had left.

"See you later," Abbie said, without any further explanation.

Mel looked after her, somewhat bemused. She'd imagined Abbie would want to chat. She was the outgoing twin, after all. Mum used to say they were like chalk and cheesecake. Abbie, with her long blonde hair and large blue eyes, versus Mel with her light brown hair and unruly eyebrows. She had blue eyes too, but they were smaller than Abbie's and more beady. Abbie was definitely the pretty twin, but that was okay, because Mel was the intelligent one. Not that Abbie was stupid, by any means; she just didn't apply herself. She liked people to like her, whilst Mel liked to be right.

Abbie gave her a little wave and disappeared out the door. Perhaps she was still pissed off with Mel for turning up out of the blue. Never mind, she'd make it up to her later. They never fell out for very long. It didn't matter how long they'd been apart or how little they'd spoken; they could always pick up again where they'd left off.

Mel's appetite had returned with a vengeance, and she opened the fridge to see what food Abbie had in. It was virtually empty aside from a few jars of jam and a carton of milk. She rooted around the cupboards and found a few tins and a box of blueberry wheats. She poured some into a bowl and doused them with milk. She was just about to take the first spoonful when she heard a whimper. She turned her head and saw that Otto was stuck outside again. Abbie must have put him out first thing. She unlocked the door and let him in. He went straight to his food bowl.

"I bet she's already fed you," Mel said, but she couldn't see any evidence of it. No empty tin sitting on the side.

"We'll have to go to the shop," she promised the dog. "That'll get me back into Abbie's good books, and I can't stand to look at your hungry eyes."

After breakfast, she took a shower and washed her hair with a bit of Abbie's peach shampoo. She dried herself off and slipped into a pair of black leggings and a red vest, pulling a grey hoodie over the top. She ran a brush through her hair and debated whether to bother with make-up, but Otto stood patiently at her side, his lead in his mouth.

"All right, all right, I'm coming."

The trees rustled in the wind as they stepped outside. There was no one about except a papergirl pedalling her bike furiously down the hill, the wind whipping her hair as she disappeared around the corner.

Otto trotted ahead of her, leading her down the footpath that led to the Duck. Mel smiled. He clearly went this way a lot.

"Too early," she told him, looking at the pub's shuttered windows. They walked on to the next pub, the Ship, and then down into the town. She passed a horse chestnut tree and paused to admire the shiny brown conkers that peeked out from spiky green cases. Otto yanked on the lead, dragging her down to the sea.

The beach seemed to stretch out for miles in an unnaturally straight line. There were more stones than sand at this end, and Otto ran straight down to the water to bark at the waves as they rushed in and out.

Mel breathed in the salty sea air. In the distance, she could make out a lighthouse. It seemed so desolate out there on its own in the mist, with nothing but the

brooding sky for company. She fantasised that she and
Otto were the sole survivors of a zombie apocalypse
that had taken over the whole of humankind.

"Otto!" she called, afraid the dog would go out too
deep.

He bounded back to her, and she shrieked as he
shook his coat out, showering her with cold water.

"How could you bear to go in that?" she asked. "It's
sodding freezing."

He gave a delighted woof. There was seaweed
wrapped around his front paw, and she bent down to
extract it, shuddering at the slimy texture.

They walked on towards the sandier section of the
beach, and her mind shifted between the way the town
used to look and how it looked now. A few new buildings had sprung up. Another shop had closed down.
Not just any shop but the games shop where she had
spent all her pocket money when she was young. For a
while, Abbie had paid her to do her homework. She'd
made a neat packet, enough to buy *Sonic the Hedgehog*,
then Mum had found out and put a stop to it. She
remembered the strop Abbie had thrown when she
realised she'd have to do her own algebra.

She put Otto back on the lead, and he galloped off
home, making her break into a run.

"You're one of those health nuts, aren't you?" she
said in disgust. The dog's tongue hung down, impossibly long and dribbly.

It seemed like every sane person was huddled
indoors with a hot chocolate or perhaps something
stronger. Mel remembered in time to pop into the corner
shop, where she filled a basket with dog food, bread,
cheese, vodka, and Red Bull. The woman at the till
raised an eyebrow at the vodka and glanced up at the
clock. Mel didn't bother to offer an explanation. It might

be eleven o'clock here, but in Australia it was late at night. She pictured Peter sitting alone in their flat, peeling an orange in that fastidious way of his, ensuring that every single piece of peel remained intact. Funny, she'd found that charming once.

She left the shop and was immediately accosted by Otto, whom she'd left tied up outside. The shop had a 'no dogs' policy, and she couldn't have him wandering off. She held the lead in one hand and the shopping in the other and let Otto drag her the rest of the way home.

"You'd make a good husky," she told him as she pulled out her key and unlocked the door. As she wiped her feet on the mat, Otto bounded past her, straight up the stairs. She dumped the shopping by the door and kicked off her shoes. Instantly, a little pile of sand formed on the carpet. This brought back memories, the way the sand got absolutely everywhere. She tasted the gritty texture of it on her tongue. She could take a shower. She could change her clothes, but when she went to bed that night, she'd still be finding those little bits of Weymouth shimmering in the sheets. It was on her skin and in her pores, and she was never going to be rid of it.

She went up to her room to see if her phone had charged. It had, and Peter had left her a flipping voice-mail. When was he going to get the hint? She'd crossed the bloody world to get away from him. She didn't need his negative energy, making her question herself.

Otto hovered in the doorway, as if waiting to be invited in. She looked up at him. "What's with you?"

The dog stood completely rigid, as if he had a rod up his backside.

She reached out and stroked his head, but he let out a little growl.

"Okay then, have it your way."

She slipped her phone into her pocket and went out onto the landing. Otto raced ahead of her. He stood at the top of the stairs, ears back, mouth pulled back into a surly expression. Then he barked. She moved towards him.

"What? What is it?"

She trod on the first stair. Otto tensed beside her, as if to say, "I wouldn't do that."

She went down a few more stairs. He didn't bark, but he didn't relax either. He remained close until she reached the bottom. Her shopping bags lay by the door; the packet of cheese had rolled onto the floor, and the tins of dog food were clearly visible, but Otto paid no attention. Every hair on his body stood on end as he peered into the living room.

Swallowing her fear, Mel took a step into the room. She couldn't see what had upset him. Everything was just as it had been, the cushions positioned on the sofa, the rug lined up neatly with the table. She glanced at the wooden shutter that separated the living room from the dining room next door. That too looked completely normal, apart from one thing. A dark shadow that shouldn't have been there, like someone was hiding there, waiting, like the Artful Assassin.

"Abbie?"

She edged towards the shutter, feeling both ridiculous and scared. When she reached it, she just stood there, too afraid to move. Was it her imagination, or was the shutter trembling slightly, swinging back and forth, as if someone was leaning against it and breathing in and out? It had to be Abbie playing a trick on her. Or maybe it was the wind. She screwed up her face and yanked it open, but it wasn't Abbie who stood poised like a statue, one gnarled finger pointing at her accusingly. The intruder's face was partially hidden by his hood, but she took in the dark angular eyebrows, the clenched lips, and the angry flare of his nose. She gaped at him, and he glared back at her. His eyes were wild.

4

S he let out a loud, animalistic cry. She didn't know what she was yelling; none of the sounds made sense to her. She just knew she had to get this man away from her. He flinched, as if she were the one intruding on him. Then he stood there, rooted to the spot, his dark eyes searching hers. It freaked her out, the way he stared at her. The way he snarled.

"Who are you?" he hissed.

With a flicker of uncertainty, she considered that this could be one of Abbie's friends, but she could see from the expression on his face that he was off-kilter. A bead of sweat trickled down his face, his chin quivered, and the whites of his eyes shone dangerously in the dim light. He had the rigid posture of someone prepared to attack.

"Get out! Get out! Get out!" she shrieked.

His eyes swirled to boiling point. She ought to have moved away, perhaps run into the kitchen for a knife, but she couldn't take her eyes off him. He kept his hands down in his pockets, and she wasn't sure, but she thought he might have a weapon. Only now did she notice that the curtains were closed, and she screamed as he took a step towards her.

At last, her survival instinct kicked in; she felt a powerful surge of energy. She grabbed a cushion and threw it at him. Then she spotted the TV remote and lobbed that too. She was a lousy shot, but it had the desired effect. He legged it across the room, his boots leaving a muddy residue on the clean beige carpet. Out of the corner of her eyes, she spotted Otto cowering under the table. She sucked down air, willing the intruder to get out of the house. He almost tripped over one of the bags of groceries she'd left in the hallway, the handle catching his foot. He kicked his way out of it and lunged for the door, but he couldn't seem to work the handle.

You have to pull up, not down.

Much as she wanted him out, she couldn't bring herself to speak. Her legs felt like they were made of wool, and her heart threatened to break out of her ribcage. At last, there was a short click, and the door flew open, letting in a strong gust of wind. He charged off down the garden path and out onto the street.

What kind of burglar doesn't have a car?

She stayed in the doorway, unable to believe what had happened. She came back in and slammed the door shut, locking it behind her. She watched frantically from the window to make sure he wasn't coming back; then she staggered back into the living room, where she collapsed on the sofa and gave in to the tears, more from relief than anything else.

"Come here, boy," she called to the dog, but Otto remained under the table, and nothing would convince him to come out. Shaken and angry, she located her phone. She went to dial 999, then hesitated. Was this an emergency? Perhaps it didn't count now the intruder had fled. She googled the number for the local police station instead. If they didn't answer, she'd…

They answered.

"I…I want to report a break-in. I just disturbed an intruder in my home."

The voice on the other end was calm and sympathetic. Mel gave out her name and address and recounted the incident in detail; then she was put on hold while she waited to speak to a police officer. She tapped one leg against the other. What was the point of this? The intruder would be long gone by now.

"Hello? Mrs Montgomery? There's no one available right now, but if you're going to be home, I can send a couple of officers round to the house later."

"Okay. Do you know what time?"

"Can't say for sure. It will probably be a couple of hours."

"Okay…" She darted a glance at the window. "What if…what if he comes back? I'm all on my own here."

The curtains twitched, throwing shadows on the wall. Her heart was still pounding, and she felt as though she'd drunk one too many cups of coffee. She walked unsteadily over to the window and yanked the curtains open, half expecting someone to jump out. She peered out at the empty road to reassure herself he hadn't come back.

The person on the phone sounded weary. "How did he get in?"

"I…" She glanced around the room. The window was locked, as had been the door. At least, the front door.

"One minute. I need to check the back."

Still holding the phone to her ear, she walked down the hallway and into the kitchen. She tried the door and found it was still locked. She went into the little box room opposite, a room as beige and minimalist as the rest of the house, and saw the broken glass.

"He smashed the window!"

"You'll need to get that fixed as soon as possible."

No shit.

She hung up the phone and wrapped her arms around her shaking shoulders. She felt cold in spite of her hoodie. She rubbed her hands together and thought about starting a fire in the hearth, but when she went back into the living room, she couldn't see any firewood and didn't much fancy going out to the shed.

Now what?

She drummed her knuckles against her teeth, waiting for the feeling of unease to dissipate. She needed something to keep her occupied, but she couldn't work. Not like this. Should she clear up the glass in the box room, or would the police want to see it? She glanced at the clots of mud on the carpet. Abbie was going to flip when she saw those. Maybe she should…

Her heart stopped. It sounded as if someone was trying to get into the house. She jumped up, clutching the phone tight in her hand. She could hear a rattling sound. Was that the wind? No, there was someone at the front door, trying to get it open.

She looked around for Otto, but he had wedged himself in between the sofa and the wall. She grabbed a sofa cushion, then rejected it, looking for something stronger, sharper.

The door opened, and she saw that it was Abbie.

"Oh, thank god!"

She ran towards her sister.

Abbie pulled back. "Er, are you all right?"

"There was an intruder! I walked in on him. God, I

thought he was going to kill me, Abbie. He had these eyes and…"

Abbie placed a hand on the base of her spine and pulled her in for a hug. Tears pricked Mel's eyes as she rested her head on her twin's shoulder. This was the closest she'd felt to her since she'd come home.

Abbie pulled back, and her eyes flicked around the room. "What happened? Did he take anything?"

"No, I don't think so. I chased him out."

"Nice one!" Abbie slapped her on the back. "What did he look like, this bloke? Can you describe him?"

Mel screwed up her face. It had all happened so fast. Conflicting images swirled around in her mind, and she had to focus hard to conjure up the right one. "He had dark, intense eyes and prominent eyebrows."

"What, thick ones?"

"More…angular, like a slash and a backslash."

Abbie looked concerned. "What else do you remember?"

"I don't know – it's all a bit of a blur." She held her head in her hands, but try as she might, she couldn't picture him.

"Come on. You must remember something."

She shook her head.

Abbie's mouth twitched as if she wanted to say something. She tilted her head back for a moment and stared up at the ceiling before focusing her eyes back on Mel.

"It's okay; take it easy," she said. "What you need to do is relax. Then it'll come to you."

Mel took a deep breath and tried again to visualise the man she'd found in their living room. "He looked… Middle Eastern, I think. I'm not sure though. He had his hood up, and the light wasn't very good."

Abbie nodded. "Good. That's good. You sit there and

see what else you can remember. I'm going to make us a cuppa."

The cup of tea Abbie made her was positively anaemic and way too sweet.

"Sugar's good for shock," Abbie insisted when she pulled a face.

"Is anything missing?" Mel asked. "I mean, the TV's still here and my laptop, but did you have anything else lying around? Any money or jewellery?"

"Doesn't look like it." Abbie got up and walked around, checking the desk drawers before disappearing upstairs to her bedroom. She was smiling when she came back down again.

"No, it looks okay. Sounds like you interrupted him in time."

Mel nodded, but it didn't make any sense to her. "Why was he hiding like that? What do you think he was after?"

"Who knows? Maybe he was just hungry?"

"Then I'd have found him in the kitchen. Besides, you don't break into a house just to steal food."

"Maybe. You never know what someone might do if they're desperate."

She picked up Mel's mug and handed it to her. "Drink up. It'll do you good."

Mel took it, shuddering a little as she chugged down the lukewarm tea.

Abbie laughed. "Come on, it wasn't that bad."

"Worse."

They sat side by side on the sofa and waited for the police. Otto finally deigned to come out from his hiding place and sat in a heap at Mel's feet, looking like a furry footstool.

"It just makes me so angry," Mel said, leaning down

to pet the dog. "I mean, what a nerve he had, breaking into our house like that."

"I can't believe this happened on your first day back," Abbie said, shaking her head. "You sure it wasn't someone you know?"

"Of course not!"

"So it wasn't, like, an old boyfriend or something?"

Mel rolled her eyes. There hadn't really been any, as Abbie well knew. She'd met Peter straight out of school, and she barely remembered the boy she'd been seeing before that. They'd just been kids.

The doorbell chimed, and Abbie jumped up. "That'll be the Old Bill."

Mel sat up straight, unable to relax as Abbie went to the door. A crazy, irrational part of her was scared it might be the intruder again, even though there was no way he'd ring the doorbell. She relaxed a little as she heard voices. Then Abbie brought the police officers into the room. Two uniforms: a tall, confident man with a long neck, and a cautious young woman with birdlike eyes. They introduced themselves as PC Farley and PC Moreland.

"Nice house you've got here," Moreland commented, tucking a strand of hair behind her ear. "What is it, four bedrooms?"

"Five," Abbie said, with a hint of pride. "Oh, and this is my twin sister, Mel. She's the one who saw the burglar."

Farley looked from one to the other. "You don't look much alike."

"I can see the likeness," Moreland said. Mel wasn't sure if she meant it, or if she was just being polite.

It brought to mind the disappointment on the faces of her school friends when they first met her twin. A disappointment that was further exacerbated by their lack of psychic powers. Their inability to read each other's minds was a total let-down as far as her school-mates had been concerned. There had been that one time when they'd gone skiing in Austria and both of them had got a nosebleed, but there had been no one around to witness that. Still, fourteen-year-old Abbie had agreed it was pretty epic.

Farley stood at the window like a crane, his sharp nose peering out at the view while Moreland circled the room, taking stock of what was there. "Did he take anything?"

Mel shook her head. "No, I think I caught him in the act."

"Mel's just got back from Australia," Abbie said thoughtfully. "Perhaps he didn't expect her to be here."

Mel bit her lip. "You think he'd been watching the house?"

The two police officers exchanged a look. "It's more probable he just happened upon your place," Farley said. "These people aren't the brightest sparks."

"Can I get you both a tea or coffee?" Abbie asked.

"Thank you," Farley said. "I'll have a black coffee with sugar. She'll have a white tea, no sugar."

Abbie nodded and headed towards the door.

"Do you mind if I take a seat?" Moreland asked, eyeing the sofa as you might a cosy bed after a long day's work.

"No, by all means."

Moreland plonked herself down. "Ah, that's better."

She flexed and unflexed her left ankle, then turned and looked at Mel with a motherly expression. "It must have been quite a shock for you, finding a stranger in your home?"

Mel nodded. "Yes. Yes, it was."

"I take it nothing like this has ever happened before? The house doesn't have a history of burglaries?"

"No."

"Was there anybody about when it happened? Any kids playing outside? Anyone mowing the lawn?"

Mel's eyes went to the window. "Not in this weather. I'd have to check with Abbie, but I don't think there are any kids living in this street. It's mostly pensioners, apart from us."

"And the intruder. Can you describe him?"

"He was male, dark eyes, slim build, olive skin."

"Tall or short?"

"I don't know. Not tall but taller than me, I think."

"But you couldn't say for sure?"

She ground her teeth together. It was like taking a test she hadn't studied for. She'd been there. She'd seen him, but recalling his face with any accuracy...well, it was almost impossible.

"He had his hood up," she remembered.

"Age?"

She saw him in her mind's eye. Dark eyes, rough, bristly skin. Was that real, or was her mind just filling in the gaps?

"Mel?"

"Sorry, yes, I think he was about my age – around forty. Maybe younger."

"Did he say anything to you?"

"He said...'Who are you?'"

He'd spoken like an angry snake. She wiped her face, convinced she could feel his spit on her cheek, but of course she couldn't. It had been over an hour ago. Maybe more. "I...I think he had an accent."

"What sort of accent?"

"Foreign."

"Can you be any more specific?"

She shook her head. "I'm sorry, no. He only spoke a few words."

Abbie barged back into the room. Tea slopped from the cups and puddled around the tray as she dropped it down on the table.

"Did he have a weapon?" Farley asked Mel.

"I don't know. The light was dimmed. I couldn't see his hands. He seemed angry. His whole energy was angry."

Farley rubbed his chin. "So you didn't actually see a weapon?"

"No."

Moreland slipped her notebook back into her pocket and popped the cap back on her pen, and Mel knew she was losing her audience. She needed to get them back. Farley actually pulled out his phone and was scrolling through it, like he had somewhere more important to be. Even Abbie was tapping her foot.

"I thought he was going to kill me," she blurted out.

The two police officers exchanged another look, and Mel felt instantly patronised.

"He was dangerous." She looked at Abbie to back her up.

"I wasn't here," she said. "But he sounds terrifying."

Mel clenched her fists. "I just feel so…violated, you know? This is our house! How dare he break in?"

"I know how you feel," Abbie said soothingly. "But the police just want the facts."

Mel rubbed her temples. She was getting a headache, and she desperately wanted to crawl back into bed and pretend none of this had ever happened.

"It sucks," Abbie said, putting her arm around her.

Mel nodded and tried to calm herself. She couldn't believe her dramatic sister was taking this better than she was. Perhaps it was just a front, but then, she hadn't been there. She hadn't seen that man. She gave an involuntary shudder.

"How did you say he got in?" Moreland asked.

"He smashed the window in the box room," Mel said. "Do you want to see it? I've left it as it was."

Moreland nodded, and they both waited as Farley took a long gulp of his coffee. He set the cup down, and Mel led them down the hall.

"Mind your step," she warned. "There's still glass on the floor."

She was suddenly aware of Otto right on her heels. "Stay back," she warned. "You don't want to tread on the glass."

It occurred to her she hadn't fed him, so she showed Farley and Moorland the room and then took a detour to the kitchen to sort him out. She could hear them taking photos and talking about what they were having for dinner. Mel opened one of the tins she had bought. Otto attacked his food with relish. She stood and watched him, taking comfort in the sight of the dog bolting down his food.

"Was your dog here, then?"

She jumped. She hadn't heard Farley come in. She recovered herself quickly and went to the sink to rinse out the empty tin.

"He was here, but he hid under the table."

"Little coward, aren't you?" Farley said, ruffling the dog's head.

Otto stopped eating and gave him a withering look.

Mel dried off her hands and returned to the living room.

"It seems like a quiet neighbourhood," Moreland was saying to Abbie.

"Yeah, boring as shit," Abbie agreed.

"Well, give us a ring if you remember anything else."
Moreland handed Mel a card with her details on it.

"Is that it, then?" Mel asked. She couldn't believe
they were leaving. Weren't they going to fingerprint
them or anything? "Do you want any more tea or
coffee?" she asked, trying not to sound too desperate.

"Thanks," Moreland said, "but we really have to get
going."

Mel's collar felt tight as Abbie walked them to the
door. A small, irrational part of her wanted to call them
back and demand they do something more.

Abbie returned and nodded at Mel. "Well, that's that
done, then."

Clearly she was happier than Mel about the way the
police had handled things. Mel bit her lip. She wished
she could feel so relaxed.

"Do you think he'll come back?"

"I shouldn't think so," Abbie said.

"We'll have to keep the windows and doors locked,
just in case. And we've got to get that glass fixed."

"Don't worry, I'll deal with that."

Abbie picked at her nails. They looked a right state.
Had manicures fallen out of vogue?

"I know the police asked this, but are you absolutely
certain that man wasn't some friend of yours?" Mel
asked. "I mean, wouldn't that make more sense than
some random break-in?"

She watched Abbie's face carefully for any flicker of
truth. It wouldn't be the first time that some bloke had
got hung up on her sister.

"No," Abbie said vehemently. "I haven't been out
with anyone for a while."

Mel regarded her with scepticism. "It couldn't be
some old flame?"

"I really don't think so. Doesn't sound my type."

Mel's eyes narrowed. "What exactly is your type these days?"

Abbie shrugged. "What's yours?"

"Don't!"

She closed her eyes for a moment, caught a flash of Bondi Beach. She saw a blond hunk with a smooth, toned body and an inviting smile. A promise of something fun and uncomplicated.

"Why don't you go and lie down?" Abbie said more gently. "You're still really pale."

Mel nodded. "Yeah, maybe I will."

She hoisted herself up the stairs and flopped down on her bed, but when sleep did not come, she pulled her laptop out and lost herself in *Artful Assassin*. Why did it always glitch on this level, just as she was about to enter the bank? What was it about this particular street? She stared at the assassin, who was currently dressed like a James Bond villain in a black polo neck and tight leather trousers. His dark eyes glowered at her. Was it her imagination, or did he resemble the intruder? Or was it that the intruder resembled him?

She circles the marketplace. A nun approaches and unravels a cloth full of wares.

"What do you desire?"

She looks over the knickknacks, her gaze lingering on the golden goblet and the rhinestone belt.

"I'll take the amulet."

"A fine choice." The nun hands it over, and she gives her the last of her coins. Now that she has the amulet, she will be able to catch the ferry to the Island of Discovery. She slips it into her pocket and takes a couple of steps towards the gate before a thought crosses her mind.

What if the nun is the assassin? It couldn't be a more perfect disguise.

She turns and frees the crossbow from its harness. Aims it at the nun. The nun is screaming, pleading for her life.

"Think of the orphans," she says, and points to the children playing in the street beyond. "I provide for them. I feed and clothe them. I beg you, for their sake, let me go."

She stares at the nun, looking for a clue. If she kills an innocent person, she'll never get to the island, but if she's wrong... She fires the arrow. Instantly the nun alters, *shapeshifting into a centurion. She whoops with delight, because this means she gets to go to the island; then the game freezes.*

Mel stared at the screen. The same bug manifested itself in different levels of the game. She had to figure out the common denominator. Why was it doing this, and how did she make it stop?

IT WASN'T the first time Mel had fallen asleep face down on her laptop, and it probably wouldn't be the last. She lifted her head and watched as the light crept over the blue brindle tiles on the house opposite. The early morning sun burned a brilliant orange. The colour made her thirsty.

She dragged herself downstairs, amazed to find Abbie already up and sitting at the kitchen table.

"Morning!"

"You look like shit," Abbie told her, looking up from her phone.

"Thanks." Mel pulled a mug down from the cupboard.

"No, I'm serious. You look worse than shit. You're like one of those flies that buzz around shit."

Mel couldn't raise a smile. The intruder hadn't hurt her, hadn't touched her in any way, but she felt as bruised as if he'd battered her over the head with a cast-iron frying pan, and Abbie making light of it wasn't helping. She plodded over to the coffee machine and switched it on, her gaze trained on the strong black coffee as it trickled into her mug. Then she headed to the fridge and pulled out a can of Red Bull. She popped it open and poured some into her coffee.

"What are you up to today?" Abbie asked.

"Work, work and more work. What about you?"

"Depends on the weather." Abbie slouched back in her chair and continued to look at something on her phone.

Mel rubbed the sleep from her eyes. "So you might as well level with me. What really happened to the harp?"

Abbie grimaced. "I gave it to the Sally Army."

Mel stared at her with incredulity. "But why? Dad loved that harp!"

Abbie drew a breath. "All right, I just couldn't bear to look at it anymore. It was there whenever I went into the living room. It was as if Dad were in the room with me. I felt like I was never really on my own. I found it kind of…creepy."

"Couldn't you just have put it in the box room?"

"I'd still know it was there."

Mel shifted her weight from one foot to the other. She didn't want to fight, but she still couldn't believe Abbie had got rid of such a beautiful family heirloom. Personally, she loved to be reminded of their parents. She'd kept a bottle of her mum's honeysuckle perfume just so she could get a whiff of it whenever she missed her.

She cast her eye around the kitchen. She'd always considered it the heart of their home. It was as cosy as a kitchen could be with its large ceramic sink, chunky butcher's block counters and weathered stone floor. The welly green cabinets were so old they'd come back into fashion. Abbie had had a modern cooker installed a few years back, but they'd had a real Aga when they were young. She had loved to watch their mum kneading bread and baking muffins in it. She wasn't much of a cook herself, but she appreciated good baking.

"I don't suppose you've got time to bake some of your lovely cheese twists?" she asked.

"Dunno. Maybe." Abbie looked unenthusiastic.

Mel perched on a chair and took a big sip of her coffee. The kitchen clock ticked loudly behind her. Instantly, she was transported back to the house she'd shared with Peter. She recalled sitting across the table from him while they each silently chewed their food. The clock on the wall ticking so loudly she'd wanted to pull it down and stamp on it.

She stood up abruptly. "Right. I'd better get back to it."

"Okay."

She topped up her coffee and traipsed back upstairs, where she climbed back into bed and opened her laptop. Derick must have seen that she was online, because a moment later, a message flashed up on her screen:

I need you to fix those bugs, Mel. I'm getting a lot of heat.

Really, what did he hope to achieve by nagging her? She was so sick of his micromanaging. She couldn't wait until she was finished with this project and finished with him. She turned her attention back to the game and was just about to get started when the doorbell rang. On hearing a deep male voice, she came out onto the landing to investigate. Was this Abbie's latest boyfriend?

"About bloody time," Abbie was saying.

"I came as quickly as I could. We've had a lot of work on this week."

"Whatever. You'd better take those muddy shoes off before you come in."

"That's all right, I've got my boot covers." He slipped some plastic blue things on over his shoes.

Abbie grunted and walked off towards the box room, leaving him to follow. Must be the window repairman, Mel realised. Did Abbie have to be so rude?

· · ·

SHE RETURNED TO BED, happy in the knowledge that the
window was being fixed. She settled her laptop on her
knees, and the face of the assassin stared back at her.
Damn, he gave her the creeps. The screen changed, and
the assassin was someone else now, a cute little girl with
pigtails and a snub nose. She had her school uniform on
and a satchel slung across her shoulder. Mel smiled to
herself. The players would get a shock when she hurled
the ninja stars.

She forced herself to focus, but intrusive thoughts
popped out at her from nowhere. Whenever she thought
about the assassin, she thought about the intruder. Why
had he chosen to target them? It was such a quiet neighbourhood. About the wildest thing that had ever
happened round here was that time a teenage boyfriend
thought it would be romantic to climb the drainpipe up
to Abbie's room. Unfortunately, he'd overestimated his
climbing skills and ended up flat on his back in the rose
bushes. He'd had some nasty cuts and bruises, and Dad
had been royally pissed off about his roses. To add
insult to injury, Abbie had dumped him a few days later
for another boy.

With the intruder on her mind, it was some time
before she was fully absorbed, lost in the code. She
worked away, Otto snoring contentedly at the foot of the
bed. This was what she loved, problem solving. Her
mind seemed to work independently of her thoughts,
and her fingers flew over the keys. When she finally
came up for air, it was dark outside, and she was
hungry. She couldn't even remember if she'd had
breakfast.

"Abbie?" she called down the stairs. "Abbie, are you
home?"

She found Abbie in the living room, watching the
horse racing. She arched an eyebrow. She remembered

Abbie had once begged their dad for a pony, but she'd never seen her watch the racing before. She'd always been hooked on her soap operas. She'd been dead jealous when Mel told her she was moving to Australia, not because of the incredible landscape or the amazing animals but because she thought Mel was going to get ahead of her on her favourite Australian soaps.

"I wouldn't even watch them without you," Mel had told her.

"You have to!" Abbie had cried. "So you can give me the spoilers!"

They had both laughed and hugged and then hugged again. Mel had been so excited then, impatient to start her adventure.

She watched Abbie now. She appeared to be totally mesmerised. She had the TV on at full volume, the commentator screaming his excitement into the room. It was a curious sight to behold.

"You want a sandwich?" she shouted over the din.

"Okay." Abbie didn't once look up from the screen. "Come on, Prince Charming! Come on!"

Mel paused in the doorway, watching with mild amusement as Abbie punched the air with her fist. "C'mon! C'mon!"

She padded into the kitchen and assembled the sandwiches. She couldn't make her speciality, as there was no salami, so she had to settle for cheese and pickle. She found some crisps in the cupboard and sprinkled some onto each plate, punctuating the dish with a pickled onion. It was her little joke because Abbie hated pickled onions, so it had to be done.

She carried the plates back into the living room and handed one to Abbie before settling in the armchair. She thought she would fling the onion at her, the way she used to, but she barely even looked at it. Her eyes remained glued to the screen as she ate. It appeared to be a different race now.

"Who are you cheering for?" Mel asked.

"The Flying Frenchman is good, but he's already had two races, so I reckon Bullseye for the win."

Mel shook her head, impressed she knew so much. They each took a bite of their sandwiches and watched the horses gallop down the field. The whole thing was over so fast, Mel missed it. Not so the commentator, who was shouting and screaming like he'd just won the lottery. It gave Mel a headache.

She crammed the rest of her sandwich into her mouth and glanced across at Abbie. The onion was no longer on her plate. She must have hidden it to mess with her. Perhaps she planned to throw it at her when she was least expecting it. Well, Mel would be ready. She was about to get up when her phone beeped. Peter had left her another voicemail. *For god's sake.* When was he going to leave her alone?

She headed upstairs and dug around in her cases until she found her noise-cancelling headphones. She was going to have to unpack properly at some point, but right now, she just couldn't face it. She lost herself in her work again, moving from the bed to the desk. Spinning around in the swivel chair helped her think.

She'd had enough by nine that evening and felt the urge to get out of the house. Abbie didn't seem to have moved from the sofa all day. She was watching motor racing now, the cars zooming round the track at breakneck speed. Mel peered round the living room door.

"You want to go to the Duck?"

"Nah."

Mel stuck out her lower lip, but Abbie didn't respond.

She perched on the edge of the sofa. "Is something wrong?"

"Nope." Abbie didn't so much as look in her direction.

"Come on, you can tell me!"

"Will you stop bugging me? I'm trying to watch this."

Mel knew when to back off. She retreated to the kitchen, where she found Otto huddled under the table. Perhaps the noise offended him too.

THE NEXT DAY was no better. From the moment she got up, Abbie planted herself in front of the TV. The motor racing was on again. The sounds of the engines got on Mel's nerves. For goodness' sake, didn't she have something better to do?

"Do you fancy taking me out on the boat later?" she asked.

"The weather's not right," Abbie said.

"Well, then how about we head to the Duck for lunch?" she suggested, but Abbie had turned up the volume and didn't appear to hear.

Mel stood her ground for a moment, in half a mind to snatch the remote and toss it across the room, but what was the point? If Abbie didn't want to spend time with her, she couldn't make her. It felt odd though, almost as if they'd switched places. Normally, it was Abbie who came up with things for them to do.

She studied her sister for a moment, trying to work out what was going on with her. It was weird – autumn was what Abbie had always referred to as the 'party season'. She had lots of friends, many of whom worked in the leisure industry as she did, tour guides, holiday reps and the like. She'd never been short of an invitation or two, but now Mel came to think about it, she hadn't heard Abbie's phone beep once since she'd been home. Her sister had always been a social butterfly, flitting from friend to friend, boyfriend to boyfriend, but the invitations seemed to have dried up.

She took her coffee into the garden, where Otto was sitting under the plastic table. She picked up a tennis ball and lobbed it, smiling as the dog tore across the lawn like his life depended on it. She threw it again and then wrinkled up her nose. There had to be at least half a dozen dog turds on the lawn. Ugh. She went and found the pooper scooper and scooped them off the grass. The smell was vile. It took a few minutes to bag them and dispose of them in the wheelie bin, and the smell lingered. She turned on the outside tap and worked up a lather with the soap. If Abbie would just walk the dog more often, they wouldn't have this problem. *God, that smell!*

"What ya doing?"

Abbie stood in the doorway, her lip curled in an unreadable expression.

"Otto's been turding up the garden," Mel said.

Abbie shuddered.

"I like what you've done with the place," she said in a more conciliatory tone. "The borders are looking great. It must have taken a lot of work to get it like this?"

Abbie nodded. "Yeah. Yeah, it has."

She stepped out into the garden, hands deep inside her pockets. They walked around the garden together, Mel admiring the flowers and trees. At the very end of the garden was a strong fence that led out onto the coastal path. Abbie pushed the little gate open.

"You won't believe how bad the erosion's got. I've told the council, but they still haven't sent anyone. Come and see."

Mel followed, shutting the gate behind her to keep Otto safely in the garden. Technically, the coastal path was a right of way for hikers, but it barely got any traffic. Part of the cliff had fallen into the sea, but there was still room enough to walk as long as you didn't wander too close to the edge. The view was spectacular. Waves danced in and out of the beach below, and she could make out ships on the horizon.

"Remember when we used to play out here?" she said, holding onto the strong trunk of an alder tree as she made her way past. "Mum and Dad would have had a fit if they'd known."

"You really have to watch your step, don't you?" Abbie said, walking on ahead.

She seemed to have forgotten she was supposed to be showing Mel the erosion. Instead they embarked on some sort of power walk. Abbie was clearly feeling energetic after all the racing she'd been watching. Mel rubbed her hands together. They were still damp from the cold water.

Abbie turned and waved to her to hurry up, then scurried off even faster. Mel followed as best she could, but she was beginning to get a bit freaked out by the proximity to the cliff edge.

"Abbie, slow down!" she called, but Abbie kept up the pace, striding confidently ahead.

Mel took care not to look over the edge. She was all right as long as she didn't look.

Her sister was almost running now, navigating the narrow path like a goat. She rounded the corner and disappeared from view. Mel knew she was just out of sight, but that didn't stop her from worrying. The path was getting steeper, and the ground was slippery with moss. A gust of wind reminded her of how precarious it was. One foot wrong and you'd go over the cliff…

"Abbie? Abbie!"

Waves lashed against the perilous rocks below.

Just keep going. Don't look down.

As she rounded the corner, Abbie jumped out at her. "Boo!"

"Argh!" Mel felt herself skid. Cold fear clutched at her heart as her right foot left the path. She grabbed onto Abbie, every sense screaming inside her head as Abbie also staggered and then righted herself. She pushed Mel away, and instinctively, Mel threw herself to the ground, landing on her bottom in the dirt. Abbie dropped down too and sat there, laughing hysterically and clutching her side.

"Jesus, that was close. We nearly went over!"

Mel didn't feel like laughing. She felt flushed and angry and perilously close to tears. Abbie clambered to her feet and put out a hand to help her up, but Mel scrambled free. She looked at her sister sharply. Abbie clearly thought Mel was making a big deal out of nothing. Mel struggled to contain her rage. She could have died. They both could. She marched swiftly back towards the house, still mindful not to look down, and this time, she set the pace.

6

M el still felt a little shaky as she returned to the house. She didn't feel truly safe until she reached the garden gate, and even then, she was very conscious of Abbie behind her, right on her heels.

It was strange, she thought as she let herself back into the house, up until now, they'd always been on the same wavelength, always found the same things funny. Like the time they'd gone canoeing with the Girl Guides and Abbie had got a bit overexcited and made her canoe capsize. She'd righted herself no problem, but when she came back up, she had a huge clump of seaweed in her hair, and Mel was laughing too much to tell her. Abbie hadn't even known what she was laughing at, but she'd started laughing too while everyone else just sat there, completely po-faced. Friends had smiled knowingly, and the instructor had said, "Must be a twin thing." Mel had liked that. It had made her feel special.

She didn't feel much of a special bond now though. She didn't know what was up with Abbie, but she was really getting on her nerves. She stomped up the stairs, back to the sanctity of her room and slammed her door.

Mum! she wanted to yell. *Abbie's not playing nicely.*

She returned to her laptop and tried to lose herself in her work. The clifftop walk had been a total nightmare, but even before that, they weren't clicking the way they usually did. Normally, they talked nonstop, at least, Abbie did. But this time, they both seemed to have run out of things to say. She couldn't work it out. Was Abbie holding some sort of grudge, or was this just what happened as you approached your forties?

Her stomach rumbled, reminding her she hadn't eaten. Stretching out her limbs, she flumped back downstairs and cleared her throat. Swallowing her anger, she tried again.

"Do you want tacos for dinner tonight? I can make my top-secret guacamole."

Abbie pulled a face. "I've eaten so many kettle chips I could puke."

"Suit yourself."

There was practically no food in the house, certainly nothing as exotic as fresh avocados. She would have to pop to the shop.

"You need anything?" she called to Abbie as she pulled on her boots. Abbie didn't even bother to answer. What the hell was wrong with her? If she didn't know better, she'd say she was on drugs, but Abbie had always had very strong views on that subject. It seemed unlikely she'd changed that much.

Mel stomped out the door. Her spirits were low as she trudged down the path to the shop, and they didn't improve much once she got there. She felt the shopkeeper watching her as she browsed.

"Do you have any avocados?" she asked.

"No."

Her shoulders sagged. What had she expected? She should have gone to Asda, but she didn't have a car, and she wasn't covered on Abbie's insurance. She needed to get her own car, but it would have to wait until she got her bonus. She'd get a convertible, she promised herself. Not that the English weather really called for it, but she'd always wanted one, and Peter had always talked her out of it.

She gave up on tacos and settled on a chicken korma ready meal instead, plus a couple of bottles of lager. She grabbed a small bottle of Prosecco for Abbie too. She didn't know what was going on with her, but she sensed she needed cheering up.

She paid the man at the counter and tried not to stare too hard as he counted out her change. He wore a black woollen jumper and thin fingerless gloves. His eyes were dark and penetrating. Could he be the intruder? she wondered. She tilted her chin upwards, challenging him to meet her eye, but he continued to fiddle with something behind the cash register, as though the pricing gun was more important than she was.

"Thanks," she said brightly as he handed over her receipt, and he nodded, without once uttering a word. He seemed a little sullen, but perhaps she would be too if she worked here.

Twenty minutes later, she sat at the kitchen table, absorbed in her work. The microwave pinged, and she jumped up to get her curry. She pulled out the tray and looked down at the bright yellow mush. She must have cooked it for too long because it had shrunk down to a baby-sized portion, and the plastic tray was bent in the middle. She attempted to eat it anyway but couldn't finish more than a few forkfuls. The lager went down better, although Otto kept pawing at the bin like he hadn't been fed. She went to the cupboard but couldn't find any more of his tins.

"Just a mo," she told the mournful dog.

She shouted over the din of the TV: "Are we out of dog food?"

"What?"

"Are we out of dog food?"

"I don't know. Are we?"

Abbie continued to watch the TV while Mel had to contend with Otto sniffing pathetically at her leftovers.

"Poor mutt!"

She opened the fridge and found a packet of frankfurter sausages in the salad tray. There were only two left, but she chopped them up and put them in a bowl for him. It was hardly an appropriate dinner, but she couldn't stand the hungry look on his face. While he ate, she refilled his water bowl and checked the other cupboard. They were nearly out of the dried food too. She shook her head. She couldn't understand why Abbie had got a dog if she wasn't going to look after him. She remembered the Christmas card she had sent the previous year, with a photo of her and Otto in matching Santa hats. Perhaps the novelty had worn off now he was no longer a puppy.

A little later, Abbie emerged from the living room and stuck her head in the fridge.

"I've got Prosecco if you want?" Mel said. "It's in the door."

"Cheers."

Abbie popped it open and took a glug straight from the bottle "So. You missing Oz?"

"I miss the weather."

"What about the men?"

Mel shuddered. "Don't."

"So what happened with you and Pete exactly?"

Pete?

Mel shook her head. "Things haven't been working between Peter and me for a while. I suppose it all just came to a head."

"How long had you been together? I've lost count."

"Twenty years."

"Damn, that's a long time."

"I know. Maybe that's the problem."

Abbie studied her like she was a freak exhibit in a museum. "You were bored. I get it, but now that you've got his attention, are you going to take him back?"

"No, that was never my intention."

"I reckon you should think about it. You had it pretty good with Pete, didn't you? Are you sure you want to throw it all away?"

Mel felt her chin wobble. It had taken a lot for her to leave him.

Abbie took another glug of her drink. "Pete's pretty hot, babe. You don't think you should work it out with him? You might regret it if you don't."

Really, who was Abbie to be giving her relationship advice? She'd never kept a boyfriend longer than a few weeks. There wasn't a man alive who could keep Abbie's interest, except perhaps for Jared Leto, whom she often referred to as her 'future husband'.

"What about you?" she asked, in an effort to deflect the attention away from herself. "You seeing anyone?"

Abbie let out a joyless laugh. "God no. Have you seen the talent in Weymouth? Half of them don't even have their own teeth."

Mel giggled. "They can't be that bad!"

"Well, believe me, they are. I've been out with all the half-decent ones. All that's left is the dross. Weymouth's so lame. Nothing ever happens here."

Mel eyed her with interest. "Then why are you still living here?"

"Oh, you know. I've got my boat, but you're not like me, I think you need someone to take care of you. Someone like Pete."

"Are you taking the piss?"

"No! No, I mean it. Come on, look at the state of you. You're going to turn into one of those crazy cat women."

"There's a plan."

Abbie was like sand, Mel thought. The way she got into her pores. She knew her better than anyone, no matter how long they were apart, and she also knew exactly how to wind her up.

She was still really hungry. The chicken curry had done nothing to dent her appetite.

"I'm going to make a sandwich. Do you want one?"

"Okay. Just don't put anything weird in it."

"Like what?"

"I don't know. You've been in Australia too long. Don't they eat Vegemite with everything?"

Mel rifled through the fridge. They were out of cheese again. Abbie must have finished it, and she'd fed the last of the sausages to Otto.

"Sod it. We really need to get some proper shopping in. Do you realise we still don't have any dog food?"

"Really? Oh, crap!"

"Yeah. You really need to get some."

She eyed her sister for a moment, wondering why she wasn't more concerned about Otto. She had been so excited to get a pup, and now she treated him like an afterthought. She'd always had such an affinity with animals. It wasn't like her.

"In the meantime, I'm going to order some takeaway."

Abbie nodded, and Mel rummaged through the

kitchen drawer for the fast-food leaflets. Only they weren't there. Of course they weren't. Abbie had chucked everything out. She'd have to look it up online.

She ordered a four-cheese pizza and a completely unnecessary banoffee pie. When the food came, Abbie was only too happy to help her wade through it. She didn't offer to chip in though, Mel noticed.

"How are your friends?" she asked as lightly as she could manage. "What are Olivia and Sharon up to?"

Abbie shrugged. "Don't see much of them these days."

"Why not?"

"Dunno. People move on, don't they?"

"So who do you hang round with now?"

"Whoever. Why do you ask?"

"No reason."

Mel sank her teeth into her slice of pizza and racked her brain for another topic of conversation. Things were awkward between them, even in the rhythm of their speech. It felt stilted and unnatural, but she wasn't sure why. All she knew was that it made her feel very sad. She'd thought that no matter how long she left it between visits, she could pick up again with Abbie, just as she always had, but perhaps she'd left it a bit too long this time. It felt like there had been a rip in the very core of their relationship, and she didn't know how to repair it.

She hid behind her glass and watched her twin from across the table. Abbie had aged since she'd last seen her. Crow's feet had appeared around her eyes, and she'd noticed that her voice had deepened slightly, losing its youthful sweetness. Mel supposed she must be showing signs of aging too, but she was sure hers weren't so pronounced.

"Cheers for the feed," said Abbie. She rose from the

table and headed straight back to the living room. It was a matter of seconds before the TV blared again.

Mel cleared away the pizza boxes. Four years, she reminded herself. People changed. She could see that it was going to take more than a takeaway pizza to get their relationship back on track.

After dinner, Mel returned to her room and watched a film on her laptop. She'd have liked to watch something downstairs, on the big TV, but Abbie was watching the racing again, and there was no way Mel was going to sit through that. Her eyes were starting to close as the film finished, and just as she had resigned herself to going to bed for the night, her phone beeped.

She glanced at it.

Are you still up? I can't sleep without you.

"Leave me alone, Peter!"

It must be morning where he was. He should be at work. At least, she hoped he was. She didn't want him guilt-tripping her like this. She wanted him to get on with his life. She switched off her phone and climbed into bed. She didn't want to think about him. She resented the way he wormed his way into her thoughts.

"MELLY!"

She turned, surprised to see Peter jogging down the street behind her.

She wiped her sweaty palms on her jacket and forced her lips to smile.

"Where are you going?" His voice sounded funny, as though he were speaking to her through the bathroom door.

"Just taking a walk."

"But, Melly..."

"What?"

"Don't you think you should stay home? Get some rest? You've been working so hard."

"I'm just getting some fresh air."

"And some more stimulants?" He nodded towards the shop on the end of the street.

"That too."

"Come on, Melly, I'm taking you back to bed."

He tried to take her hand, but she shook it free.

"I have a lot of work to do. I just need something. Some energy drinks to get me through."

"You need to take it easy, Melly. You don't want to get sick again."

"I won't. I'm fine."

He seized her by the shoulder. Made her look deep into his eyes. "Melly, I'm scared for you."

She felt her shoulders droop. The fight left her body as he took her hand and bundled her back into the house. Once there, he insisted she lie down on the sofa and brought her a cup of chamomile tea. He was being so kind and thoughtful, but she felt like he was stifling her, sitting right on her chest.

She held the tea and watched the little wisps of vapour as they escaped into the atmosphere.

"Listen, there's going to be live music at the Linden Tree tonight…"

His brow furrowed. "The Linden Tree?"

"Yeah, you know that little bar on the way to China Town?"

"I don't think it's a good idea," he said quickly. "Besides, tonight's our movie night. I've already picked a film."

She clenched her jaw. "I'd really like to go to the bar."

He closed his eyes and opened them again. "It'll be too noisy. Full of young kids. We'd feel out of place. Why don't we watch the film as planned? I've already set up the take-away order online so we don't have to bother about it later."

She let out a sigh. "Sounds like you've got it all planned."

"It'll be fun," he assured her. "Come on, drink your tea before it gets cold. It'll make you feel better."

She did drink the tea, but she didn't feel any better. She felt like her world was getting smaller and smaller, and it was all she could do not to scream.

OTTO WOKE her the next morning by dribbling down her neck. She pushed him away and tried to go back to sleep, but the dog wouldn't have it. He stood by her bed, pawing and whining until she sat up.

"For Christ's sake!"

She squinted at the clock. It was only eight. She really could have done with a few more hours' sleep.

She flung back her duvet and trudged into the bathroom. She splashed water on her face and dried off. She should probably take a shower, but it felt like too much effort. What did it matter how she looked? She had work to do.

She padded downstairs, not bothering to change out of her navy blue jogging bottoms. Otto barked with excitement as she unlocked the front door and took a cautious look up and down the street. There was no one around, not even the old bloke across the way. So why did she feel so watched?

She and Otto trotted down the footpath, past the Duck and into town. Otto led her all the way down to the beach, which was very blustery today. The light rain was still a bit of a novelty after the heat of Sydney.

Otto let out an excited bark. A deflated beach ball bobbed up and down like a dismembered head in the waves.

"Here, boy, this way!"

The water looked a little rough, so Mel needed to keep him distracted. She poked the sand and unearthed an old flip-flop. It was brightly coloured, patterned in the shape of the Union Jack. She picked it up and lobbed it. Otto ran to fetch it; then he brought it back to her, dropping it at her feet. She threw it again, further this time, and once again he returned it, his expression solemn, as if this was the most important work he'd ever done. He still had it in his mouth as they walked back up the hill and stopped at the bakers to pick up fresh bread. He wouldn't let it go, even as she popped into the corner shop to buy more dog food and other essentials, since Abbie seemed determined to run down the cupboards.

The neighbourhood was a little more alive on their return. One brave bloke was even mowing his lawn in spite of the wind. Otto trailed behind her now, as though he'd used up all of his energy. She slipped off her muddy trainers and left them on the front porch; then she took each of Otto's paws and wiped them on the mat. They could really do with a sheep dip outside the door, she mused. She could hear Abbie's voice, loud and cheerful, as though she was entertaining someone inside. She released Otto, and he rocketed into the living room, where Abbie was sitting at the computer. It looked like she was in the middle of a Zoom. Mel froze as she saw whom she was talking to. It was Peter. *Her* Peter. What the hell was Abbie doing, talking to him?

7

"**A**bbie, what the…"

She couldn't finish her sentence. Peter's piercing grey eyes stared out at her. She felt trapped, unable to move. No matter how angry she was, it was always impossible to reason with this man. He never shouted or lost his temper. He always remained calm and in control. He had a way of making himself seem so…reasonable. And a way of making her look so off the wall.

Abbie had the decency to look apologetic. She hung her head, a little too dramatically.

"Sorry, Mel, but you and Pete need to talk. You can't keep this up forever."

Can't I?

She would have loved to tell Abbie where to go, but it was awkward with Peter right there, watching them.

"How've you been?" he asked softly.

"Fine."

She feasted on the sight of him, taking in his five o'clock shadow. His face had taken on a new intensity; his cheeks had become a series of sharp lines and angles. Clearly her leaving had hit him hard. Perhaps he hadn't been expecting it, but he should have. This had been coming for a long time.

"When are you coming home?" he asked.

She felt a knot tighten in her stomach. Surely he'd got the message by now. His jaw was set in a manner that could not be argued with, so she merely shook her head.

He was still talking, but she couldn't take in the words he was saying. He was doing what he always did, charming her, confusing her. Making it seem like she was the one with the problem.

"What were you thinking, running off to England? Is this really how you think a grown woman should solve her problems?"

She thought of the man from the beach. Recalled lying with him in their bed, thrilled at the novelty of his body. His smooth, surfer's skin, his bright, playful eyes. She'd never felt so spontaneous, so alive. And then Peter had walked in. He wasn't supposed to be home yet. He wasn't meant to see, but a part of her was glad. She'd done the unthinkable, and that would be the end of it, the end of her and Peter. Except, incredibly, Peter still hadn't got the message. What did she have to do to convince him?

"I didn't want to hurt you," she said.

But she had, hadn't she?

Peter's face was solemn. "I'm not convinced you know what you want. I don't think you've thought this through. You just upped and left."

She opened her mouth to object, but how could she? He was right. It had all seemed so simple when she'd packed her bags, but now, seeing him again, hearing his voice? She didn't know what to think. Was she wrong to think it wasn't worth fighting for their marriage?

Memories of their wedding day floated into her head. It had been a wonderful day, with all her favourite people around her. Abbie had been her bridesmaid, but for once she hadn't stolen the show. Mel had been the centre of attention for the first and only time in her entire life, and then Peter had surprised her, pulling a crisp white piece of paper from his pocket.

"If it's okay, I've written a few vows of my own."

Her mum had swooned. Aunt Dot had swooned. She was pretty sure every woman in the church had swooned. Tears had slid down her cheeks as he'd clasped her trembling hands in his.

"Melly, my goddess. When I look at you today, I see not only the girl I fell in love with, but my future, my wife. I promise to honour and protect you. I promise to make you coffee every morning and take the rubbish out every week. I promise to cook for you because, frankly, everything you make tastes of boiled onions, and most importantly, I promise to obliterate any spiders that sneak into our house. I promise to share my life with you, starting next month, with our new life down under, but most of all, I promise to love you. Not just now while you're young and beautiful, but also later when you're old and wrinkled as a prune."

There was a ripple of applause during which she'd thought about her reply.

"Well, if I'd known you were going to say such sweet words, I would have prepared something," she'd said with a smile. "Peter, I…promise not to put the spoons in the fork section of the cutlery drawer. I know you hate that, and I promise never to abandon you at a party, or force you to make small talk with people you don't know."

She caught his eye, drawing him in.

"I promise to stick by you when times are hard and

pull you up when life gets you down. I promise never to go to bed on an argument, but most of all, I promise never to take you to Ikea, ever, ever again."

Peter had pulled her into a hug, and the vicar had had to break them apart, suggesting gently that they might like to exchange the rings now. She'd loved that day. The honesty of it, the spontaneity. Their love had seemed invincible, and she'd felt ready to take on the world. Difficult as it had been to leave her family and friends behind in England, she had been excited about their imminent move to Australia, and she'd considered herself the luckiest woman in the world.

"Mel?" Peter said now. "You've gone terribly quiet."

Of course she had because that was what she always did, wasn't it? Retreated back into her shell.

"Bad connection," she lied, ignoring the look Abbie gave her.

"It's okay this end. Do you want me to call back?"

"No! No, that's okay. I can hear you now."

"I miss you, Melly."

"I…" She was supposed to say she missed him too, but she didn't want to give him false hope.

"This is just how she was after your parents…" Peter said, looking at Abbie now.

Abbie nodded with understanding. She was still there, a third wheel in their conversation. Mel wished she would leave them to it.

"I'm worried about you," he said bluntly; his eyes seemed to zoom in on the dark shadows under her eyes. "You remember she had that 'wobble'," he murmured to Abbie. "She didn't take proper care of herself. She just fell to bits."

Mel felt her anger rising. The way he talked, you'd

think she'd gone completely off her trolley. The 'wobble' wasn't anything like as bad as he made it out to be. And why was he talking about her like she wasn't there?

"Our parents had just died. I was grieving!"

He smiled in that slightly patronising way of his. "It was more than that, Mel. You were hurting yourself. You took too many sleeping pills."

"That was a mistake…"

"I should have spotted the signs. You're having another stress incident, aren't you?"

She felt herself shaking slightly, with rage and indignation. "I'm not stressed," she spat. "I'm perfectly in control of my mind."

She glanced at Abbie, but she didn't say anything. Peter sat with his arms folded, as if he'd somehow proved his point.

"Well, I won't keep you," he said, much to her relief. "I just want you to know that I'm here for you, Melly. You can call me any time, night or day. You know that, don't you?"

"Yeah, right."

His face froze in place for a moment, and she felt like picking up the monitor and hurling it across the room.

"He really cares about you, doesn't he?" said Abbie once he had gone.

Mel shook her head, her body hot with anger. "I can't believe you set me up like that!"

"I had to. He was flipping out over there. He was desperate to talk to you."

"Hmm." She stared into her sister's eyes, trying to work out what the hell was going on in that blonde head of hers. "Do me a favour, Abbie, and butt out of my relationship."

Abbie's mouth fell open. She looked like she was going to say something; then she got a haughty look on her face and sloped off to the sofa, no doubt to watch more racing.

Mel stomped up to her room, feeling every bit like a moody teenager. Before Abbie's decluttering, she'd kept a dartboard on the back of her bedroom door. Dart throwing had been a great way of letting off steam, but it was gone now, along with the rest of her stuff. She walked over to her desk and picked up a small triangular gaming dice and lobbed it against the back of the door instead. It made a satisfying clonk. *Bloody Peter and bloody Abbie.* Why couldn't they both leave her alone?

Otto was fast asleep on her bed, his head tucked up comfortably on her pillow, like a wolf pretending to be a grandmother. He smiled to himself in his sleep and looked ridiculously content. She wished she could sleep like that. She paced around the room, stressing about the Zoom. How dare Peter suggest she was losing her mind, just because she'd left him! The bloody nerve of the man.

The doorbell sounded downstairs. She walked onto the landing, but Abbie was already dealing with it, accepting a parcel from a postwoman.

"All right, all right," Abbie said, signing the woman's handheld device.

"And your full name, please?"

"What business is it of yours?"

"It…it's on the form. I'm supposed to ask."

"Just give me my fucking package!"

Mel was mortified. The poor woman looked young, barely out of school. She was bright red and flustered. Mel blinked as Abbie practically shut the door in her face, then stalked back to the living room, the thin parcel tucked under her arm.

Mel was filled with unease. Once again she found herself watching her twin from the doorway. Abbie must have sensed her presence, because she swung round and glared at her. "What are you gawping at?"

For a moment, Mel thought she was joking; then she threw her hands up. Abbie had always been a little huffy and self-centred, but she'd been able to laugh at herself too. It wasn't like her to blow up like that, not without good reason.

"Something wrong?" she asked lightly.

"Not with me," Abbie snarled.

Mel gulped back a bubble of pain. If anyone should be angry, it was her. She was the one who'd been tricked into a Zoom call with her ex. She watched her twin as she plonked herself back down in front of the TV. Was this what Abbie was like now? Had she changed so much their relationship could not be saved? Mel shook her head. Her happy homecoming was crumbling around her, and she was powerless to stop it.

She snuck downstairs, grabbing her jacket from the bannister and forcing her feet into her trainers. She still had work to do, but she was much too upset to concentrate. Before she could shut the door, Otto raced out and barked in excitement at the prospect of another walk.

"All right, boy. I suppose you can come too."

She didn't bother to ask Abbie if it was okay to take her dog. She didn't seem to care about him at all. Clipping on Otto's lead, she explored her old neighbourhood, taking solace in the quiet streets. Otto tugged on his lead, dragging her towards a big muddy puddle. She pulled him away, but he still succeeded in making a splash, and a blob of mud hit her right on the nose. She turned round to tell him off, but it was impossible to be angry with him when he looked so damned pleased with himself.

She'd thought they might get coffee at the café on the corner, but apparently it had closed down. She saw that the local park had had a brand new climbing frame added and a great big spider swing. Nothing stayed the same forever. Everything was subject to change.

The cottage next to the park had a 'for sale' sign up. It got her thinking, that sign. Maybe she could rent somewhere. It didn't have to be far, but it would be great to have a place of her own. She had thought sharing the big house with Abbie would be fun, but it wasn't turning out that way.

The more she walked, the more sense it made. If she had her own place, she could stay up late without worrying about disturbing Abbie, and she wouldn't feel like a stranger in her own living room. She could watch whatever the hell she wanted instead of having the racing on twenty-four seven. Best of all, she could be independent again, because that was what she really needed. It was high time she asserted her independence, and she could hardly do that when she was living with the twin from hell.

She went straight up to her room when she got home and logged onto Right Move to look at what houses were available. She wanted something nearby, some-where small and self-contained. She was probably going to need to rent, but it wouldn't hurt to look at what was available to buy too. She'd want to buy somewhere eventually once Peter bought her out of their house in Sydney.

She entered her details. She wanted to remain in Weymouth for the time being, close enough that she could still see Abbie. Perhaps they would get along better once they weren't sharing the same space. She entered their postcode, and one house came up right away. It was probably the one she had seen on the corner. Out of nosiness more than anything else, she clicked. The décor was in neutral colours, much like their own house. All beige carpets with white or cream walls. The layout looked similar too, with the guest room on the ground floor and a dining room that was on the opposite side of the house from the kitchen. It had a large living room, with a woodburning stove and patio doors that led into a secure, private back garden with scenic views of the sea.

The garden was really similar. The two houses must have been designed by the same person. She zoomed in on the front lawn and saw there was a car in the driveway. Was that...Surely not? It looked like Abbie's car. It even had the same bumper sticker on the back. She craned her neck as she scanned through the specifications: five bedrooms, three bathrooms, bay windows. No address, but if she wasn't very much mistaken, that was *their* house. Had Abbie put it up for sale?

8

This couldn't be right. There had to be a simple explanation. The estate agent had somehow mixed their house up with the one on the corner, the one that was actually for sale. They did look rather similar on the outside, with their white walls and sloping driveways.

Abbie was still downstairs, watching telly. Mel heard a roar of approval: apparently the car she was rooting for had won its race. She chewed her lip so hard it almost bled. Could Abbie have put their house on the market without telling her? No, it wasn't possible. She'd never do that. *Would she?*

She was still making excuses for Abbie while she dialled the number listed on Right Move.

"Oh, hello, yes, this is Melanie…Otto. I'm enquiring about the house you've got listed in Weymouth. The five-bed in Evergreen Crescent."

Feeling like a fool, she nonetheless held her breath as she waited for the cheery estate agent to check the details. She hated making these sorts of calls. She hated estate agents, with their slick hair and smooth talk. They reminded her of snakes wiggling their tongues to attract prey. She gritted her teeth as this one rabbited on about the weather. If there was one thing she couldn't stand, it was small talk, but she had to get this cleared up. She had to know what was going on.

"Yes," the estate agent said after a pause. "Number fifteen Evergreen Crescent. A gorgeous property, that one. Really spacious, a quiet but convenient location, ample parking, ideal for families."

Mel's heart plummeted in her chest. "It's definitely for sale, then?"

"It is. You'd better get in quick if you're interested. We had an open house there last weekend, and there's been a lot of interest. In fact, there's already been an offer. Can't tell you how much for though…"

The estate agent gave an irritating chuckle, but she couldn't find anything funny about the situation. Abbie was attempting to sell the house out from under her, her own flesh and blood.

She hung up the phone and thundered down the stairs to the living room. She stormed over to the TV and switched it off, much to Abbie's outrage.

"Oy! I was watching that!"

Mel stared at her sister, unable to believe she was actually about to have this conversation.

"When were you going to tell me you're trying to sell the house?"

Abbie's nostrils flared the way they did when she got defensive.

"If you must know, my business is struggling, and I'm in a bloody bind, all right?"

Mel took a step back. "I thought you said the business was doing fine?"

"Well, it's not, which you'd know if you'd been around. I'm going to lose everything I've worked for if I can't raise some cash, so I thought 'why not sell the house?' I didn't know you were going to come back."

Mel fought to keep her cool. "When were you going to tell me? This is my house too. Mum and Dad left it to both of us."

Abbie's bottom lip quivered. "I just wanted to see if there was any interest. Listen, there's a lot of money tied up in this house. We could get a million pounds for it and split it fifty-fifty. Think what you could do with that money!"

Mel sank down to the floor. So it was true. She couldn't believe it. "What about the remortgage?" she asked quietly.

Abbie looked startled for a moment.

"We remortgaged it when you bought your boat, if you remember."

They'd done it as soon as their inheritance came through so that Abbie could achieve her lifelong dream. Mel hadn't minded helping her out; after all, she wasn't even living in the house. She hadn't known she would want to return.

"Of course I remember!" Abbie snapped, but she was looking at her with a slightly puzzled expression. "How much do you think we'd get, then, if we sold it for a million?"

"I'd have thought you'd have worked that out already?"

Abbie's lips twisted slightly. "I need to double-check." She stared at the wall for a moment, seemed to think hard before she spoke again. "Selling the house would still get me out of a hole. Come on, Mel. Don't be selfish here. You know how much my business means to me."

"Me? Selfish?"

"Yes! I'm the one who's been living here. The one

who's been paying all the bills. It's just been me rattling round this big house. It was too big for me on my own, and it's still too big, even for the two of us. Why not sell it and get somewhere smaller so I can save my boat and my business?"

Mel shook her head from side to side, feeling like she was going to explode. She clenched and unclenched her fists. She couldn't shake the feeling that Abbie was trying to sell the house out from under her.

Abbie flopped down next to her.

"Look, I haven't gone behind your back. Honest, I haven't. I just wanted to find out what we could get for it if we sell. I was going to present you with all the facts. Then it all moved so fast I didn't know what to do. And look at you. You've just left Peter. You're a total mess. I didn't want to lay something else at your door."

Mel swallowed. She was too angry to respond reasonably right now. She dragged herself to her feet and shuffled up the stairs to her room, where she collapsed on the bed and stared at the newly painted walls. The whole house looked as if they'd never lived there. Perhaps that was Abbie's intention. Painting it neutral, removing all their stuff, all the traces of their family so that anyone could imagine themselves living here. It was like a blank canvas.

A tear trickled down her face as she thought of everything that had happened. Why hadn't Abbie come to her if things were so dire? Why did she have to behave like this? All the secrecy, all the sneaking around. She wanted to go back downstairs, but she couldn't bear to be in the same room as Abbie right now. Even without the crap she watched on TV, it was like they had nothing in common anymore. All those years of shared memories and family traditions seemed to have faded into insignificance. But not going down, that just added to the tension. She was sure Abbie was sitting down there, resenting her just as much. They had to find a compromise. One that did not involve selling the house.

Eventually, she heaved herself off the bed. She was the older sister by sixteen minutes. She was going to have to make the first move.

She found Abbie on the sofa, eating a Cornetto, a blob of ice cream running down her chin. She was watching a different sport on TV. It looked like curling.

"Can you turn that down for a minute so we can talk?" she asked grimly.

Abbie reached for the remote. The players paused mid action, their butts sticking comically in the air.

"What is it?" she asked, looking bored.

Mel ground her teeth. Abbie wasn't making this easy for her. "If selling the house is what you really want, then I will think about it."

She looked Abbie in the eye, but she didn't mean a word of it. She could be sneaky too if she liked. Pretending to think about it would give her some breathing space. It would be a stalling tactic while she tried to talk Abbie round.

"Oh, thank you, thank you!" Abbie came and wrapped her arms around her and held her close. Mel wasn't a particularly tactile person, but she'd always found her twin's hugs to be soothing. Perhaps the close proximity took her back to the womb. But today, even the hug felt manufactured somehow. Not genuine, but designed to manipulate, to pull at her heartstrings and make her concede.

"We've been made an offer, and I think there will be more," Abbie told her. "The estate agent said there are a couple of people who seemed interested. With any luck, we'll have a bidding war on our hands."

Mel nodded, but she didn't want anything of the kind. The house was worth far more than money to her; it was the house they'd grown up in, their family home. Their remaining connection to their parents.

She released herself from her sister's grasp and walked over to the window, to look out at the front garden. Dad's roses were still going strong. They were both beautiful and hardy, with their peachy pink petals and razor-sharp thorns. Her eyes flickered to the neatly mowed grass. It had grown a little even in the few days since she'd been home, and looked lush and vibrant from the rain. Her gaze settled on the curious little hole in the middle of the lawn, and she realised with a thump what had caused it.

Birdfeeder, my arse.

It had been made by one of those 'for sale' signs. Abbie must have planted it right in the middle of the lawn, and then she'd taken it down again when she heard Mel was coming home.

9

The man Mel spoke to from the Citizen's Advice Bureau was so gentle and well meaning that she found it hard to hang up on him, even after he'd prattled on for half an hour.

"Thank you so much, but I couldn't possibly take up any more of your valuable time. There must be other people who could use your advice."

He didn't take the hint though. He sounded truly scandalised at what Abbie had done.

Mel eyed her laptop as he talked. In this incarnation, the assassin had transformed himself into a police officer and was now walking up to her, ready to strike.

"The gist of it is that you should stay in the house, no matter what," the man from Citizen's Advice droned on.

"Yes, I intend to."

"Because legally speaking, it would be best if you stay put rather than renting another place, at least until this dispute with your sister is resolved."

"Yes," Mel agreed. "Just as I thought. Thank you very much for your time. Gotta go."

She hung up before she could get pulled into any more of his musings. He was a nice man, clearly lonely. But she didn't have time.

Next, she rang the estate agent. Luckily, she reached a different one from the one she'd spoken to before. A man this time. She apprised him as calmly as she could of the situation, silently thanking him for the lack of scandal in his voice. Perhaps they heard this kind of thing all the time at the estate agents. Perhaps Abbie's behaviour was the norm.

"So you see, even if my sister accepts an offer, you cannot go ahead with it unless I give my permission."

"We wouldn't dream of it."

She'd insulted his professional integrity now. Nice one. Come to think of it, she didn't know why she hadn't just told him that the house was not going to be sold at any price. Perhaps she was afraid Abbie would find out. The TV was not on downstairs; she couldn't hear it booming through the floorboards, which might well mean that Abbie was lurking in the hallway or listening at the door. Then she heard the clinking of mugs on the stairs, and the door flew open. Abbie came in carrying two steaming mugs of tea.

"Thanks," Mel said begrudgingly.

Abbie set the mugs down and perched on the desk, her legs swinging out in front of her. She hadn't shaved in a while, Mel noticed. Little tufts of blonde hair poked out from under her cropped leggings. She clearly didn't have any social plans, then. She never went out looking anything but perfect.

"It occurs to me," Abbie said, "there is another solution, if you're not keen to sell the house…"

Mel looked up with interest. "Oh, yeah?"

"What would you say to buying me out?"

Mel forced out a laugh. "How much money do you think I have?"

Abbie got that look on her face, the one where she resembled an angry hippo. "I know you're raking it in."

Mel shook her head. "This may come as a surprise to you, but I'm not."

Abbie narrowed her eyes. "Oh, come off it, you're a successful computer programmer..."

"Developer."

"Working for a big-arse company..."

Mel felt her shoulders tense. "I won't get my bonus until I've sorted out the bugs in *Artful Assassin*, and it's not going well, Abbie. Plus I've just left Peter. I need money to set up on my own."

"Can't he sell your house in Australia?"

"I'm not going to ask him to do that. I'm going to let him buy me out, but he hasn't got that sort of money. Not straight away. It'll take time." She dropped her gaze. "Look, if you must know, I'm not exactly on top of my game anymore. I want to take a break, maybe even a year out, and really think about what I want to do with my life. I'd like to help you. Of course I would, but I just don't have that kind of cash."

Abbie slipped off the table and walked towards the door.

"Abbie!"

She turned and looked back at her. "You could help me if you wanted, Mel. You're just being selfish. You really don't care about me, do you? I could lose the business!"

Mel felt a wrench in her gut. "I do want to help," she insisted, but it was no use, Abbie had flounced out and was now stomping down the stairs, like an irate three-year-old who'd just woken from her nap.

"Don't forget your tea!" Mel yelled, but there was no response.

Mel stared up at the old familiar ceiling. This was one part of the house Abbie hadn't messed with. She traced the shell-shaped pattern of the plaster with her eyes, just as she'd done when she was a little girl. She and Abbie had argued then too, and if she remembered rightly, it had been mostly Abbie's fault.

She stayed in her room until she was hungry; then she went downstairs, creeping past the living room so as not to alert her sister. She really wasn't in the mood for another argument.

She spotted Otto in the garden and let him in. The poor dog was shivering as she poured out some food for him. Then she heated a pan of baked beans and toasted some bread for herself.

Abbie walked in, heading straight to the cupboard for a glass. She didn't say a word as she poured herself a drink, preferring to stare out the window rather than look at Mel.

"You hungry?" Mel asked.

"Not really."

It occurred to Mel that she hadn't once seen Abbie cook since she'd come home. It was like she couldn't be bothered anymore. Abbie took her drink and returned to the living room. Straight away, Mel heard the TV go on again. It was odd. Although Abbie had always liked sports, she'd been more interested in playing them than watching them. She'd been particularly keen on volley-ball when they were at school, playing for hours on the beach with her friends, and then there had been phases of tennis and swimming. Not anymore, apparently.

Mel placed her toast on a plate and poured on the baked beans and hot sauce. She ate alone in the kitchen, with Otto at her feet. The afternoon stretched out in front of her, long and lonely. There was a time when she'd had friends in the town, but they'd moved away now, and aside from the odd Facebook 'like', she hadn't heard from any of them in years. She moped about the house, her anger welling up again as she thought about all the crap Abbie had pulled. Not just trying to sell the house, but chucking out her stuff and getting rid of Dad's harp. It wasn't hers to get rid of! It was probably worth a lot of money, that harp. Google confirmed her suspicions. A harp like that in good condition with carbon-fibre strings would probably fetch a few thousand. She marched into the living room and glared at her twin.

"What did you really do with Dad's harp?"

"I…I told you, I gave it to the Sally Army."

"Like bollocks you did. You've pawned it, haven't you? Tell me where so I can go and get it back."

Abbie's eyes twinkled. "I thought you didn't have any money?"

"It's not about the money, Abbie. That was Dad's harp. It means something. At least, it does to me."

Abbie got a petulant look on her face. "Well, you're two months too late. I'm sorry, Mel. But it's done now, so sue me."

There was a hardness in her tone that made Mel retreat. She didn't remember her sister ever being so mean, but then, they'd never quarrelled about money before. She'd been fine with Abbie remortgaging the house. She hadn't had a problem with that, knowing that it would help her to set up her own business. In fact, she'd been happy to help, and now it felt as though she was throwing it back in her face.

She fought back the tears. She needed to get out of the house again. Since she'd come back to Weymouth, she'd taken more walks than she had all year in Sydney.

Things had been tense with Peter, but she'd buried her feelings, refused to admit anything was wrong. Here, with Abbie, it was impossible to pretend, so she grabbed her coat, sank her feet into her shoes and slipped outside.

The trees swayed, naked in the wind, and an empty Coke can rolled across the street in front of her. A half-eaten apple lay discarded in the gutter, and she pulled her coat more tightly around her.

She walked briskly down the footpath, unable to smile at a couple of ramblers weighed down with heavy backpacks. She was tempted to call in at the Duck for a swift half. Maybe on the way back, she told herself. First, she'd go to the shop and get a big slab of chocolate, and she'd pick up some more dog food for Otto, since Abbie didn't seem to give a stuff about him anymore. She never would have thought her sister would be so neglectful.

The bell on the door tinkled as she walked into the corner shop. The moody man wasn't working today. A teenage girl sat behind the counter, texting on her phone. Mel picked up one of the wire baskets and began to fill it with whatever caught her eye. She grabbed a box of her favourite cereal, a jar of peanut butter, some potatoes, and a big tub of olives. As she reached for the Pedigree Chum, she felt an unsettling sensation in her spine. Somebody was watching her. She turned slowly. There was a man lurking behind the tinned carrots. He wore a long trench coat, the lapels pulled up over his face. Mel's fingers twitched as she inched a little closer. He was holding a tin out in front of him as if trying to read the ingredients. He couldn't be the intruder, could he? He looked too old, and from the way he was holding the tin, he needed glasses.

He turned suddenly towards her, making her jump.

She dropped her basket, spilling potatoes all over the shop.

"Oh, dear!"

The man bent down and handed her a spud that had rolled his way. Mel shivered as their fingers touched, but this man was far too elderly to be the person who'd broken into her house.

"Thank you," she managed, her voice little more than a whisper.

She grabbed the chocolate she'd come in for and lugged her basket over to the counter, where she set it down in front of the teenage girl.

"Everything all right?" the girl asked, glancing behind Mel at the old man.

"Yes, fine," Mel said, cheeks blazing as she rummaged in her pocket for her cash card. Perhaps Peter was closer to the mark than she'd realised. Perhaps she really was losing her mind.

10

T he kid on the skateboard looks a bit wobbly. He's trying some pretty advanced tricks and seems a bit out of his depth. She watches as he attempts another jump and barely makes it. The kid clearly has a death wish. She leaps out of his path, and he crashes into the wall. She should help him. Maybe he has something useful in that bag of his, like the Orb of Destiny. Maybe he'll give it to her if she shows him a little kindness. She approaches him carefully as he yells and writhes on the ground. The fall didn't look that bad, and it gets her Scooby sense going. Is the kid really injured, or could he be the assassin? She takes a flamethrower from her bag and hurls it over his head as a warning shot. Instantly, he morphs into a wildcat and then a dragon. His skateboard turns into a block of dynamite, and then the game freezes again.

God damn it.

ABBIE WAS SITTING at the kitchen table, flipping through a tabloid newspaper, when Mel came down for breakfast the next day.

Abbie lifted her head. "Coffee's still warm."

"Good."

Mel moved towards the machine and filled her mug. She looked in the fridge, but she'd forgotten to buy more Red Bull, so she'd have to have it without.

"Not a bad day today," Abbie said. "Might actually be sunny later."

Mel looked out the window at the pale gloom. She didn't share Abbie's assessment of the weather, but she appreciated the sentiment. It was nice to be on speaking terms again.

Abbie offered her a watery smile. Perhaps she felt bad for the way she'd behaved. Abbie had never been big on apologies, so she wasn't holding her breath in that respect, but she was grateful for the renewed warmth.

Abbie closed her newspaper. "It's such a nice day. How about you skive off work and come out on the boat with me?"

Mel broke into a grin. "I wish I could. I have far too much work to do."

"Oh, come on, a bit of fresh air will do you good."

Mel glanced out the window at the cloudy sky. "Are you sure the weather's going to hold?"

"Sure as I can be."

Mel thought of Derick barking orders at her over Discord. She was sick of taking orders, sick of being bossed around. Maybe she should take the day off. She could make up some hours in the evening so she wouldn't be totally goofing off.

Abbie was watching her, a knowing smile on her face. She knew how to twist her arm.

"Well, what are you waiting for? You need to go and get ready."

Mel scurried up the stairs and dug out her purple

fleece and some waterproof trousers. She'd have to wear her trainers again – she didn't have anything else suitable. Her laptop blinked at her from its space next to the charger, but she ignored it. She wanted her sister back, and this boat trip might be just the thing to help them reconnect.

By the time she went back downstairs, Abbie was outside, packing the boot with bottled water and fishing gear. She had the car door open and the radio blaring. Mel turned it down a few notches as subtly as she could. She didn't want to start another argument, but she'd get a splitting headache if she had to put up with that racket.

She settled into the passenger seat and searched the glove box for sweets. Abbie usually had a bag of jelly babies stashed in there, but today, it seemed she was out of luck.

"Aren't you going to put your seatbelt on?" she asked as Abbie reversed out of the driveway.

"Of course. We aren't on the main road yet, are we?"

The road was completely clear, but it still made Mel uncomfortable. You never knew when some idiot was going come up and whack you from behind. Look what had happened to their parents.

"Did they abolish the speed limit, then?" she asked as Abbie whizzed down the road.

"Huh?"

Mel had hoped she would slow down, but she refused to take the hint.

"Red light!" she yelled as they approached the traffic lights.

Abbie screeched to a stop.

Mel couldn't remember the last time she'd been in a car with her sister, but she was sure it hadn't been this bad. Abbie had become very impatient with other road users, especially cyclists. She couldn't stand to sit behind them for too long and took to blaring her horn to make them get out of her way. It made Mel feel uneasy. She couldn't imagine how she got on when the tourists were in town.

She closed her eyes for a bit, and when she opened them, they were driving right past the marina.

"Hey, where are we going?"

"I keep the boat somewhere else now. I found a better place up the coast."

"Oh, really?"

"Yeah. It's cheaper too."

Mel nodded and looked out the window. Birds soared high in the sky, and the clouds looked fluffy and full. Perhaps Abbie had been right about the weather after all. It was turning out to be a warm day.

When they arrived at the new mooring place, Abbie parked the car haphazardly, not seeming to care whether or not she was within the lines. They clambered out and loaded themselves up with the supplies Abbie had stashed in the boot.

"What have you got in here?" Mel asked, feeling the weight of one of the boxes.

Abbie smiled. "Everything but the kitchen sink."

They lugged it all down to the jetty. Mel wasn't sure she'd call the new place an improvement, but she could see why it would be cheaper out here, away from the town.

They passed a row of white sailing boats, their masts rattling like chimes in the wind. By contrast, Abbie's bright blue fishing boat was easy to spot, even without the words 'Catch 22' painted on the side. She still found it ironic that the boat was named after a book Abbie had never read.

They set down their boxes, and Abbie helped her

onto the boat. She sat down quickly, always a little afraid of falling in. She wasn't the strongest swimmer, unlike Abbie, who'd been captain of the school swimming team.

The boat was looking better than Mel had expected. With all the talk of the business failing, she'd thought it would be in a more obvious state of disrepair. Instead, she found herself admiring a new canopy, and the boat seemed well equipped with spearguns and snorkels and all kinds of other fishing paraphernalia.

"Hey, you've still got the hat!" she said, finding the pink baseball cap she'd sent from Australia. It was totally tacky, the word 'Skipper' emblazoned in sparkly gold letters on the front. Abbie plucked it from her hand and pulled it on.

"I wear it all the time," she said. Mel assumed she was joking, but she couldn't be sure.

"Put me to work wherever you need," she said as Abbie busied herself with ropes and tackle. Abbie smiled but didn't take her up on the offer, so Mel sat back and looked at the clear blue waters of the Jurassic Coast. The waves looked playful but not too rough. She looked forward to getting out on the water. She knew she was in safe hands with Abbie. When it came to boats, her sister really knew her stuff.

Abbie had been interested in boats since she was a little girl. When she was about ten, she'd written to Father Christmas, asking for a speedboat, and she'd been furious when she'd received a remote-control toy one on Christmas Day. The dream had never died though. For years, Abbie had talked about 'her boat'. Aged just fifteen, she'd set up a savings account for it, and after that, she'd faithfully put a chunk of whatever she earned towards her dream. It was a bit of a family joke, really. Boats were so expensive, Mel had wondered if it would ever become a reality. Then Abbie had asked for her help with writing a business plan. She'd wanted to buy a boat and take tourists out on fishing trips to pay for it. Mel had been cautious about whether Abbie would be able to make this work, but Abbie had been so enthusiastic that she'd got swept along with the idea. She remembered her joy when Abbie rang to tell her she'd finally gone ahead and done it. She'd livestreamed the launch just for Mel. She'd even had a bottle of champagne to smash against the side, and there had been lots of fun and laughter. Their parents' absence had been conspicuous that day. It was only a year after they'd passed, but lots of Abbie's friends had been there.

Where are all those friends now?

"Lovely day for it," Abbie said as they set off. Mel nodded, enjoying the view. There was something to be said for Weymouth out of season. During the summer, there were so many other vessels to contend with, but today, it felt as though they had the entire sea to themselves.

"Hey, Mel. Can you pass me a bottle of water?"

Mel looked under her seat, where Abbie had stashed a cool box. She pulled out a bottle and got to her feet. She walked across the boat, feeling a little giddy as the waves lapped at the sides. Abbie wasn't wearing a life jacket, so Mel hadn't thought to put one on either, a decision she regretted when the boat made a sudden lurch to the right. She clutched at the railing to stop herself falling.

"Careful!" Abbie warned, with a hint of amusement. "Boats can be dangerous."

"I'm all right."

She gripped the rail with one hand as she made her way over to the console.

"Ta," Abbie said when she handed her the bottle. She downed about a third of it and set it to one side.

"This is the life, hey?"

Mel nodded and sat down behind her and tried to get used to the motion of the waves. The boat was flying over the water. It felt as if they'd left civilisation altogether. She could see nothing for miles around. There were no islands, no other vessels, not even a plane in the sky. She put on her sunglasses and looked out at the water, hoping for a glimpse of the dolphins and seals the area was known for.

"How about we get a nice big catch for dinner?" Abbie suggested.

"Great!"

Mel wasn't massively keen on the prospect of live fish flapping about at her feet, but she didn't want to be a party pooper.

Half an hour later, they arrived at a secluded cove, with dramatic rock formations and a soft golden beach. The calm crystal water looked inviting, and Abbie wasted no time in stripping off. Mel turned away to give her privacy as she changed into her wetsuit.

"You want to join me?" Abbie asked. "I've got a spare wetsuit."

Mel shook her head. She'd never fancied diving. She'd always been a little freaked out by the thought of getting trapped under water, as Abbie well knew.

"Suit yourself. It's not every day we get this kind of weather. The sea's looking really clear. It's going to be great down there. Hey, pass me that weight belt, will you?"

Mel did as she was asked. "What's it for?"

"The wetsuit's nice and warm, but it's also rather buoyant. I'll need something to weigh me down if I want to dive under the water."

"Oh, I see."

Abbie finished fastening the belt and reached for her speargun.

"How does that work?"

"Basically, you trigger a big rubber band, and it throws the spear at the fish."

Poor fish.

There seemed to be a lot of gear involved in this simple expedition. Abbie had already put on a mask and flippers, and now she was sitting on the swimming deck, attaching her fins.

"Are you sure that's safe?"

Mel regretted the words no sooner than they were out of her mouth.

"Yes, Mum."

She supposed she deserved that. She watched as Abbie donned her snorkel and dived backwards into the sea, instantly disappearing from view.

The waters were very still today, just a lazy tide lolling across the water. Mel watched as it rolled back and forth, and felt her muscles relax. She sat there for a while, hypnotised by the motion of the waves.

Where is Abbie?

She had her snorkel, but all the same, Mel felt a little nervous. Abbie knew what she was doing, but Mel would feel much better if she'd just pop up to the surface for a minute. She stared out at the water, trying to figure out where she was.

Damn it, Abbie. Will you come back up?

All at once, Abbie burst up to the surface, spluttering for breath. She turned to Mel and gave her two thumbs-up. She looked like she was having the time of her life.

"How's the water?" Mel called out, but Abbie was too far off to hear her, so she leaned back and tried to relax. Perhaps it was better if she didn't watch.

A few minutes later, Abbie brought her a fish. It flapped about madly. There was a spear embedded in its face. Mel's stomach heaved at the sight.

"Nice shot. Were you aiming for the face?"

Abbie laughed. "I always aim to shoot them in the head so as not to ruin any of the flesh."

"Yum." Mel pulled a face. Honestly, she was a little bemused at her sister's new hobby. Abbie had always loved swimming and diving, but hunting fish with a speargun? It felt a bit *Hunger Games*. Still, Mel was impressed with how well she'd picked it up.

The boat swayed a little as Abbie clambered aboard and deposited the catch in the boat's built-in tank. Mel was glad not to have to look at it anymore.

She looked with longing at the nearby cove. If the water were a little warmer, she might have swum across and explored the rock pools. She and Abbie had always loved looking for crabs and other little creatures. She remembered Abbie picking them up and chasing after other children with them. She was a little devil, really.

Abbie dived back into the water. Mel sat back and tried to enjoy the quiet. She didn't remember the last time she'd been forced to relax like this. She felt her pulse slowing slightly, the tension leaving her shoulders as she let her body breathe. She closed her eyes and listened to the gentle lull of the water. This was what life was supposed to be about, wasn't it?

She must have drifted off for a while. When she opened her eyes, she glanced out at the water, frowning as she tried to spot her twin again. There she was, holding up another fish. Looked like a big one.

Abbie swam back to the boat.

"Do you need a hand?" Mel asked.

"You can take this." Abbie held out the speargun.

"Oh, right…"

Abbie handed it to her butt first, and Mel took it cautiously. "What should I do with it?" she asked.

"Just pop it in the corner. I'll deal with it in a minute."

"Right."

The speargun felt red hot in her hands, though she was sure she was just imagining it. She'd never been keen on hunting, never liked the thought. It made her uncomfortable to be clutching the weapon Abbie had just used to kill with, especially as there was still a trace of blood on it. She'd never known fish could bleed so much.

Abbie climbed up the ladder and stepped onto the boat, then busied herself removing the weight belt.

"Anything I can do to help?"

"You could wash the fish."

"Er…"

"Just pass me that towel, will you."

"Okay."

Abbie towelled herself off before scrubbing the fish; then she scrubbed the blood from the bottom of the boat.

"Can you unzip me?" she asked when she straightened up. She stood in front of her and fidgeted impatiently. "Just give it a yank."

"You cold?" Mel asked, working the zip.

"Not really." Abbie shimmied out of the suit, first one shoulder then the other. She turned it inside out and tugged it past her hips, doing a bit of a dance as she pulled it down her legs. She dressed quickly, then brought out a thermos flask and took a big sip. Mel wished she'd thought to bring one herself. The cold air burned her lungs. Just looking at Abbie made her shiver. There was something about the way the cold air tinged her skin. The salt water had swollen her lips, and her eyes appeared to bulge slightly, like the eyes of the fish she'd caught.

"Here, do you want this blanket?"

"Yeah, okay."

She wrapped it around her sister's shoulders, the way their mum would have done. As the warmth returned to Abbie, Mel began to feel warmer too. She sat down on the seat beside her, trying not to stare as her sister slurped her coffee. It had been so long since they'd spent quality time together like this, she felt almost shy. Still, it was nice sitting there, just the two of them. Not doing anything much.

"Hey, do you remember the time we hired those canoes?" Abbie said. "And you capsized?"

"It was you who capsized!" Mel corrected her.

"Are you sure?"

"Of course I'm sure. You were pissing about as always." She smiled at the memory. "It was fun though, wasn't it?"

"Yeah. Yeah, it was." Abbie looked up at the sky. "It's almost three. We should be heading back."

"Wait…you can tell that just by looking at the sky?"

Abbie burst out laughing. "No, I also have a watch."

"Oh. Now I'm really disappointed."

"It is time to head back though."

Abbie went to the control panel and started preparing the boat. Mel watched as her hands flicked over the controls, her expression earnest. It was nice seeing her at work on her boat. This was what she had always wanted. She had earned it.

Abbie revved the engine. There was a deep line of concentration on her face as she got the boat started. They zipped off over the waves, and Mel couldn't help but smile as the wind whipped through her hair. There was something incredibly soothing about the way Abbie steered the boat through the calm expanse of water. Next time she would bring an extra jumper, she promised herself, and thicker socks and definitely a thermos.

"Stupid boat, can it go any slower?"

She looked up in surprise. Abbie had muttered the words under her breath, but Mel had caught them clearly enough.

"Is something wrong?"

Abbie looked up, like she'd forgotten Mel was there. "Oh, no, it's just getting old, that's all."

Mel blinked. She'd never heard Abbie speak of her beloved boat with anything but pride. It was the same kind of devotion their dad had shown his prized Mercedes. It seemed only fitting that that car had died with him.

There was very little conversation after that. Mel looked out at the sea and tried to enjoy the rest of the trip, her hands nestled deep inside her sleeves to keep warm. She was going to have a bath when she got home, she decided. A nice hot bath and a glass of wine. Abbie took the scenic route, slowing to point out a spot popular with dolphins. Mel nodded and smiled, but there was nothing in particular to look at. She was getting tired as well as cold. The sky was turning grey again, about the colour of an old man's beard, but the water remained reassuringly calm.

"Looking forward to a nice fish supper," Abbie said as their mooring came into view.

Mel thought of the flailing fish and forced herself to smile.

11

M el watched as Abbie expertly prepared the sea bass. The whole house filled with the aroma like a salty reminder of their day out on the boat. She had wanted to take her bath as soon as they got in, but now she felt like she should hang around the kitchen and help. Abbie claimed not to need any assistance, but Mel still felt obliged. Setting the table and emptying the dishwasher seemed like the least she could do since Abbie was going to so much trouble. She opened a bottle of wine and poured two glasses, knowing Abbie liked to have a drink while she cooked.

"Cheers," Abbie said, taking a large gulp.

The conversation seemed to have dried up again, so Mel put on the radio, and they bopped along to the music, topping up both their glasses until they'd finished the bottle. Then she opened another and watched as Abbie mashed a huge knob of butter into the potatoes. She bit back a comment about her cholesterol. It didn't do to insult the chef.

"Ta-da!" Abbie set the plates on the table, each one piled high with food.

The sea bass stared back at Mel, its eyes deadpan as it lay on the plate.

"Looks lovely!" she told Abbie.

She took a big gulp of wine and forced her fork into her mouth. The fish was delicious, but having seen Abbie kill and then gut it had not played well with her appetite. Luckily, Otto was waiting under the table, ready to take her scraps. Abbie had dished up enough mash and peas to feed an entire army, so it wasn't as if she was going to go hungry.

There had been no more talk about selling the house, and Mel was glad. She was hoping that Abbie was coming around to her way of thinking. Much as she cared about Abbie's business and did not want it to go under, the house was more than just bricks and mortar. It was their childhood home, and for Mel it was a special link to their parents. She felt like there was still an echo of her parents in the house, because of the memories it prompted. She could be grabbing a mug from the cupboard when she would be hit by a memory of Mum making tea, or she could be looking out the window at the garden, and she would hear Dad ramming the ancient lawnmower over the grass. It hurt her heart to think of giving that up.

As if to atone for their pleasant day out, the following day arrived with a crash of thunder, rain splattering down the windows, and a strong northerly wind blew through the house. Mel put on her dressing gown over her pyjamas and coaxed Otto out from under the bed. Abbie was already in the kitchen, stirring a pan at the stove. She was wearing Mum's apron, the one they'd brought back from a field trip to Basingstoke. It said 'I wish I'd gone to Venice', in curly red letters.

"Something smells good," Mel greeted her.

Abbie turned and smiled. "I thought I'd make pancakes. I don't know what it is about the sea air, but I'm always extra hungry after a fishing trip."

Mel nodded in agreement. "I take it Otto hasn't been fed?"

"What? Er, not yet."

Mel grabbed a tin and saw to the dog while Abbie plated up the pancakes. They sat down at the table, and Abbie poured on so much golden syrup that she needed a spoon to eat it.

"So, I'd better tell you that we've had an offer on the house. A very generous offer," Abbie said. She leaned in, as if to confess a great secret. "They're offering a million pounds, Mel. How do you like that?"

Abbie was beaming, as if she expected this news to please her.

Mel sucked in her breath. It was a lot of money, even with the mortgage and fees taken out.

"It's completely your decision of course," Abbie rushed on, "but promise me you'll think about it. We can't take too long, or we'll lose our buyer."

She looked very pointedly at Mel, who fought the urge to shrink away from her. Abbie had always been a little headstrong, but this was on another level.

"I'll think about it," she said, concentrating on her food. She'd really hoped Abbie would forget the idea. If her business was doing so badly, throwing more money at the problem might not help. Perhaps it just wasn't profitable. She wanted to broach this with Abbie, but her twin could be sensitive about such things, and she was afraid of stepping on her toes.

Abbie pushed the hair back off her head, smearing sticky syrup into her blonde locks. Her roots were showing, Mel noted. Wispy greys floated around her face.

Abruptly, Abbie hopped up from the table and grabbed the plates.

"Hey, I'm not quite finished," Mel complained.

"Oh, sorry."

Typical Abbie, always in a rush.

"What are you doing today?" Mel asked.

"Oh, not much."

"You haven't got any plans?"

Abbie wrinkled her forehead. "Not bloody likely. It's pissing it down out there."

Still though, Mel couldn't help but wonder about Abbie's friends. She'd had so many. What could she have done to fall out with every single one of them? She sensed there was a story there, but she was sure Abbie would tell her in her own time. There must have been a big falling-out. Perhaps she'd had a fling with somebody else's husband? Or maybe they'd all paired off and started families, leaving her out in the cold. Whatever had happened, she felt Abbie needed to get back out there again. It was one thing for Mel to mope around the house, she really had crashed and burned, but quite another thing for Abbie. Staying home wasn't in her nature. She was supposed to be the party girl – the one their parents had worried about. Never in a million years could she have imagined that her wild sister would be living such a dull life.

She picked up the plates and stacked them in the dishwasher, then wandered into the living room. Thankfully, Abbie hadn't put on the TV yet. Mel sat down on the sofa opposite her.

"How about I loan you some money?" she suggested.

Abbie's eyes widened. "Oh, Mel, that would be great. How much are we talking?"

Mel swallowed. "Well, I'm not exactly minted, but I think I could manage five grand."

"Five?"

She couldn't tell if Abbie thought this was too much or too little. Abbie's eye twitched slightly, and she sat very still for a moment, then she nodded slowly. "That's incredibly generous of you, but it's not going to be enough to save my business."

Mel nodded. She'd suspected as much.

"I thought it might tide you over for a while?"

Abbie smiled weakly. "It might keep the wolves from the door for a few more weeks."

Otto gave a well-timed bark, and they both smiled.

"I have bills to pay, Mel. I'm behind on everything." She shook her head in frustration.

"I know," Mel said, taking her hand and giving it a squeeze. She hated to see her sister upset.

Abbie let go of her hand and rubbed her eyes as if they ached. "You know I'm worried about you too, Mel."

"Me?"

"Look, I know things have been difficult between you and Pete, but are you really sure you want to close the door on him? I mean, you were married to him for a really long time. Practically forever."

Mel raised an eyebrow. This again. Since when was Abbie Peter's greatest fan?

"I think you should Zoom with him tonight," Abbie said. "Just to let him know you haven't completely forgotten him."

"Do you think?" Mel wasn't convinced this was the best idea. She was starting a new life here in Weymouth. Did she really want to keep Peter hanging on? He'd finally stopped bombarding her with messages, so she took that as a positive sign. In order for her to move on, she really needed him to move on too.

"I just think you have some unfinished business," Abbie said.

"Like what?"

"Like, you still haven't really talked. The poor man doesn't know why you've left him. Don't you think you owe him that much at least?"

Mel pulled a face. She hated it when Abbie was right, but she had a point. Maybe she did owe Peter an explanation. Ugh, talking to him was the last thing she felt like, but was she just putting off the inevitable?

She pictured him sitting alone in their house. He'd probably be having dinner around now. Unlike her, he loved to cook. But would he bother when it was just for himself? She wondered how he was filling his time. Was he getting together with friends, going to parties without her? She couldn't picture it, somehow. Neither of them were very good at parties. Somehow, they'd got out of practice, and they inevitably talked to each other all night.

Against her own better instincts, she tapped out a quick text, asking him to let her know when he was free. He replied instantly, as if he'd been waiting for her message. Oh, Lord, he wanted to Zoom now.

She darted up to her room and checked her hair in the bathroom mirror, flattening it down so it didn't look too frizzy. She didn't put any make-up on. She wasn't going to tart herself up for him. She just wanted him to know she was fine. She was a strong, independent woman.

She spun around in her chair while she waited to be connected. What was she going to say to him? She really should have given it some thought. She wanted to know if he was okay. That was the main thing. She'd left him in the lurch, after all. He'd seemed okay the last time, but how would she know if he wasn't? He never shouted, never got upset, never cried.

His face flashed up on the screen.

"Hi," she said, suddenly feeling awkward. He smiled, and for a moment they just sat there, looking at each other. It was weird; they had been married for such a long time, yet she felt like she had very little to say to this man. She was the one who had had the affair, yet she was the one who was angry.

"How are you feeling?" he asked, resting his chin in his hands.

"Me? I'm fine."

"Good. Are you getting some rest?"

"Rest? Ha!" She laughed at the idea. "You know I've got work, right? I'm not just lounging around on the beach all day. I mean, the pressure's on!"

"My little pressure cooker," he said fondly.

She stared at the screen, at the familiar contours of his face, and all at once she had the urge to reach out and touch him, to feel the roughness of the stubble on his chin.

"Peter –"

"Mel –"

"No, go on…"

"I just…I didn't mean for things to end the way they did. I mean, I didn't mean to hurt you."

There was a touch of sadness in his eyes. "You could never hurt me, Mel."

But they both knew that wasn't true.

"I don't want to lead you on…"

"Mel, you're all I care about, you know that. Well, you and Nicole Kidman, but she's not exactly hammering my door down. Perhaps you could ring her, tell her you'd be okay with it if she wants to make a move now."

She swallowed. They had serious problems in their marriage, even if he could still make her laugh.

"The way I see it, running off doesn't solve anything. You're stressed at work, and you never give yourself a break. You're making yourself ill again, Mel."

She turned away slightly. "I swear I'm fine, Peter."

"Look at me, Mel, look at me! You have to trust me. I know you almost as well as you know yourself. I was there when you had your 'wobble', remember? I remember how sick you were…"

"I wasn't that bad!"

"You were, you just refused to see it. You were losing your grip on reality. Don't you remember? You took to your bed for days. You couldn't eat or sleep. You couldn't function. I'd hate to see that happen to you again."

She attempted a brave smile. "It isn't like that. I'm fine, Peter. I know what I'm doing."

"I hope so, Mel, because I'm going out of my mind here."

She closed her eyes, and when she opened them, he was gone. She got up and paced the room, feeling embarrassed and angry. What was she thinking, letting Peter back into her life? She'd been doing perfectly fine, and after five minutes of talking to him, he had her questioning herself again, feeling like she was out of control. Well, she wasn'tshe knew exactly what she was doing. This was what she wanted.

12

A bbie knocked on Mel's bedroom door. "Did you speak to him? How did it go?"

Mel wasn't sure why she was asking. The only way she could have known she'd spoken to Peter was if she'd been out there earwigging.

"It was weird and awkward," she confessed. "I feel like I've opened up a can of worms. I mean, I ran away from him, Abbie. I came all this way because I knew if I was going to leave him, I had to put some distance between us. And here I am bloody talking to him again, like I'm just on holiday. It's confusing him, and it's confusing me."

"You might get back with him, then?" Abbie couldn't hide the delight in her eyes.

"No! Of course not!"

What the hell *did* she want? Why she even talking to him if she didn't want him in her life? Was it guilt at having run out on him like that, or was it more than that? She shifted uncomfortably, wishing she had a clue.

Abbie booted one of her suitcases out of the way with her foot and plonked herself down on the bed.

"Are you going to unpack these or what?"

"I will when I have time," Mel said. Right now, she didn't have the energy. The thought of unpacking was too exhausting. She glanced out the window. "I don't know if you've noticed, but your hanging baskets are in need of a good trim."

"Are they?"

"Yes, they are."

Abbie had her feet up on her best suitcase now. It annoyed her the way her sister trampled over her stuff.

"Come on outside. I'll show you."

Abbie rolled her eyes, but she rose from the bed, and Mel was irrationally pleased to get her out of her room. She walked down the stairs and slipped some shoes on. She couldn't understand how Abbie could bear to go out in bare feet.

"There," she said, pointing out the straggly plants.

"Why don't you trim them, then?" Abbie asked.

"They're your plants!"

"Yeah, but you're the one who cares."

It dawned on Mel that the hanging baskets were part of Abbie's campaign to sell the house, along with the clean carpets and the repaint. It all seemed rather calcu-lated, somehow, although she was impressed by the lengths she'd gone to.

"Hey, remember that time Mum and Dad took us camping and the tent blew away?" Abbie said suddenly.

Mel felt her anger dissipating. "How could I forget? The cows in the next field were all staring at us and…"

"They were mooing like crazy! And remember how Dad tried to calm them by offering them milk? Milk! They were bloody cows!"

"Cooey!"

Mel's face broke out into a smile. Their old teacher, Mrs Crowe, was hobbling up the path; her cloud of woolly white hair bobbed up and down as she walked. Mrs Crowe stopped and looked her over. "I heard you were back."

"Afraid so," Mel said with a grin.

"What happened to Australia? Don't tell me you burnt it down?"

"No, nothing like that!"

Mrs Crowe had seemed old when they were at school, so she must be positively ancient by now. She'd taken both the twins for maths.

"They're both very bright girls," she'd told their mum at parents' evening, "though I despair of getting Abbie to pay attention."

"You and me both," Mum had replied.

Mel looked at Abbie, but she had turned and was heading back into the house.

"Abbie?" she called after her, but she had already shut the door behind her. Mrs Crowe looked after her in bemusement.

"I think she left the bath running," Mel said, embarrassed. She would have liked to invite Mrs Crowe inside, but Abbie's behaviour stumped her. Why had she disappeared without saying hello? It was like she was being deliberately rude.

"What was all that about?" she asked when she came inside.

"What?" Abbie reached for the remote, poised to turn on the TV.

Mel placed herself in front of the screen. "Mrs Crowe! You totally ignored her."

"I didn't even see her!" Abbie protested.

"She was standing on our doorstep!"

"Was she?"

"Yes, and if you really didn't see her, I'd say it's about time you get your eyes tested." Mel watched her for a moment, trying to figure out what was wrong. She was a tricky person sometimes, her sister. Impossible to fathom.

"I thought she was your favourite teacher?"

Abbie snorted. "Who gives a crap about some old teacher? School sucked."

Mel narrowed her eyes. She was the one who had hated school. The way she remembered it, Abbie had had a blast. Although she wasn't particularly academic, she'd had a great social life and had always seemed happy. At least, that had been her impression. It just went to show, you never really knew what was going on inside someone else's head.

She trudged up the stairs, feeling tired enough to sleep. She lay down on the bed with her laptop. If she fell asleep working on the game, perhaps her mind would untangle the puzzle while she slept.

She heard Abbie coming up the stairs. "Knock, knock," she called before coming into Mel's room.

"What's it all about, then?" Abbie asked, peering at *Artful Assassin* on Mel's laptop.

Mel rubbed her tired eyes. "Basically, there's this bloke who's out to get you. He's an assassin. The problem is, he can make himself look like anyone, so you never know who to trust. You're always on the lookout. Do you want to have a go?"

"No, thanks. It sounds freaky."

"Are you sure? The graphics are really good. You can explore the whole town. There are shops and cafés and everything. There's even a harbour with boats."

Abbie laughed. "Have you based this on Weymouth?"

"No, of course not." The corners tugged at her lips. "Well, maybe a little."

She hadn't intended to base it on anything, but ideas had to come from somewhere, didn't they? Looking at it now, she supposed she had borrowed quite a bit from real life. The nun had the irate look of their old Sunday school teacher, and the vicar was a bit like their dad.

Abbie was looking at her in amusement. "So that intruder the other day, you sure he was for real?"

Mel felt the heat rush to her cheeks. "I'm not totally nuts, Abbie!"

"You sure? Because I think this French bloke looks just as you described."

Mel watched as the assassin made an appearance, walking along the sea front in the guise of a French tourist. In this incarnation, he had a twiddly moustache and a beret, and he was dressed all in black, just like the intruder. She folded her arms across her chest.

"The intruder was real, Abbie. I didn't imagine that smashed window, and he did not have a comedy moustache."

Abbie threw her hands up. "I'm just joking, Mel. Don't bite my head off."

Mel ignored her and carried on playing.

"What did go wrong with you and Pete, then?" Abbie asked. "You never really said."

"It hadn't been working for a while. We wanted different things."

"Like what?"

Mel thought back, remembering a conversation she'd had with Peter a few months after her parents had died, when all the colour seemed to have disappeared from her world. It was as if she'd packed the grey Weymouth skies and brought them back to Australia with her.

"I've been thinking," she'd said as they were finishing dinner. "How about we take some time off and do a tour of Australia?"

Peter said nothing, but he stopped eating, his brow furrowed.

"I reckon we'd need at least a month," she went on. "Do you think you could get that much time off work?"

"You've only just gone back to work," he objected.

"I know. I'd have to take unpaid leave, but I think I could swing it."

She'd pulled the map out and set it in front of him. "Look, I've marked all the places I want to go. I've never seen Fraser Island or Tasmania, and it would be really awesome if we could do a few of the national parks. And I've always wanted to see the Great Barrier Reef."

He looked over her plans for a few minutes, the harried look never leaving his face.

"This would cost a bit, wouldn't it?"

"We've got some money saved."

"Yes, but that's for the new kitchen."

Mel looked up at him, trying to work out how to convince him. "A new kitchen would be nice, but you can't put a price on new experiences. I've lived here for sixteen years, Peter, and I've still barely seen anything of the country. I want to get out there and explore a bit. Think of it as a holiday of a lifetime."

"We could do that later," he'd argued. "How about we do up the kitchen as planned, then save up again. We could take the trip in a few years' time."

"I don't want to wait," she'd said in exasperation. "Tomorrow might never come. Look what happened to my parents. They thought they had their whole retirement ahead of them."

Peter had steepled his fingers together. "Mel, it's tragic what happened to your parents, but that's not going to happen to us. We can wait."

He'd picked up his plate and rinsed it under the tap before slotting it neatly in the dishwasher. As far as he was concerned, the conversation was over.

FOR THE NEXT FEW DAYS, Mel worked long hours, the lines of code blurring like a road in front of her. She just had to keep going, ducking and weaving, avoiding the assassin, solving the bug that made him freeze.

One night, she had worked right through until morning. She knew it was morning, because she heard Abbie crashing around downstairs in the kitchen, banging cupboard doors and cooking bacon. It appeared she couldn't do anything quietly anymore. Mel rubbed her tired eyes and set the laptop to one side. Her hands curled beneath her as she drifted off to sleep.

She woke suddenly, her face beaded with sweat. She stared at the shadows on the wall, almost convinced there was someone there, then drifted off again, chasing an intruder she could never quite catch.

She was awoken by Otto's bark. *What was that? The doorbell?* She listened for a moment, but it seemed Abbie was still busy in the kitchen. There it was again. Surely she must have heard? Apparently not. Either she had her headphones in, or there was something wrong with her hearing.

She heaved herself off the bed and trotted down the stairs, planning to get rid of whoever it was. She opened the door, and her mouth fell open. There on the doorstep stood Peter, brown duffel bag by his side. His face looked thin and drawn, his hair flatter than she remembered, his shoulders a little less straight, but the expression on his face was as confident and self-possessed as ever.

Mel narrowed her eyes. "What the hell are you doing here?"

13

Her first instinct was to slam the door in his face, but then Abbie appeared behind her.

"Pete! Fancy seeing you here! My god, I can't believe you've come all this way! The things we do for love, hey?"

Mel stiffened. She felt as though her entire body had filled with bubbles. She couldn't stand the way Abbie was fawning over Peter.

"Let him in," she hissed in Mel's ear. "Go on, don't be a bitch."

Mel staggered backwards, and just like that, Peter steamed into the house and back into her life.

"Just give me a minute," she said as politely as she knew how.

She thumped up the stairs to her room and let loose on the scatter cushions, hurling each one at the door. Abbie really should have left the dartboard. She slumped down on the bed and found that her legs were shaking. She felt so helpless, like nothing she said or did made any difference. She had left Peter, for goodness' sake, and crossed the world to get away from him. And now, here he was, acting like nothing had happened. It wasn't fair. It wasn't bloody fair.

She took a few deep breaths. She'd have to go down there; otherwise, Abbie would drag him up here. She picked up her pillow and screamed into it until her throat was hoarse. She could hear their voices downstairs, chatting and laughing like old friends.

Come on, Mel, you can do this. You just have to talk to him, get it out of the way.

PETER LEANED against the kitchen counter as Abbie opened and closed cupboards, pulling out goodies Mel hadn't even known they had. Had she'd been out shopping that morning? It certainly looked like it. Which meant Abbie must have known he was coming. They must have planned this together, because this was the first spontaneous thing Peter had done since they'd got married.

Had Abbie told him she needed him? Was that what had happened? Damn her, this was her life, and Peter wasn't supposed to be a part of it anymore. When were they all going to get that through their thick skulls?

Peter oozed charm as Abbie flew around him, setting a tray for breakfast. If she didn't know better, Mel would have said Abbie was actually flirting with him. There was something unsettling about the way her hand brushed his shoulder as she passed him and the coy look she gave him as she reached over his shoulder for the spatula.

Abbie had cooked up an entire pack of bacon, so not only did she know he was coming, but he must have let her know exactly when he'd arrive. She didn't like this. Didn't like it at all. Since when did Peter and Abbie plan stuff behind her back? They'd never been friends. They weren't even close. What was Abbie thinking? Was she so disillusioned with the idea of ever meeting someone herself that she couldn't bear for Mel to let him go?

Abbie led Peter into the dining room and pulled out a chair for him at the nice table, the one they only used on Sundays. She set the coffee pot down on the table and pulled out the little china cups they reserved for guests.

"Do you take sugar, Pete? I can't remember."

"Not for me," he said.

"Sit down, Mel," Abbie scolded. "You're making the place untidy."

Reluctantly, Mel took the empty seat beside Peter.

She reached for the sugar bowl and heaped two generous spoonfuls into her cup. Peter raised an eyebrow. She spooned a third one in, waiting for the blister on his forehead to pop, but he turned his attention to Abbie, who was now plying him with Danish pastries.

Danish pastries! She hadn't put on this much of a spread when Mel had come home. She'd had to make do with a packet of biscuits.

"Just be a mo." Abbie walked back towards the kitchen, no doubt to fetch some other culinary delight.

"I'll give her a hand," Mel said, and hurried after her. She caught up with Abbie in the kitchen and resisted the urge to yank her ponytail.

"What the hell are you doing?" she hissed.

"Being nice," Abbie said, shooting her a look. "He's giving you a second chance. Don't screw it up."

Mel exhaled slowly. "I don't know if I want a second chance."

"Oh, come on, Mel! He's come all this way. Have a bloody heart!"

"I didn't ask him to come," Mel said petulantly. Her

lower lip went out involuntarily, and Abbie pronged it with her finger, forcing her to smile.

She glanced towards the dining room. She still felt something for Peter; of course she did. She couldn't just switch it off after twenty years, as much as she wished she could. And honestly, she was really surprised by him turning up like this. Never in a million years did she think he'd come after her.

"Take these," Abbie said, loading her up with jars of marmalade and jam. She gave her a little push, and Mel stumbled through to the dining room.

Peter looked up as soon as she came back into the room. His plate was full, but he wasn't eating. His eyes met hers pleadingly, and she felt even worse than she had before.

"What about your job?" she asked, hovering at the table.

"What about it?" he said with a shrug. "Family comes first, right?"

She sat down hard in her seat. *Was that a dig?*

She should have done the grown-up thing and talked to him about the problems they were having, but leaving had been easier. More final, somehow. She'd thought if she ran off to England, there would be nothing more to say. Apparently, there was.

"Seriously, I hope you haven't ditched your job for me. You need it. You've got a mortgage to pay."

He spiked a piece of bacon with his fork. "Is that all you want to talk to me about? The mortgage?"

"What do you want to talk about?"

"You, Mel. Us. We need to fix this."

Abbie walked in at that moment and poured more coffee. Mel gesticulated wildly, trying to get her to sit down, but she merely loaded up a plate and walked out again.

Peter reached for Mel's hand. His touch was electric, sparking a need in her that she had almost forgotten. She was still attracted to him. Still wanted him, on some level. But was it enough?

Peter pulled her closer. She could smell the cinnamon scent of his breath.

"That's better," he said. "Just the two of us. You can be yourself now. You can tell me how you really are."

"I'm absolutely fine."

She didn't pull her hand from his, but she wanted to. She didn't like feeling like this, and she didn't want him to take care of her, as he always did. She wasn't a child, she was a perfectly capable woman. Even if she screwed up from time to time.

She couldn't help but wonder where it had all gone wrong between them. It had been such a gradual thing, like coastal erosion. It had happened so slowly, she couldn't really tell while she was there, living it.

"I don't want you running my life anymore."

There, she'd said it. It felt good.

"Whatever you need, I can do it," he said. "I can be a whole new man if you want. I can change."

She looked at him sceptically, but he didn't look away. His face was so earnest that she felt the knots in her stomach tighten. He meant it. He really would do anything for her.

"Listen, I'm going to book you into a hotel," she said at last.

"A hotel? I thought I'd be able to stay here. You've got five bedrooms, haven't you?"

"Yeah, I know, but I think we need some space."

"You've had some space, Mel!"

"I mean it, Peter. If you're serious, then let me do this. I need time to think, and that's hard to do if you're right here, under the same roof."

He put his hands up. "Whatever you want. Take all the time you need."

"Okay then."

She found him a room at the Four Seasons. It was a decent hotel. A little old-fashioned, but decent. She'd got a good deal with the hotel booking website, so the room would be free for the first night and reduced for the second. She hoped she could persuade him to go back after that.

"I can pay for my own room," he objected.

She shook her head. "Let me take care of it."

He made a face. He'd never been able to handle the fact that she earned more than he did.

He looked down at all the plates of food. "Abbie went to a lot of trouble, didn't she? I feel bad that we didn't eat much of this."

"She'll understand," Mel said, stacking as much as she could onto a tray, anything to occupy her hands. He hadn't made any moves on her, hadn't done anything to make her feel uncomfortable, yet she worried about their proximity. There was a danger in being alone with him. She allowed herself, just briefly, to remember how much she'd once loved lying in bed with him on lazy Sunday mornings.

"Do you want me to ring for a taxi?"

"It's okay. I've got a hire car."

She raised an eyebrow. "Wow, that's very organised of you. Let me walk you out, then."

She wasn't being remotely subtle, but she couldn't be with Peter. She watched as he wriggled back into his shoes. They smelled like wax polish and…him. She shut the door as soon as he stepped outside. She told herself she didn't want to let the warm air out of the house. She could still smell the polish as she walked back towards the kitchen, where she found Otto under the table, with the chewed-up flip-flop in his mouth.

"Have you been hiding there all that time?" she asked, bending down to stroke him. "You softie. Some guard dog you turned out to be."

"So where's lover boy?" Abbie asked, peering into the kitchen.

Mel rubbed the back her neck. "I've packed him off to a hotel."

Abbie's smile slipped. "You've what?"

"I couldn't let him stay here." She wasn't sure why she had to explain herself. "I left him, remember? Nothing's changed."

Abbie's jaw grew tight. "He's come all this way! Don't you think you should make a bit more effort?"

"I *am* making an effort. I could have just slammed the door in his face."

"Why? What the hell has he done to deserve that? Pete's a stand-up guy. You're the one who had an affair. You're the one who hurt him."

"Right."

Mel pushed past her and started up the stairs, but Abbie followed, talking right in her ear.

"The bloke you went off with. Are you in love with him?"

"God, no." She cringed as she thought of the surfer. He was almost young enough to be her son. What on earth had possessed her?

"Then stop pissing around, Mel! Peter's willing to take you back. It's time you met him halfway. This might be your only chance at happiness."

"Abbie, I…"

Abbie laid a heavy hand on her shoulder. "Don't fuck this up," she said through clenched teeth. Her voice sounded so savage that for a moment, Mel thought she was joking.

She spun around and looked at Abbie, expecting to see light in her eyes, but all she saw was darkness. The expression on her face was so vile and unfamiliar that for a moment she had the most insane thought. It was as though Abbie had morphed into someone else, like the assassin in her game. It was in the way she looked at her, like pure evil, and the thought floated into her mind. *That's not my sister.*

14

Mel curled up under her duvet. She needed to sleep, but she was feeling unnerved by it all. It was as if the entire world was conspiring against her. She'd been so sure about leaving Peter. So sure about coming home and starting over, but Abbie was being so weird she almost didn't recognise her, and Peter was acting like a cartoon corpse who refused to stay dead.

Her phone beeped. It was Peter. Of course it was.

- Sorry. I know I said I'd leave you alone. Just want to know if you'll have dinner with me tonight? You know I hate eating alone.

She thought for a minute then texted back.

- Dinner would be nice. See you at the hotel at eight.

- Can we make it seven? I'm not sure I can hold out that long.

He never could let her have the last word.

- Seven thirty, she texted back.

She waited for him to text 'seven fifteen'. She pictured him with his finger hovering over the phone. The effort must be killing him.

She lay back against the pillows and pulled the duvet tighter around her, like a protective shell. Abbie had the TV on again downstairs, louder than ever. She reached over to her desk and grabbed her headphones. It wasn't comfortable, trying to sleep with them on, but she couldn't stand the sound of engines revving or the sound of Abbie shouting at the TV. She tried not to think about the nasty look Abbie had given her, but she couldn't get it out of her mind. It was like she had seen right into Abbie's soul, and she didn't like what she'd seen there. She didn't like it at all.

She dozed fitfully, tossing and turning like a piece of driftwood on a stormy sea. Never calm. Never still.

She sat up suddenly, unsure what had woken her. Otto was sitting on her swivel chair, tongue hanging out as he stared at her laptop. He looked like he was eager to start work. Automatically, she reached out and stroked his soft fur.

"You're a good dog."

He picked up the flip-flop and brought it to her.

"Oh, I couldn't," she said as he thrust it in her face. She pushed it away. "No, really, you have it."

She checked her phone. No more messages from Peter. He must have gone to sleep. She had an hour or so before she was due to go and meet him, so she took a leisurely shower, the first one she'd had in days. She wasn't going to have Peter thinking she wasn't looking after herself. She even dug out her hair dryer and blow-dried her hair with a touch of serum to make it shine. She wasn't sure why she was going to so much effort, but she felt a little buzz, knowing she was going out, even if it was just with Peter. She slid into her tightest black skinny jeans and a red shirt that Peter had bought for her. It was the only item of his she'd actually kept. The rest of the things he'd given her were still in bin bags in their house in Sydney. She'd left a note, telling him he could donate it all to the Samaritans, but she bet he was still holding on to it all.

Downstairs, she slid her feet into her least scruffy boots. She paused briefly in front of the living room, wondering if she should tell Abbie she was going out. Abbie had a jar of peanuts on the table in front of her and was eating them by the handful, cramming them into her mouth like some kind of animal. Even the way she was sitting struck Mel as a little odd. Since when did Abbie sit cross-legged like a child? And since when did she stay home to watch fencing?

"Just heading out," she called.

Abbie whipped her head round. "With Pete?"

"Yes, as it happens."

Abbie's face split into a huge grin. "Don't do anything I wouldn't do."

Mel shook her head. "Believe me, I won't."

IT HAD GROWN DARK OUTSIDE. The road ahead was lit with the amber glow of the street lights. Mel walked briskly. She'd never felt particularly unsafe in Weymouth, even in the high season. This was her home. She was comfortable here, at least she had been.

The wind blew around her and she now realised that blow-drying her hair had been a wasted effort. It rained softly, giving her the sensation of light fingers strumming her back. All was still, and the only sounds to be heard were the rhythmic crash of the waves as they washed in and out on the beach.

Dark clouds blocked the moon's reflection in the water, and she hurried on, eager to reach the hotel. As she crossed the car park and headed towards the Four Seasons, she felt her neck stiffen and tense. She wasn't immediately sure what was making her feel uneasy; she just felt a light tingling sensation up and down her spine. Then she noticed it, the silhouette of a man leaning against the wall. He wore a long dark coat, with a baseball cap shielding his eyes. There was something disconcerting about the way he stood there, unnaturally still, with his back pressed against the wall. He lifted his head ever so slightly, and the air caught in her throat. She recognised those strong dark eyebrows and aquiline nose, and panic spread through her body. She ran for the hotel, panting like Otto, arms flailing wildly. She pushed through the entrance, tripped and collided with the revolving doors, which send her sprawling into the hotel foyer.

15

"Bloody hell! I haven't seen an entrance like that since the *T. rex* in *Jurassic Park*."

Mel blinked as the security guard held out his hand to help her up. "Are you all right, love?"

Before she could utter a word, he hauled her to her feet, almost wrenching her arm out of its socket.

"He was out there!" she gasped. "He was watching me!"

She pointed wildly at the car park, but she could no longer see the intruder. She was aware of Peter stepping forward, placing himself between her and the security guard.

"It's all right. I'll deal with her," he murmured.

"Deal with me?" She grabbed him by the hand and dragged him outside, scanning desperately for the man she'd seen.

"What's all this about, Melly?"

"It's this bloke who broke into our house," she explained. "I just saw him again."

"Wait, what bloke?"

Mel followed his gaze to where a small, plump taxi

driver was smoking a surreptitious cigarette. "No, not him!"

She looked around again, but the shadowy figure was nowhere to be seen.

"Are you sure it was the same bloke?" Peter's calm, soothing voice did what it always did. It pissed her right off.

"Yes, I'm sure."

Peter's eyebrows moved closer together as if they were conferring with each other. "Why would he follow you here?"

"That's what I want to know!" She pulled out her phone.

"What are you doing now?"

"I'm texting Abbie to make sure she's locked all the doors and windows."

"Well, at least come in out of the rain. It's cold out here, and you're not even wearing a jacket."

She felt an irrational urge to sit down on the pavement. Anything other than follow him inside.

"You don't believe me, do you?"

"Of course I do. You obviously saw someone, but whether it was the same bloke who broke into your house, I really can't say."

Mel rolled her eyes, but he had a point about the cold, so she followed him back into the hotel, making a more dignified entrance than she had the last time.

She paused in the foyer to finish texting Abbie. Maybe she was being paranoid, but she wasn't going to take any chances.

"It was good of you to get me a room on the seafront," he said.

"Of course. It was the least I could do."

"You should come up and see it. It's quite a view."

"Peter…"

"I'm joking, of course."

He strode towards the restaurant ahead of her.

"Do you have a reservation?" the maître d' asked.

"Yes," Peter said. "It's Montgomery. Mr and Mrs Montgomery."

Mel suppressed a laugh. Now he was definitely winding her up.

They were seated by the window. They had a breathtaking view of the beach, courtesy of the full moon. Mel picked up her menu and tried to focus on the food rather than the sense of unease she still felt at seeing that man outside.

"You're cold," Peter said.

"I'm fine."

"Here." He slipped one shoulder out of his jacket.

"You don't have to do that…"

"Of course I do. You're freezing."

"Well…thanks."

It felt odd accepting his jacket. It was warm and soft, shielding her shoulders from the irritation of the air conditioning. Why did they insist on air con? It was October, for Christ's sake, and they had the sea air to contend with. She shifted in her seat. Peter's jacket was more than just a jacket. It was a gesture of togetherness. She was wearing his scent, literally. It lingered in the fibres and clung to her goose-pimpled flesh. And now, after wearing it, it would smell of her too.

Her phone beeped. It was Abbie.

- Stop worrying. I've locked the doors.

She smiled and put her phone face down on the table. A moment later, Abbie texted again.

- I hope you're wearing matching underwear?

Mel reddened and shoved the phone back in her pocket. She didn't even own any matching underwear, *so there.*

"Did Abbie seem normal to you?" she asked now as Peter tried to flag down a waitress.

"She seemed fine. Why?"

"I don't know…" She fiddled with the button of his jacket, twisting it around between her forefinger and thumb. "I'm just not entirely certain she's…herself."

"What do you mean?"

"I mean, she's Abbie, but she's not Abbie."

"You're not making any sense, Melly."

"She's more obnoxious," she supplied. "You should have seen the look she gave me yesterday. It was like she hated me."

"Of course she doesn't hate you! She's worried about you, that's all."

"No, it's more than that! She's been so different. I'm beginning to wonder if there's something wrong with her. Maybe she's depressed or something? Do you know she put the house up for sale without even telling me? She reckons she needs the cash to save her business."

"Wouldn't that be for the best?" he said slowly. "I mean, it's too big, and you might not want to stay long…"

"It's our family home, and it's as much mine as hers. She has no right to sell it."

"Well, you'll have to talk it through with her and do what you think's best."

"I fully intend to."

"But I mean, from her point of view, perhaps it makes sense to sell. I know you're fond of that house, but is it really worth losing Abbie's business?"

She shifted uncomfortably. She hadn't expected this from him. She'd thought he'd be on her side.

A waitress appeared in front of them. "Do you want to hear today's specials?"

Peter nodded, and she rattled them off faster than a

high-speed train. As Mel could have predicted, he chose the most difficult thing to eat, which was the undressed crab.

"I'll have the scampi and chips," she said, closing her menu.

"Would you like any wine with your meal?"

"We'll just have some sparkling water," Peter told her. The waitress nodded and started to walk away.

"Wait!" Mel called after her. "I'll have a glass of red, please."

She waited for Peter to say something about how red wine didn't go with scampi, but he leaned back in his chair and kept his lips firmly pressed together. Maybe he really had changed.

Their food came quicker than Mel expected. They set the steaming hot crab in front of Peter, with what looked like an entire toolkit to extract the meat. He rolled his sleeves up and looked delighted as he picked up the hammer to crack it with. She reached for her own cutlery, which was wrapped tightly in a linen napkin. Automatically, he reached across to help her.

"Let me…"

"No, I can do it."

She tore the napkin open with such force that she accidentally elbowed the waitress behind her.

"Oof!"

"I'm sorry! So sorry!" She felt her cheeks burn, and it didn't help when Peter reached over and touched her hand.

"It's okay."

"Will you stop telling me it's okay? It's not okay, Peter. Not by a long shot. I don't know what the hell is going on with Abbie, but something is. She just isn't the same anymore. Something's missing. It's like…"

To her embarrassment, she felt tears streaking down

her face. She didn't even know why she was crying, but she wanted it to stop right away. She tried to explain to him. Told him about Abbie's new obsession with racing, but instead of being concerned, he burst out laughing. "No, sorry, I can't quite picture it."

"I'm serious, she watches that stuff for hours. Do you think she might be depressed?"

"What, because she's watching shite TV?"

"No, because she hardly ever goes out anymore. She doesn't even want to go to the pub."

"In that case, she must be ill."

"I'm serious, Peter. This is Abbie we're talking about. It's not like her."

"You know what I think?"

She shook her head.

"I think you should eat your scampi before it gets cold."

"Peter!"

"I'm serious! You've forgotten how to relax. So come on, eat, drink. Chill out. You're with me now. Everything's going to be fine."

After a few minutes, she did relax. She ate her scampi while he poked and tweezed his crab as if he were performing an operation. Her mind returned to the man in the car park, and she felt unsettled again.

"Do you think he might still be out there?" she asked, setting her fork down. "The intruder, I mean? What if he's just waiting for us to finish?"

Peter leaned towards her. "I won't let anything happen to you, Melly. I promise."

"What about Abbie?"

"I won't let anything happen to her, either."

The waitress came and took their plates. "Would you like anything else?"

"Not for me, thanks," Mel said.

"I don't suppose you do a crème brûlée?" Peter asked.

"Afraid not, sir. The apple crumble's very good, and we do a range of ice creams."

"I'll just have the bill, thanks," he said.

"Certainly."

She brought it over, and Peter produced his credit card. Mel pulled out her own. "We'll go halves," she insisted.

"That's really not necessary."

"Yes, Peter. It is."

They both tapped in their pin numbers, and he left an audacious tip. She let him.

"I'm going to go now," she said, to avoid any further awkwardness.

"Of course you are."

"I did have a nice time though."

"Me too." He patted his chin with his napkin. "So will I see you again tomorrow?"

"Yeah, why not?"

"I can run you home now if you want?"

"Thanks." She could hardly refuse. She wasn't going to walk home, knowing that man could still be lurking about, waiting for her.

"I'm really tired," she said when he pulled into Evergreen Crescent. Hers was the only house that still had a light on. The rest of the street stood in darkness, silent apart from the faint rustle of leaves in the wind. She'd lived in a crowded city for so many years that the stillness was disconcerting. It left her straining for sounds of life.

Peter reached across and squeezed her hand, accidentally sounding the horn in the process. They jumped apart, which set Mel off giggling. He didn't laugh with her. There was a serious expression in his eyes.

"I'll see you tomorrow," she told him as she hopped out of the car. He wanted her to invite him in, but she wasn't prepared to cross that line. She'd had a good time. She didn't want to ruin it.

She smiled as she let herself in, taking care to lock the door behind her. It wasn't until she was safely inside that she realised she was still wearing his jacket. She looked out the window, but his car was already gone. She searched the pockets, but there was nothing in them that he might urgently need, aside from a box of cinnamon mints and a packet of tissues. She hung the jacket on the banister and wondered if he'd let her hang on to it on purpose, as a visual reminder of him.

Paranoid much, Mel?

The house was quiet, but there was a light on in the living room. Mel walked towards the door and peered in. Abbie was sitting in that strange cross-legged pose again. She looked up from her magazine. Mel was amused to see that she'd finally moved on from the *Cosmo* magazines she used to devour and was now reading about fishing.

"Well? How did it go?"

Without waiting for an answer, Abbie went to the drinks cabinet and pulled out a bottle of scotch.

"Oh, no, thanks," Mel said.

"Wine, then," Abbie insisted.

"Red."

Abbie barrelled into the kitchen and returned with two glasses of wine. She set them down on the coffee table and flopped back into a chair, looking at her expectantly.

"It went okay," Mel said as truthfully as she could. "By which I mean, not a total disaster."

She watched her sister curiously, trying to pick up on

what it was that had unnerved her before. She seemed so normal now.

"Hey, do you remember that bloke you used to go out with before Peter?" Abbie said.

Mel blinked. She'd been so young then. Just a kid, really. She barely thought about him at all.

"I remember his stupid long scarf," Abbie went on. "He looked like Doctor Who."

Mel allowed herself a smile. "Yes, I think that's who he based himself on."

"Is that why he carried a screwdriver?"

They both cracked up, remembering. He'd been Mel's first boyfriend when she was about sixteen. She'd cried for days after he dumped her. She couldn't think why now.

"What about Dean?" she said, thinking of Abbie's first boyfriend, one in a very long line. Dean hadn't broken up with Abbie; she'd broken up with him, and Mel had felt quite sorry for the boy.

"God, Dean!" Abbie threw her head back.

"I quite liked him," Mel admitted now. "Shame he only had eyes for you."

Abbie giggled. "Well, what can I say? When you've got it, you've got it."

Before Mel could protest, she topped up both glasses again, and Mel felt more relaxed than she had in days. She felt silly now for doubting her sister.

"You know you and Pete are meant to be together?" Abbie said.

"How can you be so sure?"

"You just...get each other. That and the fact that you're both so dull and predictable..."

"Dull, I'll give you, but who are you calling predictable?" Mel grabbed a cushion and scrambled to her feet. "You'd better put that wine down!"

"Why?"

"Because…cushion attack!" She launched her cushion, and Abbie only just moved her glass out of the way in time. Soon, the cushions were flying back and forth, and they were both shrieking hysterically. Mel paused to catch her breath, smiling at Abbie. She had missed this.

Abbie went off to bed at midnight, but Mel was still wide awake, feeling buzzed and nostalgic for the past. After a brief search on her laptop, she found the home video compilation she and Abbie had made for their parents' silver wedding anniversary. Had it really been eight years ago? She laughed out loud as she clicked through the photos and video clips. When she came to the one of the family camping trip, she doubled up with laughter. Hadn't they just been talking about this the other day? There were all the cows mooing, and Abbie staring back at them, trying to moo back.

"I don't think they understand you," Dad was saying. "You must be speaking the wrong dialect."

This had made them laugh all the louder.

"I miss you, Dad," Mel said, touching her father's face through the screen.

16

The ping of the phone woke Mel way too early the next morning. It was Peter of course.

- *Last night was nice. What are you doing today?*

- *Working. What else?*

- *Need any help?*

She laughed at that. Peter was about as technical as a zoo animal. She was still impressed that he'd managed to figure out Zoom.

- *Nah, I'm fine, thanks. Speak later.*

She forced herself to concentrate on her work, but then the phone pinged again.

- *Can't find the way out of my hotel room.*

She ignored him.

- *Seriously. I think I might be stuck in the cupboard.*

She smiled and picked up the phone.

- *Call reception. I'm sure someone will be happy to help.*

- *I'd rather speak to you.*

She turned back to her work. She wanted him to leave her alone. And she didn't.

Unable to concentrate, she brought up the video

compilation she'd been watching the night before and watched a few more clips. There was Abbie in her old Asda uniform. She'd been working there when Mel left for Australia. And there was Mum cooking up a storm in the kitchen. She smiled as she watched her dad flip pancakes and Abbie cheered in appreciation. She was so grateful that they still had these old clips. It felt like she was being transported back to a simpler, happier time. Oh, goodness, there was Mel with her first boyfriend. She hadn't even realised they'd got him on video, but there he was, jogging up the path with his long scarf trailing behind him. She could even make out the screwdriver in his pocket. She chuckled to herself. Hadn't she and Abbie just been talking about him last night?

AT LUNCH TIME, she headed downstairs to find Otto outside again, whining to be let in.

"Aren't you going to take pity on him?" she asked Abbie, who was sitting at the kitchen table.

"Nah, it's good for him to get some fresh air, and besides, he'll only shed everywhere. I'm sick of hoovering up dog hair."

Mel stuck out her bottom lip. "Oh, come on!"

Otto didn't shed that much, and he was such a sweet, friendly dog. She snuck a look at her sister, who was changing the batteries in the remote. She got the impression Abbie didn't want him anymore. She hadn't seen her pet him once.

"I'm going to let him in," Mel decided. "He looks cold."

"Suit yourself."

She opened the back door, and the dog bounded into the house and straight over to his bowl, which was empty. Mel didn't even bother to ask Abbie if she'd fed him. She took it upon herself to get some food out for him. He licked his lips appreciatively and got stuck in.

Abbie looked up from the table. "Mel, I hate to ask, but have you come to a decision about the house yet? Only, we can't keep the buyer waiting forever."

Mel swallowed hard. "I thought you said you were hoping for a bidding war?"

Abbie pulled a face. "That would be nice, but no one's come forward with a higher bid, so I'm thinking this might be it." Her eyes bored into Mel. "If we don't hurry up and make a decision, we're going to lose out. They aren't going to wait forever."

Mel kept her head down and walked over to the coffee machine.

"You never told me exactly what went wrong with your business?" she said as she switched it on. "You were doing so well in the beginning. What happened? I can't believe people have stopped wanting boat trips. Is there too much competition?"

She waited for an answer, but Abbie just shook her head and tucked a strand of her blonde hair behind her ear. The cheap gold earrings she was wearing had left a black smudge mark on her earlobes.

"I really don't know what to tell you. I had a slow year. I had to repair the boat. Then there was bad weather on the day of a big booking, and I had to give the clients a refund, and then…I don't really know…"

She cast her eyes around the kitchen, as if the pot plants contained the answer.

"How about I take a look at your accounts for you?" Mel suggested gently.

She had set Abbie up with a simple spreadsheet to track her outgoings and expenditures. It was nothing fancy, just simple enough to cover her basic needs.

Looking at that might help pinpoint where she was going wrong.

"You are still using the spreadsheet?"

"Of course," Abbie said. She looked a little vacant, Mel thought.

"Right, well, I'd better get some work done now, but I'll come down later and take a look, okay?"

"Okay."

She topped up her mug with coffee and grabbed a banana to take back to her room.

It was several hours later before she came down again. She had finally made a breakthrough with the game and felt in need of a little sustenance.

"Do you have time to look at my spreadsheet?" Abbie asked the moment her foot hit the bottom step.

"Give me a minute," Mel said. "I need something to eat first."

"What do you want? A sandwich?"

"Are you offering? That would be nice."

"Cheese and ham do you?"

"That would be great, thanks."

She went into the living room and sat down at Abbie's computer. She didn't have to ask for the password. There was a luminous pink Post-it note on the side of the monitor that bore the word 'CaTcH22'. She logged in and waited for the computer to wake up. It was so old and slow, she pictured herself winding it up by hand.

She fired up the spreadsheet, the only one Abbie had, and looked over her numbers. Abbie had started off well, noting every expense, every bit of profit, but then she seemed to have just given up. There were very few entries for the past four months, and the numbers she had inputted made no sense at all. It was as if she'd just plucked them out of thin air. Mel leaned closer, trying to make sense of it all. Was this really all there was? Perhaps she'd lost some of the data and tried to re-enter it. If that was the case, Mel might be able to help her retrieve it.

"Abbie?"

She was about to ask about the spreadsheet when an email popped up. It was obviously private, so she was about to close it when she saw what it was. An appointment reminder from the Chicago Brain Clinic. It looked important.

"Hey, what's this?" she called out to her sister.

"What's what?"

Abbie appeared in the doorway, carrying a tray of sandwiches and drinks. The half-smile froze on her lips.

A bbie seemed flustered as she plonked the tray down on the table. A cherry tomato rolled across the floor, but neither of them went after it.

"What's going on?" Mel demanded. "Why have they sent you this?"

She consulted the email: "If you choose to go ahead with the programme, we can promise you improved cognitive function, high-quality physical therapy and behavioural therapy as part of the six-week programme. We must receive your non-refundable deposit of £12,000 no later than Nov 1. The remaining balance of £96,000 can then be paid in monthly instalments."

She looked up at Abbie, who blinked rapidly, as if she had something in her eye.

"Tell me!"

"If you must know…" Abbie drew circles on the ground with her stockinged foot. "I had a bit of an accident. On the boat."

"What happened?"

Mel thought back to their day out on the *Catch 22*. It hadn't seemed damaged as far as she could tell, but then, Abbie had mentioned getting it repaired.

"You remember that cove I took you to?"

"Yes, of course."

"Well, I took a group of tourists there back in June. They wanted to have a go at spearfishing."

"And?"

"Well, I don't remember much, but I was up on deck, demonstrating something, when I fell backwards and hit my head. I was completely out for the count."

"You knocked yourself out? How bad?"

"I don't really remember. I conked out for a bit, and when I woke up, I had a fuzzy head, like I'd been drinking. Someone was saying something, but I couldn't make anything out, and I struggled to focus. I couldn't understand what had happened."

Mel looked at her in horror. "How did you even get yourself home in that state? I'm amazed you didn't end up in France or something."

"I was okay. I had some decent people on the boat. They knew enough to get us back to the marina. They were pretty good about it too, even though I'd ruined their day out."

"But what about you? Did they take good care of you?"

"As luck would have it, one of them was a nurse. She knew exactly what to do. Anyway, to cut a long story short, she made me go to hospital. I didn't really want to go, but I knew something wasn't right. I could hear ringing in my ears, I felt really tired, and I had a bad taste in my mouth, but still I thought she was making a fuss."

"Abbie!"

"I had some tests done, Mel, and it's not good. I've got a type of traumatic brain injury called a brain contusion. It basically means that my brain tissue is bruised."

Mel's jaw dropped. "But...but why didn't anyone ring me? I'm meant to be your next of kin, for Christ's sake!"

Abbie placed a hand on her arm. "You were in Australia! And really, I'm fine. I'm just a bit different now, that's all."

Mel stared at her, and everything seemed to fall in to place, because Abbie was right, she *was* different. She'd thought there was something off about her from the minute she'd come home. No wonder she'd been acting weird. No wonder they'd struggled to reconnect.

"I'm going to help you!" she said, immediately feeling guilty. Why hadn't she suspected Abbie was ill? It all made sense now. This was why she'd stopped socialising, and why she wasted her time watching TV. It also explained her complete lack of humour. Her lack of...Abbieness.

"How...how bad is it?"

Abbie climbed onto the sofa, sitting in that odd cross-legged pose again. "I wish I could say it was nothing, but the truth is, I have such trouble remembering things now. It's like half my memories have been stolen, and I'm just left with bits and pieces. A lot of the time I'm struggling to fill in the blanks."

Mel's eyes welled with tears, and her heart ached as her sister went on.

"I barely remember anything from school or my twenties. I just get little snatches, like I remember this red coat I used to have, or the time we rode donkeys on the beach."

Mel clicked her fingers. "Morecambe Bay!"

"Yes, I can remember the smell of the donkey, the vivid blue of the sea, but I can't remember actually being there. it's all just fragments, and it's really frustrating. I'm not even sure I feel like me anymore, Mel. I don't like the same things. The house was full of those blueberry wheat cereals, and I don't even know why I bought them. I can't stand the bloody things."

Mel bit down on her lower lip to keep it from trembling. Poor, poor Abbie. It was like she'd been completely reprogrammed, with just a trace of the person she was before.

"I remember being in hospital, and a nurse walked in, and I asked her when dinner was, and she told me I'd already had it, but I had no memory of it. I really couldn't remember."

"You don't do that now," Mel said. "Perhaps you're getting better?"

"God, I hope so." Abbie turned her gaze to the empty spot where their dad's harp used to be. How much did she even remember about their parents? Mel wondered. Although the memories could be painful, she couldn't imagine losing them. Memories were all they had.

"I thought I was doing okay," Abbie went on. "I was discharged from hospital after about a week or so. I came back home, and it was hard, but I was managing day to day. What I couldn't manage was the business. I still knew how to handle the boat. It seems to be locked into my long-term memory, but people kept calling me, telling me they were waiting for me at the harbour, and I didn't even remember making the appointments."

Mel covered her mouth with her hand. "Oh, Abbie! Why didn't you say something before? When were you going to tell me?"

Abbie wiped her eyes with her sleeve. "It's hard, all right? I don't want people to think I'm mental or something. I don't want you to think that."

"Of course I wouldn't…"

"And then you called me, completely out of the blue! When I heard your voice, my first reaction was that you knew. That you must have felt it somehow, you know, because we're twins."

Mel swallowed. "I…"

"But then I realised you had no idea, and then I felt this burning anger towards you, but I honestly can't tell you why. Had we…had we had an argument or something?"

"No," Mel said quietly. "I think we'd just grown a bit distant, that's all. After Mum and Dad passed."

A branch tapped against the windowpane, and they both looked up, a little startled.

"How *are* you feeling? On a day-to-day basis, I mean. Obviously you must be frustrated?"

Abbie's eyes closed for a minute, as if she was trying to summon up her thoughts.

"I'm ruled by my heart now," she finally said. "I feel more primal. I go with what my gut tells me. I know when I'm pissed off or hungry or…or…when I find something funny, but I don't always know why. My mind feels so blank sometimes. Like it's completely vacant. Before I was always looking forward to the next big party, but now I'm just living, trying to get from one day to the next. I can't cope with any more than that."

"And this clinic?"

"I think they can help me. I need help to improve my memory and get myself back to how I was before. Otherwise I have to wait to get a treatment plan on the NHS. It might be okay; the only problem is the waiting list."

"How long is the waiting list?"

Abbie pressed her lips together. "About three years."

"Three years?" Mel shook her head. "That's ridiculous!"

"Tell me about it. They can't do what this clinic can do anyway. They just want to fix me enough that I can get back to work, but these private American clinics, they really might be able to help. That's what my consultant said, anyway."

Mel nodded, taking this in. "So this is the real reason you want to sell the house?"

Abbie nodded. "It's not just the business that's going down the tubes, Mel. It's me as well."

Mel leaned in to hold her and felt tears trickle down her face.

"I'm here now," she whispered. "And I'm never going to leave you again."

Mel had never considered herself a spiritual person, but perhaps she had come back home for a reason. She had a purpose now, and that purpose was to nurse her sister back to health. She needed to make sure Abbie looked after herself from now on. There had been nothing she could do for her parents, but it wasn't too late for Abbie. She was determined to help her get better.

She needed time to digest this news. It was shocking, like a plate smashing on the floor, the pieces flying everywhere. She wanted to ask Abbie more, but she knew it wouldn't do to ply her with questions. She already looked tired, and she needed time to take it all in.

She also knew this version of Abbie didn't take well to being mothered. She required careful handling, because if Mel fussed too much, she was liable to blow her top. All the same, Mel felt the need to check on her every so often. She had visions of finding her collapsed on the floor, and she would never forgive herself if anything happened to her twin.

Her phoned beeped with texts from Peter, but she could hardly take them in. She felt awful that Abbie had had to go through something so traumatic on her own. But she was here now, and she was going to do everything in her power to help her get better.

She recalled a friend's dad who'd had a skiing accident when they were young. She remembered he'd always been so jolly and fun, but after the accident, he sat as stiff as a board in his armchair and didn't seem to understand the meaning behind any of their jokes. The kids at school had called him Robo Dad. She hadn't liked going round her friend's house after that. She felt bad about that now, but at the time she'd just been a kid who didn't understand.

Her phone buzzed again, but she left it charging. She couldn't think about Peter now. She got on her laptop and read everything she could about traumatic brain injuries and brain contusions. It made her feel a little sick, the thought of Abbie's brain being bruised like that. Was it still bruised? she wondered. Or had it healed now? She had so much to learn.

Later, she found Abbie doing nothing at all, just sitting in the living room, staring vacantly at the wall.

"I know you've got that American clinic lined up, but what are the doctors here doing to help you?" she asked.

Abbie let out a big yawn. "I've had lots of boring appointments where they ask me endless questions and make me walk up and down the room to see if I'm walking funny. I've seen a neurologist too."

"Was that any help?"

"Not really. She shone lights into my eyes until I wanted to punch her."

"Have they given you any advice? I mean, you've been driving around and taking the boat out. Is that safe?"

Abbie looked insulted. "That's all muscle memory. I'm sure I'm no worse than some of those other idiots on the road."

"No, of course not…"

But thinking back, she *had* noticed a difference in Abbie's driving. Her impatience, her lack of attention to detail. Was she really allowed to be driving? She supposed the doctor would have notified the DVLA if not.

"And this clinic in America – when are you supposed to go?"

"At the end of next month."

"Where is it again?"

"Chicago."

"Isn't there anything nearer?"

"Apparently not."

Mel stared at her for a moment. "You weren't going to tell me, were you? I mean, what would you have said when you actually went for the treatment?"

"I was going to say I was going on holiday."

"You were going to go on your own?"

"You were in Australia," Abbie reminded her. "I've got used to doing things on my own."

Mel slapped herself round the head. "I've been a crap sister, haven't I? Abbie, if you need help, then I'm going to see that you get it."

Abbie smiled weakly. She seemed tired, so Mel left her and wandered into the kitchen, where she boiled some spaghetti and heated up a tin of meatballs. They could both use a decent meal. When the food was ready, she took a plate in to Abbie in the living room. Abbie didn't even thank her, but Mel hoped she would remember to eat it. Then she returned to the kitchen and sat down with her laptop at the table. She could eat while she worked. The more she thought about things, the more stupid she felt. She should have known something was wrong with Abbie from the minute she went on that social media detox. She hadn't been on Facebook or Instagram in months. It wasn't like her. And where were all Abbie's friends? Had they all abandoned her the minute she went quiet? She felt angry on her sister's behalf. How could they be so fickle?

Abbie came in just as she was swallowing the last mouthful of spaghetti. Mel watched as she dumped her plate in the sink.

"It's changed me, Mel."

Mel looked up at her. She still found Abbie's hard stare a bit unnerving. Even if she understood now why she looked like that.

"It's like the things I care about don't matter anymore. Not even the business, if I'm honest. Not my friends, either. They've stopped calling and inviting me to go out with them, but I don't care as much as I should. I've found I quite like my company. Does that sound weird?"

Mel shook her head. "Look who you're talking to! If you tell me you've developed an interest in computer games, I might cry."

"Not going to happen. Look, I'm sorry if I seem difficult and unlovable. The doctor told me my moods would be different now. Things that didn't used to bother me make me see red, and things I used to care about don't seem to matter. But I should warn you, Mel. You need to be more careful around me and do your best not to upset me, because I'm not myself right now, and I honestly don't know how I'm going to act from one moment to the next."

She stared right in Mel's eyes as she said this, and Mel was struck again by how different she appeared.

18

"What's the name of this doctor, the one who's been treating you?" Mel asked.

Abbie thought for a moment, but she couldn't recall.

Mel looked at her with concern. "You must have it written down somewhere?"

"Yeah, probably. Give me a mo."

She pulled out her phone and scrolled through it for a few minutes. "Ah, here it is, Dr Patel at the Dorset Clinic. Dr Monica Patel," she clarified.

Mel made a note of the name. She wanted to speak to this Dr Patel for herself. Perhaps she could tell her if Abbie was okay to drive. Or drink. She needed to know more too, like what she could do to help.

Abbie had already lost interest in the conversation. Mel followed her into the living room and watched as she flicked through the channels, no doubt looking for something loud and obnoxious to watch. Mel silently berated herself. She had to stop thinking this way. It wasn't Abbie's fault her taste in programmes sucked. She wasn't herself.

Abbie picked horse racing, and Mel promptly returned to her room to shut out the noise. She didn't want Abbie to overhear anyway. Even though she was trying to help her, she had a feeling her sister wouldn't appreciate her making calls on her behalf. She had been so up and down lately, who knew when she might fly into a rage?

She looked up the number for Abbie's doctor's and dialed.

"Hi, my name's Mel Montgomery. I understand you're treating my sister, Abbie Thompson, for a traumatic brain injury? Can I speak to Dr Patel, please?"

The woman on the other end of the phone spoke with a public school accent. Mel pictured her, prim and white haired with wire-rimmed glasses held in place with a cord. "I'm awfully sorry, but the doctor won't be able to give out any details."

"I get that, but we can talk in a general way, can't we? I need to know what I can do to help with her recovery."

There was a pause. "I can put you in touch with some support groups if you like? They'd be better placed to help."

"Thank you," Mel said quietly. She gave out her email address and set down the phone. It was so frustrating. She supposed it made sense that they couldn't discuss Abbie's case over the phone, but how was she supposed to help her if she didn't have the full picture? Abbie might be able to tell her more, but she was hardly the most reliable person to ask.

Her phone pinged, and she saw that the receptionist had sent her an email with links to some useful information. It was all very general, but she waded through it anyway. Knowledge was power, wasn't that what Dad had always said?

It seemed as though Abbie was likely to need lots of different therapies: psychological therapy, physiotherapy, occupational therapy, even speech therapy. She paused at this last one. Abbie could talk just fine, but now she came to think about it, she sounded a little different than before. Her voice was huskier, and her choice of words was more basic, plus she was constantly swearing at the TV.

She clicked on a link to a brain-injury forum and soon lost herself in the posts. There were so many heart-wrenching stories of lives ruined by traumatic brain injury. Most of the posts were written by family members who were struggling to come to terms with the way their loved ones had changed. There were mothers who said their children were like strangers and husbands who no longer recognised their wives. The way one woman put it, it was as if her brother had lost his soul. He didn't look any different, but he moved more sluggishly, and his facial expressions had become surly. There was a picture of him staring into the camera like he wanted to smash it. It gave Mel the chills.

Someone else had posted about how his wife had gone from timid to aggressive overnight. She had been kind and thoughtful before, but now she was mean to the children and angry with him, accusing him of not loving her anymore.

"The worst part is that she's probably right," he'd written. "She's not my Julie anymore. The woman I loved is gone."

It made Mel weep, not just for Abbie but for herself too. She turned and stared out the window. It was as quiet as ever out there, not so much as a dog barking to disturb the stillness of the street. She reached for her coffee and found that it was cold. She could heat it up in the microwave, but she'd only forget to drink it again. Her head was all over the place.

She ran her hands through her hair, thinking about what she was going to do. She felt as if she had to get to know this new Abbie from scratch. For all she knew, this was what her sister was going to be like from now on. It was a sobering thought.

She took a deep breath and went on with her research, looking up the treatment Abbie had told her about. However, a brief read of the programme available at the Chicago Brain Clinic told her that it was completely unsuitable, geared towards people who needed significant physiotherapy, whilst Abbie's main issue was her memory. She jogged downstairs, clutching her laptop.

"How did you find the Chicago clinic?" she asked Abbie. "Did your doctor recommend it?"

Abbie looked up from her racing and blinked like a hedgehog in the fog.

"The doctor said the best treatment programmes were in America, so I thought that one sounded about right."

Mel shook her head. "Well, it's a good thing I'm here now because, believe me, this is not the one you need."

Abbie's face altered slightly. "I'm the one with the bloody brain injury! How am I supposed to know what's best?"

"Let me help you," Mel said gently, hoping her voice would soothe her. "I can take a look at some alternatives. We need to make sure you get the treatment that's right for you. I don't want them putting you in with people who can barely remember their own names. You might have had a lot of memory loss, but you're still talking and functioning well."

"All right," Abbie relented. "I thought the Chicago

one looked good, but if you think you can find me a better one, knock yourself out. I get the last say though. I'm not going on some weird hippy retreat. I need proper modern medicine."

Mel laughed. "What do you take me for?"

"I don't know," Abbie said. "I can't bloody remember."

AFTER A COUPLE of hours on Google, Mel had come up with a list of private clinics that she thought could treat Abbie. Whichever one they went with, it was going to be expensive, but she couldn't worry about that now. Like she'd told Abbie, they'd find the money. All that mattered was helping her get better.

"There's a clinic in San Francisco that has internationally renowned doctors, and they're doing some groundbreaking work," she told Abbie. "I think it might be the one."

Abbie rubbed her temples as if they hurt. "How much is it?"

"Let's not worry about that right now."

"But is it any cheaper than the other one?"

"It's more expensive," she admitted. "But I don't think that's what we should be focusing on. We need to get this right, Abbie. The right treatment could make all the difference. We'll need to speak to them on the phone, and then I think we should fly over there and meet them, see if they can help you."

"Okay."

Of course, they could do it all over Zoom, but she wanted to take an active part in her sister's treatment, and this way she would. Besides, Abbie was going to need a lot of support with her recovery. Mel needed to make sure she got up to speed. She didn't want Abbie to feel like she was in this alone. She wanted to give her sister the best possible chance of success.

"Look, I've come to a decision," she said. "About the house."

Abbie looked at her hesitantly. "Yes?"

"If it means getting you the treatment you need, then I'll sell. It's what Mum and Dad would have done and —"

Abbie jumped on her and hugged her so tight Mel couldn't breathe. She wriggled out of her sister's grasp.

"Careful. You nearly made me puke."

"Sorry, Mel. I'm just so grateful. You won't regret this!"

"Of course I won't! You should have told me about your brain injury from the beginning. Of course I'm on your side. After all, what could be more important than your health?"

19

Mel wrapped her arms around Abbie and wished she could take her injury away. It was funny, she even smelled a little different, as if the damage to her brain had somehow caused a chemical reaction in her body. She held her tight, wishing she could take back the years of distance. This was her sister, her twin, and she'd almost lost her.

Eventually, Abbie pulled away and headed to the kitchen, returning with a bottle of wine and two glasses.

"Should you be drinking that?" Mel asked as Abbie poured the wine.

"Huh?"

"The wine. From what I've read, you shouldn't be drinking."

Abbie pulled a face. "Life isn't worth living if I can't have a drink."

Mel bit her tongue. The more she argued, the more Abbie would want to drink. The only thing she could do was not bring alcohol into the house in future.

She waited until Abbie was settled back in front of the TV; then she grabbed a couple of bottles from the wine rack. She'd smuggle them upstairs to hide in her room and drink them herself if necessary. The things she did for her sister!

She worked for a while; then she went down to check on Abbie, who had barely moved from where she'd left her.

"Don't stay up too late, will you?" Mel said. "It's important you get your rest."

Abbie's head whipped round so fast it made her jump. "What the fuck do you think I've been doing?"

"I…"

Abbie drew a breath. "Sorry! Sorry, I can't help it."

"I know you can't."

Abbie grabbed her hand, causing her to flinch. "For god's sake, I'm not going to hurt you!"

"I know."

Their eyes locked, and Mel felt an irrational tingle of fear. She was being stupid. This was her sister. Abbie would never hurt her. Abbie pulled back and ran a hand through her hair, the way she always did when she was fighting to find the right words.

"Just stop fussing over me, Mel. It doesn't help, and meanwhile, poor Pete's sitting alone in his hotel room, waiting for you to call. You're not being fair to him. Why don't you take him down to London or something and show him the sights?"

"Maybe," Mel said. But she could hardly leave Abbie alone for the day. Besides, she had work to do. She was close to fixing the bug, but she'd barely made any progress since she'd found out about Abbie's accident. She was too busy researching traumatic brain injuries, and the more she read, the more she realised she didn't know. Would Abbie's change of personality be permanent? Could she get worse? There was so much to think about.

Her phone buzzed, and Abbie looked at her pointedly.

"He's come a bloody long way to see you. The least you can do is talk to him. You owe him that."

Mel brought the phone to her ear. "Peter, hi. Sorry, I've been busy."

He didn't sound annoyed, but his patience rubbed her up the wrong way. She didn't want his understanding, she wanted his fury, his passion.

"Listen, I know it's late, but I'm getting cabin fever, cooped up at the hotel. How about a moonlight stroll along that fabulous beach of yours? We could even have a go at the arcades."

"I'm afraid you're a bit late for the arcades. They're already closed for the year."

"Are they? Pity. I had my hopes pinned on winning a pocketful of change. Never mind, I'll have to make do with your company instead."

She smiled in spite of herself. A moonlit walk might be just what she needed.

"Do you want to come?" she asked Abbie as she grabbed both her coat and Peter's.

"And play gooseberry to you pair? I don't think so."

"It's just a walk," Mel said, but Abbie waved her away.

"I DON'T THINK I've ever been here out of season before," Peter mused half an hour later. "Weymouth feels all wrong in the autumn, without all the loudmouths and the traffic."

"I like it better," Mel admitted as they set off down the footpath.

In the summer, the town had a thriving nightlife, but now the pubs were empty, only the locals propping up the bar. The pier looked a bit sorry for itself with all the rides fenced off and the lights dimmed, and powerful waves thrashed against the sea wall, threatening to spill over the edge.

"Stop!" Peter said. "Stand there!"

"What?"

"I want to take your picture!"

"Here?"

It was so windy, Mel's coat had puffed up like a mushroom, and she had to hold it down. Her scarf sailed in the air above her head.

"Smile!"

She did, baring all her teeth like a mad dog.

"Beautiful, lovely!" Peter called. "A seaside snap. Wait till I show all my friends!"

He'd said 'my', not 'our'. Mel felt a slight dip in her stomach. Was he finally accepting that they were two separate people, living two separate lives?

They strolled on. The deserted pier felt a little treacherous, but she felt safe enough with Peter beside her, knowing she could grab onto him if need be. Of course, if he slipped, they were both screwed.

He looked at her fondly. "Admit it, you were a bit rash, the way you ran off like that."

Mel glanced at him out of the corner of her eye. "I don't know. I didn't see any other way out. I'd brought that bloke home. I thought we were finished."

Peter ran his tongue around his teeth. He didn't like her mentioning the affair. He wanted to pretend it had never happened, but it had. She remembered the anguish on his face when he'd caught her. His entire face had trembled. She'd thought he was finally going to lose it. She'd expected yelling and screaming. Perhaps the smashing of glass. She'd deserved nothing less. But he'd just turned around and walked out the door, like he'd just popped home for his glasses, and it had struck her then that nothing she did really ever mattered, because he was always ready to explain it away. That realisation had been the final straw.

For a while, neither of them said anything. They walked as far as they could in one direction and then turned and walked back, heading up the hill towards Mel's house. Mel paused outside the Duck. Would she be stringing Peter along if she took him to her local? She'd been itching to go there, and she could hardly take Abbie now that she knew about the brain injury.

"Do you…fancy a drink?" she asked, feeling a little foolish.

"Yeah, why not?"

She felt a flash of irritation that he'd agreed so easily. Back in Sydney, it had never been this easy to get him to go out. All he ever wanted to do was stay at home and watch Netflix. All her hints about trying out new restaurants and bars fell on deaf ears. If they went out at all, it was always to one of two cafés. Perfectly nice cafés, it was true, but never anywhere different, anywhere interesting.

She led him inside the Duck and found her favourite nook, tucked into one of the side rooms. There were shelves of crumbly old books and wooden tables that had been fashioned out of barrels.

"Bit smoky in here," he remarked.

Despite the decade-old smoking ban, there was a distinct smell of hops and malt and cigarettes ground into age-old ashtrays. The scent was soaked into the carpet and curtains, ingrained in the wooden surfaces and trapped between the pages of the musty old books. Mel found it nostalgic. It reminded her of carefree nights out with her family and friends.

Peter went to the bar and came back with a cranberry juice for himself and a double Baileys for her, plus a share-sized bag of cheese and onion crisps, the posh ones. Instead of cheddar they were flavoured with Stilton, and instead of onion it was shallot. They sat and nursed their drinks for a while, comfortable in each other's company. It could have been a nice way to spend an evening, relaxing in the cosy armchairs, drinking and talking. Laughing about old times. Why couldn't they have done this in Sydney?

She felt Peter watching her, his throat contracting as she swallowed her drink.

"Something's bothering you," he said after a while.

"Yes," she admitted. Drawing a breath, she told him about Abbie. He listened with concern.

"You mustn't say anything to her," she warned. "She's very sensitive about it. She doesn't want anyone to know."

"Nor would I."

She narrowed her eyes. "What do you mean?"

"Well, people would look at you differently, wouldn't they? Like you weren't in your right mind."

She almost laughed out loud. Ever since her 'wobble', she'd had to deal with people fussing over her and judging her. Colleagues at work, Derick, but most of all Peter. He didn't even see the irony.

"Anyway, Abbie's going to need an expensive course of treatment in America, so I've decided to sell the house after all. I'll speak to the estate agent in the morning."

"I think you're doing the right thing," he said. "You don't need that house anyway. We've got a perfectly good house in Sydney."

"Peter!"

"I'm just kidding! Trying to lighten the mood."

She smiled weakly and took another sip.

"What about you? Do you think you should go to a doctor?" he asked.

She shook her head. "Abbie's already got a doctor, and we're looking at getting her into a clinic in the states."

"No, not for Abbie," he said, "for you. I told you, I'm worried about you."

She shook her head in frustration. Felt his eyes circling the glass as she swallowed the last of her drink. "And I've told you, I'm fine. Now, I'm going to the bar. Can I get you another?"

"No, thanks. One's enough for me."

She got up anyway. They were going to have to have the talk. They couldn't keep putting it off just because they enjoyed each other's company. Only, she didn't know how to talk to him, even after all these years. She was pretty awesome at appeasing him, avoiding the subject, saying what he wanted to hear. But she'd never really learned to say it like it was. He was too nice. Too thoughtful. He never seemed to fight back. It never felt like a fair fight. Whenever she told him something he didn't want to hear, he gave her that look like a wounded puppy, or he pretended she hadn't said anything. He'd go off to bed or busy himself with some household chore. Always left her feeling like an utter shit.

"Do you want to know why I did it?" she said when she returned from the bar. She set her drink down on a beer mat. A triple Baileys this time.

Peter blinked. "I already understand. You weren't yourself, Melly. Given the circumstances, I'm willing to overlook the… All that matters is getting you well again, and getting things back on track."

He lowered his gaze and gave her a smile that would once have liquified her insides. "If anything, it's made me realise just how much I love you. Just how much I've missed you. I never want to be without you again, Mel. I know things haven't been perfect, but we belong together, you and me..."

It was tempting, this explanation of his, and easier for him to accept. She hadn't been in her right mind. She'd been depressed, on the verge of a nervous breakdown. That was what he was suggesting. Why else would she cheat on a loving partner for a man she'd only just met? A man whose name she couldn't recall?

"No," she said firmly. The vehemence in her voice seemed to startle him.

"Mel..." He was already trying to cut her off. He seized the packet of posh crisps and tore into them, holding the bag out in front of her. She pushed his hand away, and she saw his eyes dart around the room, looking for another distraction.

"Hey, they've got Pac-Man! You used to love that game. You want to play?"

He jumped up from the table and rummaged desperately in his pocket; then he glanced at her, begging her for a lifeline. "You got any change?"

"Sit down, Peter. We need to talk. I need to explain myself."

"I told you, I understand."

"I don't think you do."

His eyes betrayed him. She stared into them, found comfort in those dark pools of marmite.

"Peter, I wasn't happy."

"Are any of us really happy?"

"Yes, I'd like to think so."

He raised an eyebrow, like what she was saying sounded unreasonable.

"I mean it, Peter. We were stuck in a rut. For the past twenty years, I've woken up every day to the same bloody view of the flat opposite. We never saw anyone. We never went anywhere. We never did anything."

"Holidays are expensive."

"Life is expensive! I wanted us to try salsa dancing or take French classes."

"I'm not interested in any of those things."

"We might have had a little fun!"

"I was having fun!" he said. "I was perfectly happy with things the way they were. I liked our nights in. I liked our Sunday walks and our shopping trips. I thought we had a great life together. I didn't realise you were getting sick again."

Mel gritted her teeth. "I'm not sick."

"You have to be. That's why you did it. You'd never cheat on me otherwise. You're not like that." He couldn't look at her as he said this. "Not unless you weren't in your right mind."

There was a certain hopefulness in this last sentence, and his intention was clear. Accept his version of the truth and they could both pretend it had never happened.

Maybe if he'd got angry, there might have been a chance for them. But Mel couldn't do it. Not this time.

"I'm not sick," she repeated. "I knew perfectly well what I was doing. It was wrong, Peter. Certainly not the adult way to handle things, but I knew what I was doing."

She watched as his shoulders and stomach sagged, and his chin fell to his chest. It was horrible, breaking his heart all over again, but at least he knew where he stood now. Perhaps they could finally move on.

20

There was no conversation as Peter walked her back to her house. It felt awkward and awful, and Mel was sure he would be straight on the phone to the travel agent when he got back to the hotel, booking his flight home. Peter never had got in the habit of using online booking forms like other people. He still preferred to do everything in person.

She felt bad for causing him so much pain, but she wasn't sorry she'd been honest.

The lights were on in the living room when she got in, but she wasn't in the mood to talk to Abbie. She peered in briefly to check she was all right, then grabbed a wine glass from the kitchen and headed upstairs to her room.

She slept in late the next morning despite Otto's best efforts to get her up. She'd fallen asleep dreaming about the game again, dreaming about the assassin. Derick had messaged her again, much to her annoyance, wanting to know when she'd be finished. Soon, she hoped. She wanted this thing done as much as he did.

· · ·

IT WAS around lunchtime the next day when she went downstairs and checked on Abbie. She found her sister fast asleep in front of the TV, which was showing some kind of motorbike stunt course with lots of tyres screeching and people cheering. How she could sleep through that racket, Mel had no idea, but at least she was getting some rest. She was glad Abbie was asleep because she wasn't ready to talk about Peter. The last thing she needed was Abbie berating her for 'throwing away a good thing'.

She let Otto in from the garden and poured out some food for him, then she made herself some toast and returned to her room, but she soon felt like punching the screen. Not only was her concentration shot to pieces by the sound of Abbie's motorsports downstairs, but the internet seemed to be powered by a sloth. She heard Abbie moving around downstairs. Clearly she was awake now, but what was she doing down there? Mining Bitcoin?

She packed her laptop into her bag and grabbed her wallet. She spent too much time in the house anyway. An afternoon in a café would make a nice change. Growing up, she had often packed up her books and decamped somewhere quieter so she could study. Back then, the problem had been Abbie's friends. There had always been at least two or three of them in the house, talking loudly and generally being irritating. Abbie was always barging in and trying to get her to 'join in' or 'wear something more colourful' as if she could just morph into a more socially acceptable version of herself.

The sun was shining as she trudged down the hill, laptop bag swinging from her shoulder. She smiled as she caught sight of her favourite little café wedged between the bookshop and the bank. The Hideaway looked exactly as she'd left it. Even the staff were the same: trendy, worthy types wearing oversized aprons and garish wellies. They seemed to be competing with one another to see who could pierce the most parts of their body, and their hair was a delightful assortment of red, purple, and blue.

The top level of the café was devoted to yoga, and soft piano music wafted down the stairs. Mel plonked herself down at her favourite table in the darkest corner and read the menu by candlelight. When the waiter came over, she ordered a large latte and avocado on toast. It came with a side of beetroot. They served beetroot with everything here. They even snuck it into the cakes. She munched on her toast as she worked.

SHE STANDS *on the railway line, looking over the valley at the mists of Heaven's Hill. The train driver gets into his cab, and all the passengers scurry aboard. She has a choice to make; she can either join them or investigate the driver. He hasn't cropped up in the game before, which makes his presence suspicious. Should she light her remaining stick of dynamite in case he turns out to be the assassin, or should she board the train, which could take her to the Heaven's Hill and the End Zone?*

MEL SIGHED. It had to be the dynamite. It was always the dynamite. She lit the fuse and threw it into the driver's cab. For a moment, the entire train was lit green; then she saw the driver morph into a frog, followed by a handsome prince; then the game froze once again.

Two lattes and a beetroot cookie later, a gust of wind blew down her neck, and she looked up, startled.

Someone had left the door open, and it was flapping about in the wind. She rose from her seat to go and close it, but the purple-haired waitress got there first, tutting loudly at whoever had just walked out. Looking around, Mel realised she was now the only customer. The café owner was making obvious hints about wanting to close.

"Sorry," she muttered, shutting her laptop.

She was surprised to see that it was almost dark outside as she shoved everything back into her bag. She left a generous tip to make up for outstaying her welcome and set off for home. She knew these roads well, yet there was something slightly otherworldly about the way the leaves vibrated, almost as if they were whispering to her. She was hit by an odd, sinking sensation in her stomach, and a warning light lit up in her head. Something was off.

Behind you.

Look behind you.

She did not want to look behind her. Her legs felt a little heavy, like she was dragging them through thick mud. She crossed the road, taking the opportunity to swing her head slightly to the left. She caught the shadows of the sycamore trees and noted the delicate progress of a cat as it tiptoed along the pavement.

Look again.

She risked another glance over her shoulder, too quick to take much in. She could just make out a shadowy figure moving towards her, footsteps uneven. She squinted into the darkness. He wore a dark coat and had the hood up, partially obscuring his face. She was certain it was a 'he'. There was something about the way he held himself, as if he owned the street.

She picked up speed, listening intently. Soft footsteps

echoed hers, the sound of shoes scuffing the pavement behind her. Getting closer.

She whipped her head round and saw him clearly now, in the dusty glow of the street light. He kept his head down, the hood obscuring his forehead. He was slightly flat-footed, she noticed, and his feet seemed to glide along the pavement. He had his hands stuffed in his pockets, but those eyes…those were *his* eyes. The eyes of the intruder. They had heat in them. Anger. Menace.

Her legs felt unnatural as she began to run. Running had never been her strong suit. She was a desk jockey, a lounge dweller. She hadn't so much as run for the bus in years, and here she was tearing along like the pavement was on fire. She glimpsed the darkened windows of the holiday houses as she passed. All the curtains and blinds were drawn. No one actually lived in them out of season. She patted the pockets of her coat and trousers. If only she'd put her phone somewhere handy, but she must have thrown it into her bag along with the laptop, having no idea she'd need it on the way home.

She kept moving, one foot in front of the other. She focused on her breath, in and out, until the sound of her breathing felt like the loudest sound in the street. Then she heard a new sound, and she knew then that he was right behind her, his breathing synched with hers.

She spotted an alley and remembered running down there with Abbie when they were kids, past a row of allotments and out onto Cedar Road. The alley was dark and filled with dustbins, but if she could just get out onto the allotments, she'd be home and dry.

She ran. He ran. She stumbled over the rubbish, her bag swinging at her hip. The bins seemed to be every-where. It felt as though she were running through a slalom. He was getting closer. Too close. She grabbed a dustbin lid and hurled it towards him. *Where was the shortcut?* The gap between the fence? She ran her hand along the wall, knowing it should be there. Instead, her fingers scraped against brickwork. There was no gap. Someone had built a house on the site of the allotment, and now there was no way out.

21

S he felt his sour breath on her neck. She pulled her laptop bag over her shoulder and thrust it towards him, trembling as she spoke:
"Here, take it!"

"I don't want your computer!" His voice was sharp and hostile, his accent unfamiliar.

He wasn't English, that was for sure. He spoke carefully, overenunciating each word.

He thrust the bag back at her, and she grabbed it, held it like a shield, separating his body from hers. The sweaty, leathery smell of his jacket filled her nostrils. He was even more pungent than the chicken bones and vegetable peelings that spilled from the bins. She needed to get past, but he blocked the way. She held the laptop bag out in front of her. She couldn't bear to brush past him. She just needed to get away.

"Wait! I need to talk to you."

She didn't know what he wanted. In her mind, his face had become synonymous with the assassin. Panic tore at her insides. He was going to kill her. She was going to die. The whiteness of his teeth stood out in the dim light. He was missing one, right in the front, and another looked badly chipped.

What would she do, if this were her game? In the absence of dynamite, she threw back her arm and punched him as hard as she could, catching the side of his nose.

"Ahh!" His hand flew to his face. He seemed disorientated, staggering against the wall. She tried to run away, but her foot collided with a bin, sending her sprawling.

He grabbed her, catching her before she fell. She wriggled and kicked, but his next words made her stop.

"It's about your sister."

She turned and chanced a look at him. "What about her?"

He held up his hands, indicating that he didn't want to hurt her. She glanced up the alley. She should take the opportunity to flee, but she was intrigued now. She wanted to know what he had to say.

"My name is Cyrus."

His English was not fluent, but it wasn't bad either. "I know your sister, except she doesn't call herself Abbie. She goes by the name 'Lynette Parker'."

If they weren't standing in a dark scary alley, she might have laughed. He was clearly deluded.

"What are you talking about?" she asked, edging sideways, towards the street. She didn't want to be here with him, but she wanted – needed to hear this.

"She first made contact with me through a Facebook group."

"Abbie doesn't use Facebook," she told him.

A few more steps and she would be out of the darkness. He was still very close, but it would be safer out there on the street, where someone could walk by.

"Not anymore, perhaps. But she did then. She was

on this page I used to visit. For Iranians living in England. That's where she advertised her services."

"Her services?" *What is he suggesting?*

She wrinkled up her nose. He gave off a strong earthy scent, a combination of sweet cherry tobacco and intense, bitter coffee.

"I paid her ten thousand pounds."

"For what?"

"To transport my family over from Calais on her boat."

Mel stared at him. "Calais?"

She knew about the migrants in Calais. Thousands of people who came from countries like Afghanistan, Iran, and Syria, many fleeing war and persecution. People who arrived with little more than the clothes on their backs. She sensed that desperation in Cyrus. The way his eyes constantly flicked back and forth, like a man who'd seen hell.

"I arrived in England a year ago. I wanted to come first, to make sure it was as safe as people said it was. To see for myself that it was okay, and once I was sure, I wanted my loved ones to join me."

"Right."

"So I arranged with Lynette Parker to bring them across. I thought it was better to deal with a woman. I thought she'd be kinder. Not like those heartless thugs. She seemed so strong and capable. I thought I was putting my family in good hands."

He paused for a moment and screwed up his face as if waiting for a stab of pain to pass. Mel couldn't tell if the pain was physical or emotional. She inhaled grimly, steeling herself for the next bit of his story.

"My wife, Safa, rang me to say they'd boarded the boat. Her and our three children."

He pressed his hand over his mouth; his eyes were

filled with such sorrow that she was afraid to hear his next words. "Except they never arrived."

Mel felt the colour leave her cheeks. "No!"

"I think your sister overloaded the boat. I think she drowned my family."

"Abbie wouldn't do that," she said with certainty. "This Lynette person. She's not my sister."

Cyrus glared at her. "Your sister has a boat, yes?"

"Yes, but she just takes people out on pleasure trips. They go diving and spearfishing. She doesn't do anything illegal. She wouldn't…"

"I want you to see this." He pulled out his phone. The screen was bright in the dim light, and he held it so close to her face that she had to move back, her hip pressing against the overflowing dustbins.

"This is Safa, my wife. Look at her. Look at her face! I want you to see her."

Mel looked. Bright, intelligent eyes peered out from under a fringe of dark hair. Her lips were ruby red, the colour of pomegranates, and around her neck, she wore a distinctive necklace made from a large turquoise stone with a shell in the middle.

"I gave her that necklace," he told her. "It's very special to me. It belonged to my mother. I told Safa to wear it every day while we were apart. She said she couldn't accept such an important gift, but I told her that it was my promise to her. She would wear my mother's necklace and keep it safe until we could all be together again."

He swiped the screen, and she found herself looking at another picture of Safa, now with her arms around two children, with another taller one standing beside them.

Cyrus looked down at the picture, stroking the faces of the children.

"I want to know what happened to them. I need to know so I can lay their bodies to rest. That's why I need you to help me. I need you to talk to your sister and find out the truth."

She shook her head, her entire body shaking with emotion. This poor man, and his poor family. They must have been duped by some heartless human trafficker.

"I'm so sorry, but I don't think I can help you. Abbie would never do anything like that. Abbie's a good person…"

Her mind jumped to Abbie's recent brain injury, but she pushed the thought away. She glanced out at the street. He was no longer blocking her. She could make a break for it and run, but she no longer felt the urge. What she needed now was to make him see that her sister was not the cause of his suffering.

"When did this happen?" she asked.

"Mid-June."

She nodded slowly and felt a lurch in the pit of her stomach. Mid-June. That was around the time of Abbie's accident.

She opened and closed her mouth, unsure what to do. She didn't know this man, but the pain in his eyes was obvious. Someone had done this terrible thing to his family, but not Abbie. It couldn't have been Abbie. Could it? Even with a brain injury, she would never do anything so awful, and if she had, she'd be ridden with guilt. She would have told her. She would have asked her for help.

"Have you actually spoken to my sister?" she asked.

"No."

"Why don't we arrange a time for you to meet her properly? I'm sure we can clear this up."

"Please…no…"

He clenched his jaw and saw the fear that flickered across his face.

"Find out," he told her urgently, pressing a card into her hand. "This is my number. When you find out, you call me. Even if the truth is every bit as bad as I think it is. I just want to know."

She slipped the card into her coat pocket and blundered down the alley, wondering if he was really going to let her go. She kept her feet moving, one in front of the other until she was sure he was no longer behind her. Her breathing was still a little uneven, as if the sand that permanently invaded her clothes had somehow seeped into her lungs. She should have asked him why he'd broken into her house. Had he been expecting Abbie that day? That would explain the shocked expression on his face, and why he'd fled when he saw her.

She walked on towards the Duck and sat down at one of the wooden tables in the pub garden, keeping an eye out the whole time, to ensure Cyrus hadn't followed. Although he had seemed genuine, you never really knew, did you? There were some really screwed-up people in the world. She hesitated for a fraction of a second before she phoned Peter. She needed someone to talk to. Someone she could trust. She wished her knees would stop knocking together.

"Peter," she said without preamble, "something really weird just happened."

"Melly? What is it? Are you okay?"

Quickly, she filled him in.

"Where are you now?"

"I'm just on my way home from town."

"Right. I'll meet you back at your house."

She should have told him that he didn't need to come over, but she couldn't bring herself to do so. She clambered to her feet and walked towards the footpath;

then she stopped and looked around. Turning back on herself, she walked downhill until she reached the road. It was a fair bit longer, the road way, but less secluded, and the way she was feeling right now, she didn't want to take any chances.

A couple of cars passed in quick succession, forcing her to press herself into the prickly holly bushes that lined the road. She was about to set off again when the headlights of a third car lit up the lane. The driver slowed and honked his horn. She glanced at it nervously. Then the passenger door shot open.

"Get in!"

"God, Peter! You scared me."

"Sorry, Melly, didn't mean to make you jump. Do you want a lift or what?"

There was only just enough room to squeeze into the car.

"You're shaking!" he said as her fingers struggled to fasten her seatbelt.

She allowed him to reach across her and snap the belt into position. "Thanks."

Her whole body felt limp and heavy, yet she still felt the adrenaline coursing through her veins. She looked out the window as he drove up the lane. The holly bushes disappeared, replaced by a length of barbed wire with fuzzy bits of wool caught in it. They used to hold fun fairs there in the summer. She recalled running across that field, hand in hand with Abbie.

"Hurry up! I wanna go on the bouncy castle!" Abbie said.

"I'm hurrying!"

"Hurry faster!"

Abbie was pulling her faster than she wanted to go. Mel's feet had slid about in her plastic jelly shoes. Her hands were slick with sweat. She was losing her grip. She could feel Abbie slipping through her fingers.

"Abbie, wait!" she'd gasped, but Abbie was already running ahead, charging down the field.

"Mel?"

She turned to find Peter staring at her.

"Are you all right?"

"Yes, yes, I'm fine."

He watched her warily as he pulled into the driveway.

"That's weird. Abbie's car's not here," she said.

"Why's that weird?"

"Because she hardly ever goes out! You don't think she's taken her boat out this late?"

"I don't know." He switched off the engine. "If you're worried, why don't you give her a call?"

"Already on it."

Mel held the phone to her ear, impatient for Abbie to answer, but it went straight to voicemail.

"She's not answering. God. Does that mean she's out of reach?" She cast a glance skywards. In the past, she wouldn't have worried about Abbie taking the boat out so late. She would have assumed she'd know what she was doing, but that was before her accident.

She grimaced as she thought of the things Cyrus had told her.

Where are you, Abbie? And what are you doing?

"Can you drive me down to the marina?" she asked.

Peter pressed his lips together, the way he did when he disagreed with something but didn't want to say. "Perhaps we should give her a few minutes? She might have just popped to the shop or something."

"God, I hope so."

She pulled out her phone again. "We'll give her fifteen minutes," she decided. "Then I want to go and look for her."

She pulled the key from her pocket and opened the

door. The house was a little too silent, like the day she'd found Cyrus there. She heard a whimper.

"It's just the dog," Peter said, striding towards the kitchen. Poor Otto was trapped outside in the garden again, in the cold and dark. He unlocked the back door and let him in.

"Poor dog's freezing," he said, rubbing his fur.

Otto darted over to Mel and wrapped himself around her legs.

"Likes you, doesn't he?" Peter noticed. "Hey, there's a note on the table."

"What does it say?"

"She's gone shopping."

Mel felt the tension in her shoulders relax. Of course, they were out of food. She'd been doing little top-up shops, but they were long overdue for a proper shop. It appeared Abbie had finally gone to do it. She shouldn't come to too much harm at Asda.

"Well, that's that, then," Peter said. "How about I make you a nice cup of tea?"

Mel smiled, but she couldn't get her encounter with Cyrus out of her head. It haunted her.

"I'm going to have a look in Abbie's room."

"What? No, Melly! That's an invasion of privacy."

"I'm worried about her."

"I'm inclined to think the simplest explanation is the most likely one. It sounds to me like a case of mistaken identity. I mean, what you're describing is people smuggling! Abbie would never do anything like that. Those people are vile, risking human lives for profit."

Mel licked her lips. "The old Abbie would never do such a thing, but she's different now, Peter. I don't know what to think."

She glanced out the window. "Give me five minutes.

If Abbie comes back, I'm going to need you to distract her."

"With my stunning good looks and magnetic charm?"

"Whatever comes to you."

"Okay."

She left him in the kitchen and hotfooted it up the stairs. She hadn't actually been in Abbie's room since she'd come home, but she wasn't surprised to find the same minimalist style that characterised the rest of the house. Abbie had taken down all her photos and cleared her clutter off the shelves. Where there had once been teddy bears and ornaments and all manner of other junk, there was now just a simple shelf with three nondescript candles on it, and a selection of fluffy cushions on the bed. It looked like a page from a magazine. Neat and tidy, but completely devoid of personality.

Mel checked under the pillow. As children she and Abbie had both hidden their diaries there so the tooth fairy could watch over them, but there was nothing there now. She tried the wardrobe and gasped. Where were all of Abbie's party dresses? Her collection of Prada handbags? Surely she hadn't sold them all? She loved her clothes. *Had loved her clothes.* She went to Abbie's chest of drawers and pulled each one open only to find them empty. She took a step back and almost tripped on the rug. As she pulled it back into place, she noticed Abbie's bedside drawer was slightly open. Instinctively, she pulled it out and peered inside. Gone were all the lotions and make-up and bottles of nail polish. All that was left was a simple nail kit, a hairbrush and Abbie's passport.

Outside, she could hear the crunch of a car on gravel. Was that Abbie?

Without quite knowing why, she picked up the passport and opened it, half expecting a plague of locusts to come swarming out. She flipped to the back page, to find Abbie's picture staring back at her. It looked like a recent one, judging by the haircut. In the picture, Abbie had cold, steely eyes. She looked a little unnatural, probably because you weren't allowed to smile for the passport picture, and Abbie was always smiling, at least she had been before the accident. Mel's eyes went to the words printed below the photo. Where Abbie's name should have been, it read 'Lynette Parker'.

22

W *hat the hell is Abbie doing with a fake passport?*
        "Bought enough to feed an army!"
        Peter's voice boomed; then he let out a loud, deliberate laugh accompanied by the rustling of shopping bags and feet stomping through the house. He sounded fake, but she knew this was just his clumsy attempt to warn her Abbie was home. Yet she was glued to Abbie's passport, unable to let go. Abbie could come in any moment. She needed to do something, but all she could do was stare.

Pull yourself together, Mel!

Her heart thrummed in her ears. Quickly, she pulled out her phone and took a picture. Then she shoved the passport back into the drawer. Had it been that way around? She couldn't remember, but there was no time to mess about. A brief glance around the room told her that everything was just as she'd found it. At least, she thought it was.

She hurried out of Abbie's room and shut the door softly behind her. Just in time. Someone was coming up the stairs. Crap! Her own bedroom was at the other end of the landing. How could she explain being up this end? Thinking fast, she dived into the bathroom and pulled the ancient lock across. She heard someone stomp into Abbie's room next door. Had she seen her? Could she tell she'd been in her room? Mel stood with her back to the door, waiting for her breathing to regulate. It sounded as though Abbie was ripping something, tearing up rubbish. Or just making her presence known.

She stood at the sink and turned on the taps. For all she knew, Abbie was standing on the other side of that wall, listening. She needed time to think, to figure out what the hell was going on. There was no denying it now; there had to be at least a grain of truth in what Cyrus had told her. It seemed that Abbie had somehow got mixed up in people smuggling, and it had all gone horribly wrong.

She caught her reflection in the mirror. The strain showed in her face. She looked washed out and grim, unable to smile. She leaned against the wall, struggling to regain her composure. She had to do better than this, or Abbie would notice something was up. She splashed some water on her face and dried off with a warm fluffy towel. She could hear Abbie closing her bedroom door again and making her way back downstairs.

She heard her chatting away to Peter. What if he put his great size elevens in it? It was important not to upset Abbie. She didn't think they should confront her about this. Not yet anyway.

She took the stairs slowly, listening. Peter was passing groceries to Abbie, who was stocking the fridge and the cupboards. Otto jumped between them, with great excitement, as if this was some wonderful game.

"Wait a minute there, boy. I bet there's something juicy in here for you."

Peter looked at Abbie.

"Damn. I knew I forgot something."

Peter looked at the dog regretfully. "Sorry, mate. Never mind, I'm sure you'll be happy to chow down on the leftovers."

He looked up as Mel walked into the room. "How about I make my famous lasagne?"

Mel smiled uncertainly and glanced at Abbie. "Sounds great. Let me help unpack."

"Okay, thanks." Abbie gave them both a wink and disappeared into the living room. They soon heard the roar of engines as she immersed herself in the TV.

"I found something," Mel told Peter as quietly as she could.

"What?"

"There was a..."

She stopped short as Abbie bounded back into the room and snatched a can of beer from the fridge. "Don't mind me!"

"Why'd you shop at Sainsbury's?" Peter asked. "There's a big Asda just around the corner."

"She's probably had enough of that place. She used to work there," Mel said.

Abbie nodded vaguely, and Mel wondered if she even remembered. She waited until she'd disappeared back into the living room; then she showed Peter the picture she'd taken of Abbie's passport.

"Looks a bit of a fright, doesn't she?" he said as he assembled celery, carrots, and garlic for his lasagne.

"Look at the name!"

Peter looked again. It took him a moment to process it.

"Strewth! I thought that Cyrus bloke was full of it, but Abbie must have been up to something. I mean, why else would she have a fake passport?"

Mel shook her head. "I don't know. Would she be held responsible if she did kill those people?"

"I would think so. At the very least, it's manslaughter, isn't it?"

"But if she wasn't in her right mind?"

"I'm no lawyer, but I doubt a brain injury would get her off the hook." He rubbed his forehead. "Can you hand me that chopping board? Ta."

"You were saying?"

"I think she'd be in a lot of trouble. She'd probably have to do time."

He was probably right. The law lacked compassion. It didn't care if someone had had a life-changing knock on the head. A crime was a crime, even if the old Abbie would never have dreamed of doing such a thing.

"This Cyrus bloke. How much do you think he knows?"

"I don't know. He doesn't have any proof," Mel said. "That's why he came to me. He's desperate to find out the truth, but I can't help him, can I? Even if I can get Abbie to confess, I can't tell anyone. I can't let my sister go to jail!"

Peter was assembling ingredients, pulling out mince and pasta sheets. Mel leaned heavily against the countertop. What if she was still at it? Transporting migrants across the channel? Risking lives for profit.

"Put me to work." She needed the distraction.

"All right. You can chop the veggies."

She slumped down at the table, with the chopping board and a knife.

"Remember to keep them nice and –"

"Even," she finished for him.

He nodded and set to work opening the tinned tomatoes.

She enjoyed watching Peter cook. It was probably

the thing he was best at, creating a meal from raw ingredients. It ought to have been a pleasant way to spend the evening, but her worries ate away at her. What if Abbie was arrested? She couldn't bear it if she went to jail. She would be worrying about her night and day. It all seemed so unfair.

She took her anger out on the carrots, chopping them mercilessly until they were nothing but a pile of squares.

"Nice work," Peter said when he glanced over.

"Thank you."

She started on the celery. The old Abbie disliked celery so much she had once buried it at the bottom of the garden. For all she knew, the new Abbie ate it with everything.

"How's that celery coming?"

"Nearly done."

As she attacked the last stalk, she felt a sharp pain in her finger.

"Ow!"

Peter was at her side in an instant. "What is it? Did you cut yourself?"

"The knife slipped," she said, sucking her finger.

"Let me see."

He pressed her finger against a wad of kitchen paper, her blood spreading out like a blot of ink.

"Looks nasty."

"It's fine," she said, feeling annoyed. She never cut herself when she was alone in the kitchen. This had only happened because her mind had been on Abbie.

"Where's the first aid kit?"

"I...don't know. Abbie used to keep it in the cupboard next to the dishwasher, but she's moved everything around now..."

"Got it."

He pulled out the green box and rummaged around until he came up with a bandage.

"A plaster will do," she protested.

He took no notice and bound it tight.

"I hope the sauce isn't burning?"

"It won't. I took it off the heat."

When they'd been together, he would have kissed her injured hand. Now, he finished up and returned the first aid box to the cupboard while Mel stirred the sauce.

"Looks like it's all under control here," Abbie said, heading to the fridge again.

Mel bit her tongue as her sister poured herself another beer. She caught Peter staring and gestured to him to cut it out. Abbie walked out again, and she breathed a sigh of relief. It was exhausting just being around her these days. She felt like she was constantly walking on eggshells.

When the food was ready, Mel went to the living room to call Abbie. She was sitting crossed-legged again, a slight scowl on her face as she stared at the TV.

"Abbie, dinner's ready."

Abbie said nothing, so Mel wasn't sure she'd heard. "Abbie?"

Suddenly, her sister turned on her, her face flushed with irritation. "I'm coming, I'm coming. Keep your fucking hair on."

Mel felt a sob rise in her throat, and she blundered out of the room. She took a few deep breaths and returned to the kitchen. She kept her head down as she pulled out the cutlery. She didn't want Peter to see how badly all this was affecting her.

They sat in the dining room, at the good table, even though it meant carting all the food in from the kitchen. Mel sat next to Abbie with Peter across from her. Then she wished she'd sat opposite Abbie because she wanted to watch her without being too obvious. She desperately wanted to ask her about the passport, but it didn't feel right with Peter there.

"So what have you got on for the week?" she asked, in what she hoped was a light-hearted manner. "I don't suppose you've got any more boat trips planned?"

Abbie shrugged. "The weather might be all right this week. It just depends on whether I can find any clients. Most of the tourists have gone home now."

She reached for the salt and added tons of it to her lasagne. Then the pepper.

"I did season the food," Peter said.

"Yeah, cheers." Abbie went on grinding.

They fell silent again, and Mel couldn't think of anything else to say. She cast her eyes around the room, the same room where she and Abbie had sat for thousands of long Sunday dinners. She remembered Abbie and Dad arguing about politics, Mum making polite little interjections, trying to steer them onto safer topics. Invariably, Mel would go and fetch the harp, and then they would all relax to the soothing notes of 'Scarborough Fair'.

"Is it still mainly the fishing trips you do?" Peter asked Abbie.

"Yep," Abbie said, taking a forkful of lasagne. "Fishing and diving."

They fell silent again, and the only sound was of cutlery scraping against plates and the rhythmic chewing of food. Mel looked at her sister, waiting for her to say something. She'd never known her to be so quiet.

She and Peter might sit in silence. They often had, back in Sydney. For the last few months of their marriage, it had been as though they'd run out of things to say to each other, or more accurately, that they'd run out of safe topics. Neither one wanted to start an argument, so it had been easier to say nothing. But Abbie – Abbie had always been so talkative, feeling the need to fill silences with stories about men she'd been out with, or other entertaining anecdotes. She had always felt a need to impress on everyone how exciting her life was. Well, not anymore. She shook her head when Peter offered her a second helping and failed to pick up on his implicit request for praise.

"That was lovely," Mel said as she placed her knife and fork together.

Abbie looked from Mel to Peter.

Say something, Mel willed her. *Anything*.

Abbie speared a piece of celery and chewed it methodically. "Remind me how you two got together. I haven't heard it in a while."

She doesn't remember, Mel realised. She looked at Peter, thinking of their talk their day before. "We don't have to rehash all this."

Peter looked at Abbie and smiled. "I was supposed to be on a blind date," he said. "I was a tad late, so I walked into the restaurant looking for a woman sitting on her own. It was kind of crowded in there, and it seemed to me that all the tables were taken. I walked all around the place until I spotted the only woman sitting on her own. She had sparkling, intelligent eyes, and when I smiled at her, she smiled back. I made an assumption and sat down opposite her. She must have been pretty surprised."

Mel laughed. "I thought he had a right nerve! But he was funny, and I liked his accent. So when he said he was hungry, I just assumed he couldn't get a table. I had no idea he thought we were on a date."

"And that was that," Peter said. "Our entire relationship was all based on a misunderstanding."

Abbie grinned. "I bet the woman you were meant to meet was pissed off."

"I never heard," Peter said. "When I found out I'd got the wrong woman, I tried to ring her to apologise, but she wouldn't answer the phone."

"You snooze, you lose," Abbie said.

Peter shrugged. "Maybe."

Mel looked down at her plate, wondering what would have happened if Peter hadn't approached her that night. She'd spent over twenty years with this man. Did she regret it? Looking at him now, she didn't think so. She couldn't imagine how her life would have been without him, but she wouldn't take it back now. She wouldn't want to erase the past.

"Well, cheers for that," Abbie said, once she'd finished. She stood up from the table and walked off without even bothering to take her plate out to the kitchen.

"You can see it, can't you?" Mel asked. "How different she is."

Peter nodded. "She's so quiet and distracted. I haven't seen her lose her temper yet, but I think I should stay tonight, just in case."

"No, we're fine," Mel protested, gathering up the plates.

Peter picked up the lasagne pan.

"Melly, Abbie isn't right in the head, and you're a little fragile yourself right now. I really think I should stay."

Mel was about to object, but she realised that she wasn't looking forward to the prospect of another evening alone with Abbie.

"You can stay in the spare room," she told him.

Peter was grinning like he'd won something, and she already regretted her decision.

The spare room was downstairs, just across from the living room. Mel went in with him, to check he had enough pillows and blankets. She found the bed already made up, with a large double duvet and frilly cushions scattered about the room. Abbie had placed another wooden boat on the windowsill. Mel wondered if she'd won a job lot of them on eBay.

She went to the window and checked outside before closing the curtains. Even now that she'd talked to Cyrus, she couldn't break the habit of looking out for him. Her body was in a continual state of hypervigilance, always anticipating the worst. Besides, for all she knew, Cyrus *was* out there. He'd been understandably angry, and if she didn't get back to him soon, he might well take matters into his own hands. Her heart lurched at the thought that he might harm Abbie. Perhaps she should warn her, but then she'd have to tell her how much she knew. It wasn't a conversation she was looking forward to. Abbie would be outraged that she'd been nosing about in her business, and Mel doubted she could make her see sense.

Peter plumped himself down on the bed. "I was thinking."

"What about?"

"Well, we're assuming that if Abbie is involved in this people-smuggling business, then she did it after the accident."

"Yes."

"But what if she did it before? I mean, has it occurred to you that she might have injured herself *whilst* she was transporting people? Maybe even on the night she was supposed to bring Cyrus's family across?"

"Why would she do that?"

"You said her business was in trouble. She needed money. Well, people smuggling is a pretty lucrative business, Melly. I'm sure she didn't mean to hurt anyone, but…"

Mel felt an unpleasant sensation, like cold jelly sliding down her back.

"No," she said with certainty. "I know my sister. If she has done this…this thing, then it's because of her brain injury. She would never have done it before."

She waited for Peter to contradict her, but he merely nodded his head.

Still, she couldn't get Cyrus's family out of her mind. It must be awful not knowing what had happened to them, but if they had drowned, then there was no way of getting them back. Did Abbie have to suffer too?

23

M el let out an elaborate yawn. "I'm bushed."

"What, already?" Peter said.

"Yeah. I've been working long hours trying to fix the game." She fiddled with the frilly edge of one of the cushions.

"You work too hard."

"Derick reckons I don't work hard enough."

"Derick is a plonker. I can't believe you're still working there."

"I won't be for much longer. I'm giving my notice as soon as I get my bonus."

"Really? That's…wow!"

"I know."

She edged towards the door, knowing she should leave but not quite wanting to. It had been good to have him around today. She wasn't sure how she would have held it together without him, but she didn't want to fall back into the way things had been before. It would be so easy to do.

"Goodnight then." She forced herself to turn away.

"Goodnight," he called after her.

She went out and closed the door behind her. She hoped he would be able to sleep with the din coming from the living room. Abbie had the TV turned up again, and she was laughing loudly at something she was watching. Mel hurried past and up the stairs to her own room. She hadn't lied when she'd said she was tired, but there was no way she could sleep.

She lay in bed, googling news reports about people smuggling. The trade in illicit channel crossings seemed to be at an all-time high, with hundreds of people making the trip over from France every day, most of them in tiny boats even smaller than her sister's. Some people made it, some drowned, but they all parted with a lot of money in order to make the journey. She could see how lucrative it must be.

At midnight, she sat back from the computer, wishing she could rewind time. If only she could have come home six months ago, she would have stopped whoever it was who'd talked Abbie into transporting migrants. Because there had to be someone, didn't there? She couldn't have come up with this all by herself.

She heard Peter's trumpet-like sneeze from downstairs. The guest room was directly under hers, and the sound went right through the ceiling. He was awake too, then.

A loud creak told her that he had left his room, probably heading to the bathroom. No, the kitchen. She heard Abbie's voice. A little high and giggly. *Is she flirting with him?*

She sucked on her knuckles. She wished Peter wouldn't talk to her sister. What if he asked her outright about the people smuggling? She wouldn't put it past him. Although they'd agreed not to say anything, Peter always thought he knew best.

She climbed out of bed and tiptoed halfway down the stairs, listening to the voices that drifted up from the kitchen. They definitely sounded friendly.

"Have you won her back yet?"

"Give me time, Abbie. I've only been here a couple of days."

"Put on the charm, Pete. You've got to sweep her off her feet, the way you did in the beginning. Make her feel special."

"She is special."

Mel's cheeks burned. He could be so sweet when he wasn't being bloody infuriating.

"Take it from me, Pete. She only had that fling because she felt unloved. You've got to show her you still care."

Mel cringed. If Abbie wanted to get them back together, then bringing up the affair was not a wise move. It bruised Peter's fragile male ego. Still, Abbie was about as subtle as a sledgehammer. Even more so now, it seemed.

"Let me do this my way," she heard him murmur. Perhaps he was aware that she might be listening. The house was awfully echoey now that Abbie had got rid of half their stuff.

"I know what's best for Mel, but she needs to realise that she still needs me. I don't want to scare her off."

Scare her off? What the hell was he talking about? She wasn't some nervous schoolgirl, she was a grown woman with her own mind. Her nostrils flared with indignation, and she almost forgot herself. The way she was feeling right now, she wanted to march downstairs and confront him.

Instead, she took a couple of deep breaths. They'd both gone quiet now. She crept back to her room just in time. The next minute, she heard Abbie thumping up the stairs, slamming her bedroom door behind her. She seemed to have lost the ability to do anything quietly.

Mel closed her eyes, but her sleep was far from restful. She dreamt of Abbie's boat tossing and turning in the sea. She saw hands reaching up from the water, desperate for help. Voices calling "Abbie! Abbie!" In the dream she thought she *was* Abbie. It wasn't the first time she'd played the part of her twin in her dreams. Her identity was often fluid, switching from one to the other. They were like two sides of the same coin.

At around two in the morning, when the house was silent and she still couldn't sleep, she crept downstairs and made herself a hot drink. Abbie had bought some salted caramel hot chocolate, and it looked really good. As she carried it back towards her room, she noticed Abbie's computer blinking at her from the living room. She eyed it thoughtfully. Would she be overstepping the mark if she had another look at that email she'd received? Abbie would be fast asleep now, so it wasn't as if she could wake her and ask her permission.

Feeling a little guilty, she went and sat down at the computer. She smiled as she saw that Abbie had also been watching the silver anniversary video compilation. Then it occurred to her that perhaps she had been trying to refresh her memory. It looked like she'd recently viewed the clip of Mel's first boyfriend, the wannabe Doctor Who. Was that why she'd mentioned him out of the blue? And there was a clip of the canoe trip. Hadn't she mentioned that too?

She logged into Abbie's email account. There were dozens of unanswered emails there. Abbie clearly wasn't keeping up with any of her friends. She wasn't even opening their messages. She saw several Facebook notifications too. The world hadn't completely forgotten her, then; she was just choosing not to be a part of it.

She worked her way down the list until she came to the email about her appointment. There was very little information contained in the email, so after several minutes' deliberation, she crafted a careful reply, asking for a video consultation. She was fairly certain that the treatment she'd found in San Francisco would be more suitable than this one, but perhaps they could advise her. It was important she got this right. She was about to send the email when she noticed something odd in the email address: appointments@chicagobranclinic.net. She squinted at the screen. Chicago *Bran* Clinic. The 'i' was missing. Why would that be? She did a quick search for the domain.

Chicagobranclinic.net. Registered on the twelfth of October. That was the day before yesterday.

She sat back in her chair. Whoever had registered the domain had kept their details private. She took another look at the email. It was short and straight to the point. A demand for money. Mel felt her throat contract.

They're trying to spear phish us?

The wording was convincing. They'd used just enough medical jargon to appear credible, but that domain name – that was the tell. It had to be a scam. She couldn't believe she'd nearly fallen for it. They must have got wind of Abbie's accident and were now trying to get money out of her with the promise of making her better. They were probably making a fortune, preying on vulnerable people. Well, they'd messed with the wrong family this time.

She drummed her fingers on the desk for a moment, then ran a DNS lookup of chicagobranclinic.net. Her chest tightened as she looked at the IP address. It was the same as the one her internet company served her, but for a few digits. This was local. Like this street local. She glanced out the window into the dark night and considered her neighbours. The white-haired man across the street and the old granny who walked with a frame. They couldn't have done this. An unsettling sensation grew in the pit of her stomach as she realised what all this pointed to. The email had come from this house.

24

Mel's first instinct was to march up to Abbie's room. She wanted to wake her up and demand to know what was going on. Had she sent the email herself? It didn't make any sense. Why would she do that? Was it just easier than telling her about the accident?

She thought about waking Peter, but loud snores were coming from the guest room. The poor man was probably still jet-lagged. It wouldn't be fair to disturb him. It would have to wait until morning.

Only Otto seemed to understand her turmoil. She didn't know where he'd been hiding, but he appeared from nowhere, demanding to be petted and loved. She took him back up to bed with her, not caring that his breath smelt like garlic. She needed company tonight. She also needed answers, but she didn't know how to get them.

There was really nothing she could do but go to sleep. She lay under the covers, but there was so much adrenaline pumping around her body that she felt like she would explode. It wasn't a warm night, but sweat soaked her pillow, and every time she drifted off, something made her jerk awake. She felt as though her mind was busy unravelling a deep and difficult puzzle, yet every time she came close to solving it, she woke up and couldn't remember what she'd learnt.

She went downstairs to Peter at first light. There was no point knocking on his door or calling his name. Peter was a deep sleeper who only responded to earthquake-level shaking. She would have to go in.

He slept as he often did, on top of the covers. He was wearing the stripey boxers she'd given him last Christmas. He wore them because he thought she liked them, but in actual fact they'd been a last-minute panic buy. She hadn't known what to get him. She never did. He'd always smiled and made out that he was pleased with whatever she chose, but in reality, he never was. Even after so many years of marriage, it was still a mystery to her what he really wanted.

Peter opened his eyes slowly, squinting in the morning light.

"Melly!" He smiled up at her, clearly misinterpreting her unexpected appearance in his bedroom. He reached for her, and she felt herself go stiff in his arms, but he did not let go.

"Peter…"

"I just want to hold you, Melly. Nothing more."

He kissed the top of her head, and she forced herself to relax. Being with him had once felt as natural as breathing, but now she felt the weight of his expectations crushing her chest.

"Peter, listen, there's something weird going on with Abbie. That clinic she told me about in America? It's not real. I mean, there is a Chicago Brain Clinic but that's not who sent her the email. I checked the IP address, and I think she sent it herself."

He shifted himself up, onto his elbow. "Why? Why would she do that?"

"I don't know."

He thought for a moment. "The house?" he said. "She could be after your money."

"No, Abbie would never..."

She stopped. The old Abbie would never do something like that. But this new Abbie? "She needs treatment," she insisted. "It doesn't make any sense. If she doesn't want the money for her treatment, then..."

"She might not care about getting better. You're the one who wants the old Abbie back. Maybe she's happy with her new personality. Maybe she doesn't see the need to change back."

She swallowed. "But why would she go to the lengths of fabricating an email? It all seems so convoluted..."

Peter cricked his neck. "Could she be faking the traumatic brain injury?"

She collapsed onto the bed. She hadn't meant to sit down, but her legs seemed to give way from under her.

"No, I...She's so different. It has to be true. Why else would she have the fake passport? And all that stuff Cyrus said..."

She glanced at the door, nervous that Abbie might overhear. "I'm going to ring Cyrus. He gave me his number so I could contact him if I found anything out."

"But we haven't really found anything. All we have are more questions."

"I know. I'm hoping he might be able to tell me more. Something I can actually use."

Peter nodded and looked thoughtful. "You do that. Now, if you'll excuse me, I really have to pee."

She went outside to make the phone call. There was no sound from Abbie's room, which probably meant she was still asleep, but she wasn't going to risk it. Something was very wrong here; she just wished she knew what it was.

"Hello?" Cyrus sounded hesitant when he answered.

"It's me, Mel."

"Okay, good. Do you have any news?"

"I need more information. Is there anything else you can tell me? Did you actually meet my sister?"

"Yes, yes, of course. I handed her ten thousand pounds. It was everything I had."

"Wow! When was this?"

"I told you, four months ago. I took it to her at the marina."

"In Weymouth?"

"No, in Hull."

"Hull?" Mel's eyes widened. "Kingston Upon Hull?"

"Yes."

"That's, like…five hours away."

"Yes."

"What was she doing up there?"

"That's where she said to meet. She had her boat there."

"Do you remember the name of the boat?"

"No, I'm afraid not."

She thought for a minute, the cogs turning. "If you met her in Hull, then how did you trace her back to Weymouth?"

"With the internet," he said. "She made a video blog for her business. The minute I saw it, I knew it was her. I had been looking for her for weeks, and there she was, on my Facebook newsfeed, advertising Weymouth boat tours. So I came down here to find her. I was going to confront her, to ask for the truth about what happened to my family, but instead, I found you."

Mel bit her lip, not wanting to think about the day she'd encountered him in the house.

"OK, leave it with me. I'll speak to you again soon."

"Thank you, Mel, and stay safe. Peace be with you."

"And with you."

She slipped the phone back into her pocket and looked at Otto, who had scampered out the door behind her. He was now tearing it up, racing around the front lawn. Dead leaves had fallen like snow overnight, and the dog was having the time of his life, chasing them around the garden. His paws were covered in mud, but he was wagging his tail with pure joy, and she wished she could have even an ounce of his happiness.

She popped back into the house and grabbed his lead, then led him down the footpath for a quick walk while she thought about what Cyrus had said. As far as she knew, Abbie had never been to Hull. Or if she had, she'd never mentioned it. It would have been a bit of a boat trip. She'd almost certainly have been away overnight, and for what? To smuggle migrants over from Calais? It all still seemed so unlikely. It had to be a case of mistaken identity. Yet, she had that passport…

Otto tugged against the lead as she tried to steer him back to the house. The poor dog spent too much time shut up in the back garden. She lured him inside by throwing him the manky old flip-flop; then she led him into the kitchen for a well-deserved meal.

She found Peter sipping a glass of orange juice at the kitchen counter.

"Is Abbie up yet?" she asked in a low voice.

"No. I don't think so."

"Good. I want to go on a road trip."

He raised an eyebrow. "Where to?"

"Kingston Upon Hull."

. . .

It wasn't ideal, dragging Peter along, but he was the one with the hire car. She could hardly borrow Abbie's. She didn't want her to know what they were up to.

"I just need to shower and change," Peter said, taking another minute sip of his juice. Mel fought her frustration.

"Can you skip the shower just this once? I want to hit the road before she knows we're gone."

Peter blinked. "A bit secret squirrel, isn't it?"

Mel nodded, but she was in no mood to joke. It was time to get some answers.

Peter insisted on stopping at the corner shop for provisions. Mel gritted her teeth while he piled a basket high with rice cakes, seaweed crackers, and bottles of mineral water because he didn't trust the 'muck' that came out of the tap.

"Want anything?" he asked.

She shook her head. She couldn't think about food right now. She just wanted to get there. If they left now, they could make good progress before the roads got busy.

"What are we going to do when we get there?" Peter asked as he drove. "Do you want to start with the marina? We could show Abbie's photo around and see if anyone recognises her."

"I don't know," Mel said. "I mean, what are the chances? She might not have been back there since it happened."

She consulted her phone. "A Lynette Parker is mentioned in an article about a fish shop in Hull town centre. A family business, apparently."

Peter took his eye off the road for a fraction of a second. "What are you thinking? That there might be a real person called Lynette Parker, and what... Abbie stole her ID?"

"I don't know, but I think we should check it out."

"How do you even know this is the right Lynette Parker?"

"We won't know that unless we find her."

She found the Facebook page Cyrus had mentioned, and looked through the old posts, but there was no mention of people trafficking or any other illegal activity. Of course, the post could have been deleted. After that, she trawled through all the Lynette Parkers on Facebook. The majority appeared to be American, and none looked anything like Abbie. She consulted the census data. It seemed Lynette wasn't such a popular name in the UK, given to only a handful of babies born in England and Wales each year. If there was a real Lynette Parker living in Hull, then chances were, this was her.

THE FURTHER NORTH THEY WENT, the more countryside and open spaces they saw. There were still the big cities, built up and smoky, but in between was lush and often hilly pea-green terrain, dotted with grazing animals.

"I thought Australia had a lot of sheep," Peter muttered.

"Welcome to Yorkshire!" Mel said with a smile. "You should feel right at home."

It felt like they'd been sitting in the car forever. Peter had refused to stop, preferring to do the journey in one long five-hour stint. Still, she was grateful she hadn't had to navigate the unfamiliar roads on her own.

The sun sparkled on the water as they crossed the Humber Bridge.

"Are we nearly there yet?" she asked, just to wind him up.

"Almost."

She'd checked the satnav in Abbie's car before they'd left, but there had been no trace of Hull in her saved journeys, so there was no easy way of figuring out if she'd been there. She tried to hone her twin senses, but it wasn't like they had a shared consciousness. They weren't the Borg.

Peter parked in the town centre car park, and they walked out onto the street. It just looked like a standard English town. It had the same chain shops, like Boots and Marks & Spencer, but the phone boxes were white rather than the usual red. She didn't think she'd seen that anywhere else. Peter strode in front of her, his long legs putting him yards ahead. Mel scrambled after him. Would it kill him to slow down a little and match his pace to hers? He didn't once turn round to see if she was still with him, not until he reached the main thoroughfare. It wasn't hard to find the fish shop. The sign above the door said 'The Happy Halibut', and a large brown fish peered out from the window with creepy dead eyes. A customer opened the door, and a strong smell of fish wafted out. Instinctively, she covered her mouth and nose with her hands.

Peter gave her a sympathetic smile. "Maybe I should go in?"

She got another whiff of fish, tangy and potent, and remembered Abbie holding up the fish with the spear through its head.

"Mel? You look like you're going to barf."

"All right, all right. You go in, but remember, we're here to get information. Don't tell them who we are."

She watched as he walked into the shop and made a show of admiring the display of fish and seafood at the counter. She couldn't hear any of his conversation, but there was clearly a bit of back and forth with the jolly-looking woman serving. She was gesticulating wildly, and Peter was nodding. Presently, he came out clutching a small tub of something fishy smelling. "Whelk?" he offered.

Mel shoved him away. "What did she say?"

"That was Lynette's mum, apparently. She said she's gone to Croatia, but I think she was lying."

"Why?"

"I don't know, something about the way her eyes darted to the right. People do that when they're lying, don't they?"

"Maybe…"

"You get a sense," he insisted. "She wouldn't look me in the eye."

"So let's say she *is* lying. Why would she do that?"

"I don't know. To cover up for Lynette."

"But why?"

"I don't know."

"So what do you want to do?"

Mel scratched the back of her neck. "Let's go and grab a coffee," she suggested. "We can show Lynette's picture around, see if anyone recognises her."

"Okay. What about that place over there?" He pointed to a little café called the Greasy Spoon. A couple of hardy blokes dressed in shorts and T-shirts leaned against a small plastic table outside.

"Looks all right," Mel agreed.

They went inside. While Peter ordered, Mel pulled out her phone and showed Lynette's picture to the young lad behind the counter. "I'm looking for this woman. Have you seen her?" she asked. He looked at her like she was a bit mad and shook his head.

"Take another look," she insisted. "Are you sure you haven't seen her?"

Peter turned towards her. "Why don't you go and save us a table?" he murmured.

Mel gave him a look. It wasn't like the café was overrun with customers. He just couldn't bear for her to make a scene. Still, she sloped off and plonked herself down at one of the laminate tables. It had rickety legs, but they probably all did. She watched as vapour rose from the industrial-looking coffee machine.

A few minutes later, Peter set a bacon butty down in front of her.

"Thought you might be hungry."

"Thanks."

They ate and drank in silence. Mel was still trying to work out what to do. Here she was in Hull, and she didn't really have a plan. She needed to find out who the hell this Lynette woman was.

Peter took a careful sip of his coffee and chewed on his bacon butty. Mel toyed with hers, but she couldn't eat it. Her worries gnawed away at her, making it impossible to sit still. Peter narrowed his eyes.

"So is this what was missing in your life? A road trip? A bit of adventure?"

Mel gave him a look. This was hardly her idea of an adventure.

A bored-looking waitress approached them; her eyes settled on Mel's untouched plate.

"The food all right for you, love?"

"Yes, thanks. I'm just not hungry."

"You want owt else?"

"No, but could you just take a look at this?" Mel pulled her phone from her pocket.

"What, you want me to take your picture?"

"No." She pulled up Lynette's passport photo. "Do you by any chance know this woman?"

The waitress peered at the picture. "Yeah, that's Lynette Parker."

"Are you sure?"

"I ought to be. I went to school with her."

Peter stared at her. "You're certain? You went to school with this woman?"

She took another good look. "Oy, Tricia!"

Another waitress came out of the little room at the back. "Get your arse over here!"

She came over, and Mel showed her the picture too.

"Tell them who that is," the first waitress said.

"Lynette Parker," Tricia said it like her mouth tasted of fermented fish. "She was in the year above us at school. She used to smoke on the bus."

The other one giggled. "That's right, she did! She didn't give a shit."

Mel looked at Peter.

"Are you absolutely sure this is Lynette Parker?" he said. "Take another look at the picture."

The waitresses did as he asked. They looked bored now. "Yeah, that's her."

A man in a black bomber jacket looked up from the table in the corner. He had a flashy gold chain around his neck and a face that looked sunburned and peeling.

"Why do you want to know about Lynette?"

It wasn't a friendly question. He had a very gruff voice, and Mel could just smell the testosterone coming off him.

"She's an old friend," she said lightly.

"Oh, yeah? She's an old friend of mine and all."

25

He took a step towards them, and Mel heard a low hum in her ears.

"Time to go," Peter said, but Mel couldn't break her gaze as the man murmured something to the bloke at the next table, and now they were both giving them the eye.

"Mel..." Peter spoke as though his lips were fused together.

She felt the full force of their stares as she and Peter rose to their feet. She'd made it three or four steps before the men started after them. Thinking fast, she grabbed a chair and shoved it across the room. It skidded across the wooden floor, blocking their path. Then she and Peter darted for the door. Peter grabbed her hand as he found the door handle and almost yanked the door off its hinges. A rush of fresh air greeted them as they stumbled outside.

The street was crowded with shoppers, but Mel wasn't stupid enough to think they were in the clear. She took a quick glance behind her. Yes, they were definitely being followed. There were three of them now, all wearing those distinctive black bomber jackets, like they were in a gang.

It was hard to move very fast because there were so many people out on the street, gathered around little vans selling seafood and ice cream. They wove their way around a group of teenagers taking acrobatic selfies. One had her leg raised above her head, and another jumped and did the splits in the air. All very impressive, but they were drawing quite a crowd, and Mel and Peter needed to get past.

"Quick, get in that phone box," she hissed.

"What?

"The phone box, Peter!" She tugged his arm and pulled him inside, shutting the door after them. They stood in the confined space, puffing and panting.

"Your cheeks are bright red," he told her.

"So are yours. I can't see them. Can you see them?"

"They're still looking for us."

Mel looked around the small enclosed phone box. Either she was a genius or a total idiot. If those men went past, they'd be fine. But if they spotted them, they were for it. She pictured herself being dragged out, or worse, one of those awful men punching his way in.

"Who the hell were those people?" she asked.

Peter frowned. "Maybe she owes them money."

"What's that got to do with us?"

"I don't know. Maybe they think we're good for it."

A round of applause broke out. The teen acrobats had finished their show. The crowd was dispersing now, going their separate ways. They both fell silent for a moment, watching, waiting to see what would happen. She was very aware of Peter's breathing.

"I'm sorry I got you into this," she said. She searched his eyes with hers.

He wiped the sweat from his forehead. "I'm not

sorry. There's nobody in the world I'd rather be trapped in a weird white phone box with."

He reached out and caressed her cheek. His touch felt electric, but she forced herself to turn and look out at the road. "I think they've gone."

"Strewth, I thought they were going to cook us and stick us on spikes or something," he said.

They wandered towards the marina and found a bench, then sat there, facing the water. The salty air was filled with the sounds of squeaking masts and the squeals of seagulls. Boats bobbed calmly on the water, and the waves rolled gently in and out. People milled around, but no one seemed to be in any particular hurry. There were a number of older boats like Abbie's, but also newer, more expensive models with gleaming white paint.

She took his arm and clung to it, filled with an irrational fear of falling into the water.

"Are you all right, Mel? You've gone a bit green around the gills."

"Don't you get it, Peter? That…that person living in my house. She's not Abbie!"

Peter's frowned deepened. She could see him struggling to come up with something rational.

"So…Lynette Parker is real," he conceded. "She's a real living, breathing person. And she looks like Abbie."

"I'm telling you, she's the one living in my house. She's not Abbie! I knew as soon as I came home. I just couldn't believe…"

Peter rubbed her arm. "You were born up north, weren't you?"

"Yeah, Sheffield."

"Is that far?"

"About an hour from here."

"So this Lynette Parker. Could she be related to you?"

"I don't think so. I've never heard of her."

"Do you have any family round here?"

"Only Auntie Dot. She's still lives in Sheffield."

"Why don't you call her? See what she knows."

"Might be an idea."

She scrolled through her phone, praying she still had Dot's number. She didn't remember the last time she'd talked to her, though they'd always exchanged birthday and Christmas cards.

She found the number and dialled. The phone rang and rang. Mel pictured Dot shuffling along, her face set in grim determination. She wasn't sure how old she was now, but it must be close to a hundred. They'd always called her Aunt Dot, but she was really her great-aunt or possibly her great-great-aunt. Mel wasn't entirely sure.

"Hello?"

Dot's voice echoed down the phone as if she were shouting down into a hole in the ground. Years of working in a noisy factory had affected her hearing, and she was incapable of speaking quietly.

"Hi, Dot, it's Mel."

"I beg your pardon? One minute, I need to switch my hearing aid on."

Mel waited a moment and tried again. "Can you hear me, Dot? It's Mel."

"Mel! So nice to hear from you! How's that hunky husband of yours?"

Mel shot Peter an amused glance. "He's right here, Dot. Listen, the reason I'm ringing…" She faltered, wondering what to say. "I don't suppose we have any other family up north, do we, say, in Sheffield?"

Dot paused for a moment. "I wouldn't think so, dear. Eddie and I moved up here after we got married, but his people were from Glasgow, and mine were from Coventry, as you know."

Mel nodded. She'd thought as much. "Are there any other living relatives?" she asked.

"Well, no, dear, your auntie Maureen died years ago, and she didn't have any children, and your dad was an only child, wasn't he?"

"Yes, he was." She glanced at Peter. This was starting to look like a dead end. "Why was I born in Sheffield?" she asked. "I mean, my parents never lived up north, did they?"

"Oh, no, your mother was visiting me when she went into labour early. It was all a bit unexpected."

"I see."

She vaguely recalled her mum giving her a similar explanation. It hadn't seemed important at the time. She said goodbye and hung up, staring out at the water.

"Would it be worth talking to Dot properly?" Peter said. "I mean, she's the only one who's still around."

"You really think this Lynette is related to me?"

"I don't know what the hell is going on, but clearly something is."

"Okay, I'll ring her again. I just need a minute."

She rested her head on his chest. She needed to do this. She needed to know the truth, but a part of her was really scared of what she might find.

When she called Dot again, her aunt sounded delighted. "Two calls in one day! To what do I owe the pleasure?"

Was that a backhanded way of pointing out how little she called? No, Dot wasn't like that. She was a good sort. The best. Always happy to hear her news. She was probably lonely, poor thing.

"Hello, Dot, I forgot to say before that we're in

England. Quite close to you, actually, and I wondered if it would be okay to call in?"

"Oh, that would be lovely! When can you come?"

She glanced at Peter. "We can be there in about an hour. Is that all right?"

"That would be wonderful! What a lovely surprise. I'll have the kettle on."

Mel ended the call and closed her eyes.

"Are you sure you're okay?" Peter asked.

She nodded. She didn't have the energy to explain everything that was going on in her brain. She felt as though her thoughts were all firing at once, shooting off in different directions, and she had to do whatever she could to get the situation under control.

MEL HAD ALWAYS associated Sheffield with smoggy factories and industry, but as they drove closer to Dot's house, she was reminded that it also boasted a lush green landscape with rolling hills and wide-open spaces.

"Is this the place?" Peter asked as they turned into a street lined with tall, thin lime trees.

Mel squinted at the sign. "Yes, that's it!"

"What number?"

"Er…"

For a moment, she thought of calling Abbie. No, she couldn't do that. She scanned the row of buildings, hoping one would pop out at her. Then she spotted a simple stone terrace with a navy blue door.

"I think it's that one."

Sure enough, there was Dot at the window, a frisky smile tugging at the corners of her mouth.

The garden gate creaked as they pushed it open and walked up the path.

"Come in, come in," Dot bellowed. "Don't stand on ceremony. You'll catch your deaths out there."

It wasn't that cold, but Mel smiled anyway. She was only too glad to get inside.

Dot's house smelled of a combination of talcum powder and lemon sherbet. It was about ten degrees too warm, and Mel could see Peter was itching to take off his jumper.

"I'm afraid my curtain rail's fallen down," Dot apologised as she led them into the living room.

"Oh, I'm sure I can fix that," Peter said.

"I don't want to put you to any trouble."

"It's no bother."

Dot fussed about, setting out tea things and plying them with cakes and biscuits. Mel wondered what sort of feast she would have drummed up if she'd known they were coming.

She sat and chatted with Dot while Peter fixed the curtain rail. She knew he wouldn't mind. There was nothing he detested more than small talk.

"So what brings you up here?" Dot asked curiously.

"We were just visiting Hull," Mel said, watching carefully to see if she showed any reaction.

"What's in Hull?"

"Ah, you know, boats and things."

Dot took a careful sip of her tea. Her hand shook so much, Mel was terrified she was going to spill it. She sat poised, ready to help, but knowing Dot would hate her if she did.

Mel's eyes trailed along the bookcase, taking in the various little knickknacks and memorabilia: the little Lilliput cottage, the statue of a boy having a wee, the silver spoons polished and displayed with pride. Why did old people collect such things?

Peter sat down beside her on the sofa. "I think that'll stay up now," he said, referring to the curtain rail.

"You are good," Dot said, reaching out to ruffle his hair.

Mel squirmed with embarrassment, but Peter took it well. "No worries," he said. "I think I'll have that cuppa now, thanks, Dot."

"Of course, dear. Here you are."

"I wanted to ask you what you remember of my birth?" Mel said. "You said Mum was staying with you when Abbie and I were born?"

"That's right," Dot said with a smile. "She needed a little break, so I suggested she come and visit. She wasn't due for several more weeks, so it was a bit of a surprise when her waters broke. I seem to remember she was quite cross about it."

"She was?"

"Well, yes, because she never got to have her holiday!"

Mel managed a smile. She could just imagine her mum grumbling.

"So Dad was back in Weymouth?"

"Yes, he couldn't get the time off work."

"So did you go with her to the hospital?"

"I did, but they didn't let me stay. Your mum was quite poorly. She had very high blood pressure. Wasn't allowed out of bed for a couple of weeks."

Mel clasped her hands together in her lap. "And did you see us? Abbie and me?"

"Oh, well, you were both in special care because you were so early. I had a little peek through the glass, but I wasn't allowed in. You were in incubators, you see."

Mel nodded.

"Did you want to see the photo albums? I might have some pictures."

Without waiting for a reply, Dot shuffled over to the cupboard and pulled them out, planting a heavy tome in each of their laps.

"I just got these down from the loft," she said. "Goodness knows how long they've been up there. Eddie had packed them away with our old camping equipment."

"Wow, you did a lot of cycling, Dot," Peter said, flicking through some black-and-white photos of Dot and her late husband posing with their bikes.

"That we did."

Mel looked over his shoulder and smiled. They'd looked like 1940s movie stars, with their stylised hair and vintage clothes. She turned her attention to the album on her own lap.

"Those are your baby pictures," Dot said, leaning over to open it. The album made a rustling sound as it creaked open. Layers of tissue paper lined each page, keeping the old photos separate. Mel had similar albums at home, at least she used to. She was unnerved to realise that with Lynette's recent clear-out, they might not have them anymore.

The pictures looked old, a little faded and brown around the edges, but rather good, really. Dot pointed a shaky finger at the photo she was studying.

"That's you and Abbie. Your mum sent me that one from the hospital."

Mel stared at the picture. She didn't recall ever seeing it before, although she'd seen some pictures of her first birthday. She looked from one baby to the other. One was large and healthy looking, the other smaller and a bit yellow.

"You were a little jaundiced," Dot said. "Or was it Abbie? I can't tell the difference. I remember one of you was born bigger than the other, took all the food in the womb and squashed the other one a bit." She slipped on her reading glasses and took a closer look, but she still shook her head.

Peter looked over her shoulder. "They look identical."

Mel nodded as a sinking realisation came over her. He was absolutely right. They were.

26

"Are you all right?" Dot asked as Mel's head lolled forward. The album almost slid out of her hands, but Peter caught it and set it down on the table.

Mel glanced at him, but he looked unfazed. He evidently hadn't got there yet, hadn't reached the horrifying conclusion she had.

"I'd love to see the garden," she told Dot, and without waiting for a response, she strode across to the patio doors. Her confused fingers couldn't work the lock.

Peter came up behind her and opened it for her, and Mel burst out into the fresh air. She felt as though there was a beetle trapped in her brain. She tipped her head one way, then the other, expecting something to fall out of her ears.

"Are you all right?" he asked.

"Give me a minute."

She circled the small garden, pretending to admire Dot's flowering ginger, but her mind was running rampant, examining the evidence and trying to come up with another conclusion. When she couldn't, she clutched the fence, stars dancing before her eyes.

"What is it?" Peter asked.

Mel exhaled. "You said it yourself, they were identical."

He looked like he was going to object, but she silenced him with her hand.

"I've seen baby photos of Abbie and me. We don't look anything alike. People often joked about it."

"So what…"

"I know this is going to sound crazy, but what if we were triplets, not twins? Three instead of two."

Peter burst out laughing.

"I think your mum would have remembered if she'd come home from hospital without one of her babies."

"What if she didn't know? She was very ill at the time, remember? She thought she was having twins, and we were born by caesarean section. What if the third one came as a surprise?"

"But why would they take one?"

"I don't know. I just don't know what else to think."

"Wouldn't you all look alike if you were triplets?"

"I don't think so. I remember someone at work had triplets. Two of them looked really alike, and the other was quite different. What if we're like that?"

"No," Peter said. "It's still sounds crazy."

"Does it? Then how else do you explain Lynette Parker? That passport I found could be genuine. Cyrus identified her, and let's face it, she's been acting nothing like Abbie."

Peter looked like he was going to say something; then he thought better of it. He reached for her, and she didn't resist. They stood together, so close she could feel his heartbeat. "I don't know," he murmured into her hair. "I don't know what to think."

They remained like that for several minutes until Mel finally peeled herself away.

"Come on, we'd better go back indoors. I don't want to freak Dot out."

Dot had made a fresh pot of tea, and Mel gladly accepted another cup. Her hands were as shaky as Dot's now. She felt like she was slipping off the edge of the world.

As she set down her cup, her phone rang. She looked at the name on the display. It was Abbie. Or should she sayLynette?

Bile rose in her throat, and she struggled to keep the tremor out of her voice as she answered. "Hello?"

"Mel, where are you?" The voice was different, similar to Abbie's but not quite right. A little too husky. Mel fought to keep her own voice as casual as possible.

"Didn't I say? Peter fancied a road trip, so we've gone to visit Auntie Dot."

There was a long pause, probably owing to the fact that Lynette wouldn't have a clue who Dot was.

"Do you want to speak to her?" Mel prompted. "Say hello?"

"I...er..."

She could practically see Lynette squirming on the other end of the phone. She didn't need to worry. Dot was too deaf to have much of a conversation over the phone. If Lynette did speak to her, she doubted she'd rumble her.

"Got to get something out of the oven. See you later, Mel."

"How is Abbie?" Dot asked as she set down the phone.

It was a good question. Mel felt a trickle of perspiration run down her face.

"She's fine," Peter said quickly. "Busy as ever with her boat."

Mel shot him a grateful look.

"She should get herself a nice young man," Dot said. "Such a lovely girl. I'm amazed no one's snapped her up."

"I think she's quite happy as she is," Mel said, gathering up her handbag.

At least, she had been.

They thanked Dot for the tea and stood in the doorway, ready to leave.

"Before we go, Dot, do you happen to remember the hospital where I was born?"

"Well, it would have been the Mary Seacole hospital here in Sheffield. It was quite new then."

"The Mary Seacole? Okay, thanks."

They said goodbye and walked back to the car. They got in, but Peter didn't drive. He was scrolling through his phone. He nudged her, and she glanced over his shoulder.

"It's got a lot of hits."

There were indeed. Pages and pages.

She began scrolling through her own phone. "Sounds like the hospital was hit by a scandal." As she read on, she began to feel as though her throat muscles were closing up, and it became increasingly difficult to swallow.

"You all right, Mel?"

"Yes. Yes, I just... Have you seen this? Scandal at Mary Seacole Hospital. Multiple babies switched at birth."

She read aloud: "It was revealed today that a nurse working at the Mary Seacole Maternity hospital near Sheffield may have maliciously switched a number of babies at birth. Emily Kitt, eighty-two, is thought to have switched babies from poorer homes with those with wealthier families in a misguided attempt at giving the poorer babies a better chance at life. In a startling death-bed confession, Miss Kitt, a former nurse at the hospital, claimed she switched dozens of infants between 1978 and 1989. Three families have so far come forward to say that they believe they might have been affected, and DNA testing is under way. All the babies involved would now be in their thirties and forties. South Yorkshire Police are working with the hospital to establish how many infants might have been switched, and a hotline has been set up for the families concerned."

Peter stared at her. "Are you going to call the hotline?"

Mel shook her head. "This article is five years old already."

They sat in silence for a moment. Mel's mind was whirring, making leaps she wasn't ready to comprehend.

"If this was all over the news, then why didn't we hear about it?" she asked.

"We were in Australia," he reminded her. "Perhaps it never made the international news."

"Well, it should have!"

Her mouth felt as dry as a lotus leaf. "We were in Australia, but the rest of my family were here. My parents should have known about it. And my sister."

"But what does all this mean?"

"It means that there were no triplets, Peter."

"Then what..."

"What if Lynette and Abbie were the real twins, and I was just some random who was born in the same hospital? Lynette and I could have been switched. I think we both went home with the wrong parents, and now Lynette has found out, and she's…she switched with Abbie."

"But why?"

"So she can take over her life!"

Even as she said these words, she couldn't take in the full horror of their meaning.

She let out a puff of air. She still couldn't believe she'd been taken in. All this time, this doppelganger had been living a parallel life, like Abbie but not Abbie. How long had she been living in her house? The thought made her queasy. She'd sat and talked to her, had meals with her, discussed her intimate thoughts…

"That whole brain-injury thing really had me going," she admitted. "I knew something was off, but it seemed so plausible."

Peter screwed up his face, and she could see he was still struggling to keep up.

"This Lynette Parker. She must have known that I'd figure her out. Because I saw through her straight away, Peter. I knew she wasn't Abbie, even though she looks just like her. It's just taken me a while to get to the truth."

She leaned against him and tried to pinpoint what was bothering her the most. It was so disturbing, this whole thing, so impossible to comprehend. She got a flash of Abbie in her head. The last time she'd been in England, for their parents' funeral. It hadn't been the greatest visit, but at least it had been real.

Peter slipped an arm around her shoulders. He knew her well enough not to interrupt her, to let her gather her thoughts in her own time.

"This is real, then," she said at last. "It really happened. I was switched at birth. Lynette is Abbie's true twin, which means that my mum and dad weren't even my real mum and dad."

She looked at him, daring him to contradict her.

"But she is like Abbie, isn't she?" he said. "I mean, you said she took you fishing. How did she know how to handle Abbie's boat if she's not Abbie?"

"You've seen where she comes from." Mel thought of the fish shop and the marina. "You hear of stories like this, don't you? Twins who've been separated at birth but led remarkably similar lives. The thing is, if Lynette Parker is a real living breathing human being, then where the hell is Abbie?"

27

The fact was, she hadn't heard from Abbie in months. It was hard to pinpoint exactly when Lynette had taken her place, but she had to think it had been around the time of the social detox back in the summer. So where had Abbie been for all that time? What had happened to her?

"What next?" Peter said. "We could go to the library and see if we can find any news articles about the people smuggling? If Cyrus's family drowned, then it's possible their bodies were washed up on the beach."

Mel shook her head. "I already did an extensive search online. I'm sorry, Peter. I know we've come a long way, but I just want to go now. I don't feel good at all."

He paused for a fraction of a second and frowned deeply, little lines appearing on the bridge of his nose.

"So now what?" he asked. "We can hardly go back to your house, can we? Not with Lynette there."

"Oh, god, Lynette!"

He reached for her, and she didn't object when he stroked the tears from her eyes.

"It's a long drive back. How about I get us a hotel for the night? A good night's rest ought to do us good. We need to think clearly before we confront her."

"I'm not sure we should confront her at all. This is a police matter."

"You want to go to the police?"

"Yes, and I'm hoping Cyrus will come with us, or at least provide us with some more evidence to back up our story. I'll speak to him again when we get back. I think the police will take us more seriously then."

She lay back against her seat while Peter fossicked with the satnav. She felt as though she were in a trance.

"According to the satnav, there's a little inn just round the corner. Shall we try there?"

"Yes, okay."

He could have suggested they sleep in the car, and she probably would have gone along with it. She was too upset to care.

The Wayfarer's Inn was a little further than Peter had thought, and a lot more basic, judging by the state of the building. It felt odd showing up without any luggage, but he was right. It was much too far to even think of driving back to Weymouth tonight.

"Do you think it's open?" Peter asked as he locked the car.

"Hard to tell," Mel said, looking at the cracked light on the front of the building.

Then he took her arm and steered her across the car park, and she was grateful because there was an unnatural heaviness in her limbs, as if she were pulling Abbie's weight along as well as her own.

They walked around the building until they found the reception. The sign was missing its 'R', and some genius had scrawled the letter 'D' in its place. A young man sat at the check-in desk, playing on his phone. He was playing *Artful Assassin*, Mel noted, but she didn't tell him she'd created it. She was too tired to get into all that.

Peter cleared his throat. "Do you have any rooms available?"

The receptionist looked up and blinked. "For tonight?"

"Yes, tonight."

He scrolled through the screen in front of him, frowning intensely, as if he'd been asked to land a plane. "Ah, here we go. You're in luck. There's one room left."

"I would have preferred two," Mel said weakly.

"It's just for one night," Peter muttered.

"Yeah, I suppose."

She barely registered as he handed over his credit card. All she could think about now was crawling into bed and resting her throbbing head, so she let him lead her up two flights of stairs and down a dark, dingy corridor.

They found their room, and he pushed in the key card.

"What do you know? It works!"

He held the door open for her. She went straight into the bathroom. She'd been considering a bubble bath, but quickly changed her mind when she saw the filthy tile grout.

"I suppose I'd better text Lynette, or she'll be wondering where we've got to," she called to Peter.

"Good point. You can say we're staying at Dot's."

Mel smiled at the idea of them camping out on Dot's sofa, but for all Lynette knew, Dot might live in a mansion.

When she came out of the bathroom, Peter had already slipped off his shoes and was lounging on the bed. Mel headed straight to the minibar. "Do you want a drink?"

"I'll take a lemonade."

She found a plastic bottle and tossed it to him. The bottle skittered across the floor, landing under a small wooden table that was missing one of its legs.

"You still throw like a girl," he told her, ducking as she lobbed another one in his direction. She missed him by miles.

He retrieved the drinks, then returned to the bed and flicked through the channels on the remote. Mel felt a wave of irritation as snooker came on.

"No, we're not watching this!"

He shrugged and switched to soft music. She turned her attention back to the minibar. She had a memory of Abbie mixing one of her fancy cocktails, and as she pulled out all the little bottles, she arranged them in the order she wanted to drink them, starting with her favourite, the Tia Maria.

"You look like you're on a mission," Peter said.

"Too right." She was going to need this lot to knock herself out.

He gave an exaggerated yawn. "Aren't you tired?"

She shook her head. "No, I'm wired. I can't believe I was sharing a house with that…that person and I never twigged. I mean, I knew something was wrong. I just never…"

"You mustn't beat yourself up about it. You weren't to know."

"But I should have! She's my twin, Peter. How could it take me so long to realise it wasn't her?"

In fact she *had* realised. If only she hadn't fought against her own instincts. The brain-injury story had seemed so plausible. But she had known from the minute she'd arrived home that something was out of whack.

"Do you mind if I get comfy?" he said. "I can't very well sleep in my jeans."

"By all means." She tossed aside the bottle she'd just finished and started on another. She really ought to pour them out into the plastic glass, but she didn't feel like doing that. She just wanted the drink to do its job so she could stop feeling so completely rubbish. Guilt throbbed inside her, and she couldn't sit still. She just wanted something to take her away from this nightmare.

Peter stripped down to his boxers. He looked a little cold, she thought, lying on top of the covers like that. She pulled her hair out of its ponytail, letting it fall loose around her shoulders. There, that was better.

"Do you want me to brush your hair?" he asked.

There had been a time when she'd enjoyed the sensation of his hands caressing the back of her neck.

"I haven't got a brush."

She opened a bottle of peach schnapps and necked it. She didn't have a toothbrush, either. Her mouth was going to be rancid in the morning.

"Pity," he said. "I thought it might take your mind off things."

She turned and looked at him.

"With respect, it wouldn't have worked, Peter. Unless you can rewind the clock four months and stop that monster from taking over Abbie's life. Unless you can prevent me from being switched at birth and...no, I don't want that because then my family wouldn't be my family, and that woman in the fish shop would be my mum..."

Peter's eyes widened. "Oh, god! She probably is, isn't she? You know, come to think of it, she did look a bit like you. She had your eyes and your chin. I didn't notice it at the time. I suppose I wasn't looking for it."

"Will you shut the hell up?"

She reached for another bottle, a miniature Jack Daniel's, and took a large gulp, making herself shudder. Her parents were dead, but they had been her parents. She couldn't imagine anyone taking their place.

Peter huddled under the duvet. The cold must have got to him. Mel ran a hand over the radiator. It was broken. He switched off the TV.

"Are you coming to bed?"

"In a mo."

She set the Jack Daniel's aside and drank the Baileys instead. She felt a warm flush as the alcohol hit her bloodstream. Finally, she moved on to the sweet Disaronno. She was feeling it now all right.

Peter had turned out the light, leaving her with just the little side lamp. She made her way over to the bed and climbed in. He was on his side, she noticed. He had always slept on the right, while she had always slept on the left. Even in all the days since they'd been apart, she had continued to sleep closer to the left than the right, as if her muscles remembered.

She slipped under the covers and rolled on to her side, facing away from him. Immediately, she felt him spoon her, his knees forming a chair under her buttocks, one arm draped protectively around her waist. She didn't shrug him off, nor did she encourage him. She felt his hand in her hair, and he traced a finger down her back. Then his mouth was on her neck, kissing, nuzzling.

"I've missed you so much."

She rolled over to face him. Looked into the face that was almost as familiar as her own. He smelt slightly sweaty, but in a good way, and his eyes were liquid with desire.

She barely had time for a gulp of air before she felt his wet lips on hers. She hadn't thought about this, hadn't had any intentions of letting things get physical, but as she lay there in his arms, she found herself responding. There was comfort in being here with him. She felt safe and warm and wanted. The kiss was unexpectedly passionate. He caught her hair in his fingers as it grew more intense. Their lips seem to fit perfectly together in a way they never had before. She closed her eyes and lost herself in the moment. He tasted just the way she remembered, but they had never kissed like this when they were together, not since the early days of their relationship.

"I missed you, Mel," he whispered, but she shut out his words. She didn't want to talk, didn't want to think. She just wanted to get lost in his arms.

AFTERWARDS, he rolled onto his back, and they both lay there, enjoying the warmth of the afterglow. He reached for her and squeezed her fingers. She squeezed back, but niggling doubts marched across her skin like an army of ants. She rolled over, cold now, and looked down at the puddle of clothes on the floor. Miniscule grains of sand fell from her T-shirt as she pulled it back over her head. "We shouldn't have done that," she whispered into the darkness, but Peter was already asleep, snoring like a bulldog.

She lay beside him, haunted by memories of herself and Abbie skipping together across the beach. She reached out to hold Abbie's hand, but even in her dreamy state, her sister slipped like sand through her fingers.

Peter was shivering on the edge of the bed when she woke up. Somehow, she'd ended up with all the duvet. She pulled it back over him, then swung her legs over the edge of the bed.

"Ugh!"

Her stomach spasmed painfully. As she set her foot down on the floor, she felt a carpet of little bottles. She bolted for the bathroom and vomited violently into the toilet as the events of the previous day before came rushing back to her.

Abbie! Oh, god, Abbie.

"Are you all right?" she heard Peter outside the door.

"I'm fine," she called back. She stripped off her clothes and turned on the shower. On second thoughts, she locked the bathroom door.

The shower sucked as much as the rest of the room. She got a blast of icy cold water that went from arctic to burning in ten seconds. She played with the dial until she found a setting she could live with, and even then, the water smelled liked pond weed.

Peter went into the bathroom straight after her. She heard him whistle a tune, and she wanted to slap herself for being so weak the previous night. She wished she could blame the alcohol, but she'd known exactly what she was doing. For her, it had been like indulging in tub of ice cream or watching a favourite TV show. But for Peter, it had meant something more, and now he had the impression that they were getting back together.

Peter had opened the curtains while she was in the bathroom, and the light shone painfully into the room. She stumbled over to the window and yanked them shut again, then found the last of the lemonade and glugged it down. She didn't care if it was £3 a bottle. Her throat was like sandpaper. She would have killed for a Red Bull, but the minibar didn't have one. All that was left was the remainder of the Jack Daniel's and a sorry-looking packet of Bombay mix.

She flopped back on the bed, but lying down made her head throb. Her cheeks were hot, and her heart felt like it was marching to its own rhythm. The longer she lay there, the more aware she became of an unpleasant odour in the room. Probably, it had been there the night before too, but she'd been too stunned to notice. Now, the combination of the smell and the inner gurglings of her stomach made for an unpleasant combination. She sat up slowly and slipped on her shoes.

"See you downstairs," she called to Peter, and she hurried out into the corridor. She staggered down the stairs to reception, where she insisted they put the bill on her card. It was the least she could do.

The reception smelt even less appealing than their room. Down here, someone had attempted to disguise the musty smell with heavily perfumed cleaning products that made her want to hurl.

"Did you have a nice stay?" the receptionist asked as he processed her payment.

Mel forced her head to nod up and down, and then she stumbled out the door.

THE MORNING AIR was like a bucket of cold water, instantly sobering her up. She waited by the entrance, leaning heavily against the wall, one hand shielding her eyes from the sun.

"You might have waited for me," Peter grumbled when he eventually made it outside.

"Sorry. I'm not feeling too hot."

"Do you think you could manage some breakfast?"

She shook her head. "Can't face it."

"Let's hit the road, then."

They started to walk across the car park.

"Last night was amazing," he said. "Even better than before."

She swallowed, unable to come up with an appropriate response.

He tried to take her hand.

"Peter…"

"We'd better get going," he said.

He must have sensed it, her reticence. It would be impossible not to.

"You didn't like it?"

"It was great," she admitted. "It just…I just. It's not what I want anymore. You and me, it's not going to work."

Colour flooded his face. "So, what? You think the last twenty-odd years were a mistake?"

His chin quivered, and for a horrifying moment, she thought he was going to cry.

"No, I'm not saying that at all. I was happy most of the time, Peter. It's only been the last few years that I've —"

"Last few years? You've just been…putting up with me that long?"

"No, I…I didn't know what I wanted. The last few years were tricky for me. After my parents…"

He pulled her hand towards him and held on tight as if he could somehow hold them together. She ached to pull away, but she didn't know how to without hurting him even more, so they just stood in front of the car until he was ready to let her go.

28

I t was a quiet journey back to Weymouth. Peter didn't say a thing when she called out the counties' names as they passed. He focused all his attention on the road, staring at the road with a grim expression on his face. For her part, she felt like utter crap. She leaned her head against the window, and the world seemed to spin every time she closed her eyes.

"I suppose I'd better ring Cyrus," she said after a while.

Peter didn't respond.

These fits of silence were by no means unusual. He'd always favoured silence over discussion. She had not forgotten how infuriating it was to spend time with someone who acted like they could see right through you. She took out her phone. It was a relief to speak to Cyrus, to have someone else to give her attention to. She arranged to meet him at his place. He was squatting in one of the holiday homes near the Hideaway café.

"You mean he just broke in?" Peter said, overhearing.

She shot him a look. Did he have to be so judgemental?

"I keep it very nice," Cyrus was telling her. "I take good care of the house for the owner. I'm like a friendly ghost."

Frankly, she didn't give a toss about the owner. That wasn't important right now. All that mattered was Abbie. And Cyrus's family, of course.

"I am very concerned to hear about your sister," he went on. "But your news brings me fresh hope. It means we may at last be able to get some answers."

He didn't say justice, she noted. Because how could there ever be justice for his family? If they had drowned, then nothing would ever bring them back. She just hoped it wasn't too late for Abbie.

"What time can you get here?"

Mel glanced at the satnav. "In about four hours."

"Very good, I will speak to you then. Peace be with you."

"And you."

She tried to sleep after speaking to Cyrus. Her head was throbbing, and her empty stomach rumbled, reminding her of what an idiot she'd been the night before. Peter reverted to silence, saying nothing until he pulled in at a service station close to home. Then he nudged her awake.

"You might want to stretch your legs."

She opened her eyes and sat up. She hadn't really been sleeping anyway, just drifting in and out, her mind torturing her with images of Lynette and Abbie. Where was her sister? What the hell had Lynette done with her?

She got out of the car and followed Peter into a self-service café.

"You go and sit down," she told him. "I'll go and queue."

He sat with his head in his hands and didn't even raise a smile when she brought him a doughnut with his coffee. She reached out and squeezed his shoulder. He could go on like this for days, sullen and miserable. She should never have shared a room with him. She should have known he'd only get hurt.

"Tell me what you're thinking," she said. She looked at him steadily, willing him to speak.

"I came all this way. I chucked in my job, Melly."

"Oh, Peter!"

"I really thought things would be different."

She wanted to put her arms around him, but she didn't want to give him false hope. She rubbed the pain from her temples. She didn't want to seem ungrateful after all he had done for her, but she couldn't go back to him. She knew that now. Life was too short.

THE AIR WAS STILL thick with tension when they arrived at the address Cyrus had given her.

"Here's what you should do," Peter said. "You've still got the number for those cops who came to the house, haven't you?"

"I think so."

"Right then, so call them and tell them about your mate Cyrus and what he knows. You've just got to keep him there till they come. The police are good at making people talk. That's their job. If he knows anything more, they'll get him to talk."

Mel was appalled. "We can't do that! He'll get into trouble. They might even deport him!"

"So?"

"For god's sake, Peter. Do you think he'd have risked

his life and his family's lives to come over here if every-thing was fine at home? If they send him back, he could be killed."

"He can claim asylum, can't he?"

"I don't think it's that easy. A lot of people slip through the net."

He folded his arms. "Fine, do it your way."

"Aren't you coming in with me?"

"No. You clearly know what you're doing."

"Don't be like that. I thought we were in this together."

She reached out and touched his arm, but he shrugged her off.

"I have to go, Peter. Cyrus is expecting me."

"Go on then."

She reached for the door handle. "What about you?"

He let out a sigh. "I tell you what, I'll go back to your house and see if Lynette's still there, and if she's not, I'll grab her passport. The police will have to take us seri-ously then."

"Don't confront her," Mel warned, fumbling in her pocket for her house keys. "We don't know what she might do."

"I think I can handle myself, thanks."

Mel looked down at her knees. "This isn't Abbie, remember. We don't know what she's capable of."

He made a noise like a deflated balloon. "Yeah, all right."

She hesitated for a moment, wondering if she should say something more. But no, nothing she said was going to make any difference. It was over between them. She needed to be clear about that. No more leading him on.

She got out, and he drove off, leaving her standing in front of an imperfectly formed terraced cottage. The sunlight fell directly on a bush of violet chrysanthemums, and a fat ginger cat was curled up on top of an old coal bunker.

She let out a sigh. It was probably for the best that Peter wasn't with her. Cyrus was skittish, and she had a feeling he'd clam up at the sight of him. She walked up the stone path and knocked on the door.

"Cyrus?" she called.

When there was no answer, she walked around to the back. A rake lay on the lawn, beside a neat pile of leaves. She went up to the back door and peered inside, wondering if she'd got the wrong cottage. That was when she saw him through the frosted glass. He lay at an unnatural angle, face down on the kitchen floor.

29

P anic rose in her throat as she battled with the door handle. God damn it, it was locked.

She picked up a large rock and lobbed it at the door, but the glass did not break. She retrieved it and tried the window instead, aiming for the lower right corner. This time, the glass cracked, fanning out like a brittle spider's web. Panting from the exertion, she threw the rock again, swinging her arm back to hit the fractured window at full force. There was a cracking, crunching sound as the remaining glass shattered, and jagged fragments rained down on the windowsill. She grabbed a rake that had been lying by the leaves and used it to clear the stray pieces of glass from the frame; then she put her arm through and felt for the door handle. She pulled it down and felt the door move. This was it. She was in.

She rushed inside, covering her mouth and nose with her hand. Cyrus lay in a puddle of blood-streaked vomit. It made her retch, but there was nothing inside her to throw up. Her head pounded as she considered what to do. She didn't want to touch him. She didn't want to get too close, but she was his only chance.

Breathing through her nose, she reached out and shook him. "Cyrus, wake up! You've got to wake up!"

He was still warm. Surely he was still in there?

She wrapped one hand underneath him, the other on his shoulder blade and heaved him onto his side. He was as heavy as if he were actively resisting, and the second she let go, his body flopped back down again.

She picked up his wrist and felt for a pulse, but couldn't find one. She tried his other wrist, then his neck.

"Cyrus!"

She tried again to roll him over, and this time he fell onto his back, and she found herself staring into his dead eyes. There was a look of absolute terror in those eyes. They were wide open, bloodshot, frozen in time.

Fumbling in her pocket, she pulled out her phone and dialled 999. It was only then that she noticed the discarded syringe lying beside him.

"God, Cyrus. What did you do?"

It didn't make sense. He'd sounded so hopeful. They were so close to getting the answers they needed. She shrank back against the wall as the truth hit her.

Lynette was here. Lynette got to him first.

"Which service do you require?"

The person on the other end of the phone was waiting for her to respond.

She looked again at the body of the man she'd known so briefly, and her voice, when it came, didn't feel like her own.

"I think there's been a murder."

· · ·

IT FELT like forever before the police and ambulance arrived. In all that time, it was just her and Cyrus sitting in silence in the perfect house that wasn't his. She tried not to think about the owners and how they would feel when they discovered someone had been killed here.

Paramedics buzzed around the body, swiftly followed by the police. There were a number of them, but she was mainly aware of the two detectives. One looked close to retirement. He seemed unruffled by the sight of the body, his keen eyes taking in the scene, as if it fitted exactly with what he'd expected. He was accompanied by a ginger-haired man with a very fair complexion. He had small green eyes that looked like two peas rolling about on a plate, and she wondered if this was his first dead body.

"I'm Detective Dankworth," the second one told her. "Let's step outside, shall we? We can wait in the garden while my colleagues see to the body."

Process the crime scene, you mean. But she was only too glad to do as he suggested.

She walked up the garden path and sank down on a wooden bench that overlooked a small fish pond.

"Did you know him well?" Dankworth asked.

"No, I've only spoken to him a couple of times."

"Then why are you so certain he was murdered?"

She took a deep breath. "I think he was killed by Lynette Parker. She's been living in my house, impersonating my sister. I –"

"It looks as though Cyrus overdosed on heroin," the other detective interrupted. "Did you know he was a user?"

"Like I said, I didn't really know him, but for what it's worth, he didn't strike me as an addict. What I do know is that he came here looking for answers. His wife and family went missing after he paid a woman called

Lynette Parker to bring them across the channel from Calais. I don't believe he would have killed himself. Not yet, anyhow."

"You say his family are missing?" Dankworth was scrawling furiously in his notebook. "Sounds like he had reason to be depressed, then."

"No! He wanted answers, and we were so close to getting them. Listen to me, you need to arrest Lynette Parker. She's staying at my house, pretending to be my twin –"

"Jeanette Parker, you say?" She couldn't miss the look that passed between them.

"Lynette," she correct. "L-Y-N-E-T-T-E. I believe she and I were switched at birth."

Dankworth shook his head. "Okay, slow down. I think we're going to have to start at the beginning."

Mel swallowed down her frustration and began again. Dankworth listened attentively, yet as soon as she brought up her allegations against Lynette, she seemed to hit a wall. If her life were a game, she would call this a bug. It all sounded so outrageous that no one would take her seriously.

She pulled up the photo of Lynette's passport picture on her phone and made him look at it. He didn't seem as impressed by this piece of evidence as she'd hoped. Perhaps because she'd zoomed in to get a good shot of Lynette's face. You couldn't make out the rest of the page. Just the picture and the name.

"You need to come round to my house," she told him. "You can speak to her yourself. And you can speak to my husband, Peter. He'll back up what I'm saying."

She gave him Peter's phone number, and he assured her he'd give Peter a call, but he didn't seem in any rush to do so.

"Tell us again how you came to find the body."

She repeated how she'd had found Cyrus and why she had been there. She supposed it didn't matter much now to admit that he was in the country illegally. No one could help him now anyway.

"Thank you for reporting the death," Dankworth finally said. "You can go home now if you like. I know it's been a tough day."

"You don't know the half of it," she muttered. "But what about Lynette Parker? Aren't you going to speak to her?"

"We'll be looking into that."

"You know, some of your colleagues have already met her," Mel said. "When they came to our house about a break-in."

"Did you tell them about your concerns then?"

"No." She looked down at her feet. "I still thought she was my sister then. It was only later that I realised the truth."

Dankworth's mouth twitched a little, and he scratched the stubble on his upper lip.

"I'll need the names of those officers."

"Yes, of course. It was…"

She thought hard. What had they been called? She remembered the woman's birdlike eyes. Damnit, why couldn't she remember?

"Wait, they gave me a card."

She searched through her handbag, but she must have left it at home. "I…can't recall right now. I'll have to get back to you on that. Or I can let you know when you come round."

He nodded, but he looked as if he was thinking about something else.

"Listen, it's imperative that you speak to Lynette. I think she's got Abbie."

Dankworth seemed to come back into focus. "Have you filed a missing persons report for your sister?"

"No. I didn't realise she was missing."

"Right, well, I suggest you come down to the station tomorrow morning, and we'll do it then."

"Why not now?"

"You've had a shock. I think you need to take a little time to recover. Then we'll go over it all in the morning when you're feeling fresher. Now, do you need a lift home?"

"No, that's all right. It's not far."

TEARS OF FRUSTRATION trickled down her cheeks as she set off for Evergreen Crescent. She couldn't believe Cyrus was dead. It had been just hours since she had spoken to him. What had happened in the short time since? And why wouldn't the police take her seriously?

She walked on autopilot, the wind blowing leaves across the street in front of her. The sky was an ominous shade of grey, and she felt tension in her head, as if a storm was brewing. She pulled her phone out and saw she had three missed calls from Peter. She'd been a long time. She really should have called him. She dialled his number, but he didn't pick up. She quickened her pace as she entered her neighbourhood.

Peter's hire car was parked a little way down the street. He hadn't been stupid enough to park right outside the house, then. He wasn't in the car, nor was Abbie's car in the driveway. She must have gone out. She raced up the garden path.

"Peter? Peter, are you there?" She tried the front door and found it unlocked. "Peter!"

She ran to the stairs, her heart thumping as Peter appeared on the landing.

"Where the hell have you been?" he asked, looking all hot and bothered. "You've been bloody ages. Hey, what's wrong?"

She shook her head. She would tell him about Cyrus later. Right now, they needed to get what they'd come for and get the hell out.

"I can't find the passport," he said. "Are you sure it was in her bedside drawer?"

"It was."

She followed him up the stairs to Abbie's room. He had pulled the entire drawer out and set it down on the bed. She rifled through it, convinced he wasn't looking properly, but she was wrong. It wasn't there.

"Damnit, she must have moved it."

She walked around the room, checking every nook and cranny. She tried the wardrobe, the windowsill, the gap between the wall and the bed.

"This is useless!"

In her frustration, she kicked Abbie's bed, and another drawer slid out unexpectedly. She bent down and had a look, moving a pile of pyjama bottoms aside.

Please let it be in here.

She emptied it all out on the floor, but there was nothing hidden there. Nothing but a pile of clothes. Peter was fussing about, trying to put things back the way they'd found them.

"There's no time for that," she told him. She flipped back the rug and checked the loose floorboard, but the passport was nowhere to be found.

"Could she have hidden it somewhere else in the house? Down in the cellar maybe?" Peter suggested.

"We don't have a cellar."

"The attic, then?"

"It's all blocked up."

"Well, where, then?"

"I'm beginning to think she's got it on her. Do you think she's left, Peter? She might have realised we're on to her."

They left Abbie's room and hurried through the house. She tried not to see Lynette's influence everywhere. How she hated those plain walls and drab carpets. It was as if Lynette had sucked the essence right out of their house.

Suddenly, she realised Peter wasn't following.

"Peter? What are you doing?"

"Just a minute, Mel. I need to use the dunny."

"For god's sake, we need to get out of here!"

"I'll just be a minute."

She tapped her foot impatiently. There was no stopping him once he had his mind set on something.

"Peter…"

She stopped. Held her breath. There was a noise at the front door. She heard the squeak of the letter box and relaxed a little. It was probably the post. Then the door flung open, and she found herself staring into the cold, calculating eyes of her enemy. Lynette was back.

"Peter!"

There was no time to hide. Lynette was clumping through the house. Mel looked at her, hoping and praying that this time it would be Abbie, but she knew instantly it wasn't. It was in the way she held herself: shoulders slumped, stomach out. It was in the permanent snarl on her face, and even in the lines around her eyes and mouth. She could see that Lynette had lived a hard life. Far harder than her and Abbie.

She heard the sound of the toilet flushing; then Peter came out of the bathroom, shaking the water off his hands. "Couldn't find a towel…"

He stopped and stared at Lynette.

"Oh, hi, Pete," she said, with a toss of her hair. She

fluttered her eyelids at him, and Peter gawped at her. He seemed unable to look away.

"You look so much like her!" he said.

"Peter!" Mel hissed, but it was too late. Their cover was blown.

Lynette swivelled her head and locked eyes with Mel, mocking her with her smile. There was no fooling anyone anymore. All pretence was gone.

30

"What do you think you're looking at?" Lynette asked, her eyes trained on Mel. "Think you're going to stop me, do you?"

Mel fought to keep her voice calm. "Look, I just want to know what you've done with Abbie. Just tell me where she is."

Lynette tipped her head to one side, the same way Abbie always did. "I'm going to go now. You haven't got the guts to stop me."

Mel took a step towards her, but before she could stop him, Peter charged at Lynette as if he were on the rugby pitch, head down, arms balled. Too late, Mel saw the flash of metal.

"She's got a knife!"

The edges of her vision greyed as Lynette embedded the boning knife into Peter's thigh. His anguished scream ripped right through her, tearing at her heart. Peter dropped to the floor as a fountain of blood spurted from his thigh. He was screaming in panic and pain. Mel stared at Lynette and saw that she was watching with a curious expression on her face. Not concerned, not apologetic, merely inquisitive, as if she hadn't known stabbing him would cause this much pain. Lynette was still watching him as she edged away. Her hand knocked into the wall, and the knife slipped from her hand and skittered across the kitchen. Mel made a dash for it, but Lynette was faster, swooping down like a pterodactyl. Her eyes danced as she brandished it at Mel, daring her to come closer.

Mel took a step back, and Lynette headed down the hallway. She reached the front door just as Otto came bolting down the stairs, slobbering and snarling. Mel had never seen him like that before. He lifted his lips, baring his pink gums and teeth. His ears were up, his posture rigid, his tail moving rapidly from side to side. Lynette yelped and rattled the door handle as the dog threw himself at her, giving vent to months of neglect in a rabid volcano of fury. There was a loud tearing sound as he sank his teeth into her backside.

"Fuck!"

Lynette twisted this way and that, trying to get him to release her. Mel edged forward, afraid she would stab the dog, but Lynette kicked him instead, sending him flying backwards, hitting the bottom stair. He recovered quickly, but Lynette was already out the door. The dog tore back to the doorstep, alternately growling and barking as she made a dash for Abbie's car. Mel put a hand on his collar.

"She's not worth it," she told the dog as the car engine started. Lynette would not think twice about running him down.

Lynette glowered at her as she reversed down the drive at breakneck speed. There was a crunch as the car clipped the wall, and then she was gone, leaving Otto to bark furiously at the empty road.

Mel heard a stifled moan from the kitchen.

"God, Peter!"

She found him slumped to the floor, clutching his wound. His breathing was hard, his hands bloody with the effort of containing the blood. She pulled the first aid kit down from the cupboard and helped tear his jeans off so she could get at the wound. His skin felt cool, and he whimpered at her slightest touch.

"Peter, you've got to let me see."

"It hurts!"

"I know."

She kissed his cheek, and reluctantly, he moved his hand away so that she could see the damage.

His thigh looked swollen and tender, and the wound gaped open, blood spurting out. It made her want to retch, but she forced herself to focus. Peter gripped her shoulder with his right hand as she cleaned the area as gently as she could. She wrapped it tight with a thick layer of bandage. She wasn't sure how much he needed, so she used it all.

"How does it feel?" she asked once she'd finished.

"A little numb."

She grabbed a blanket from the sofa and covered him with it. Then they both looked at Otto, who was still snarling in the doorway. Blood dripped from his muzzle.

"You let her get away," Peter said.

Mel's eyes searched his. "I had to, didn't I?"

"I was talking to the dog."

"I think he did great."

She jumped to her feet and rifled through the kitchen drawer. "You got your phone? I need you to call 999."

She found the Swiss army knife and slipped it into her pocket.

His eyes widened with alarm. "Mel…"

"Give me your keys. Hurry. I think I know where she's heading."

"Where?"

"Abbie's boat. The *Catch 22*."

He pulled the keys from his jacket pocket, but when she reached for them, he wouldn't release his grip.

"Peter, I have to do this. Call 999."

She tore the keys from his hand and then ran towards the door.

"Melly, don't go! Look what she did to me!"

She turned around briefly and tried not to worry about the paleness of his skin or the stricken expression on his face.

"I'm sorry, Peter, but I have to go after her. I have to find out what happened to Abbie."

She dashed out to Peter's hire car and got behind the wheel. The lights came on automatically. All she had to do was check her mirrors and go. Too late, she realised she could barely reach the pedals. She let the car roll as she fumbled under the seat for the lever. There was no time to pull over. She had to catch Lynette before she made off on Abbie's boat.

She tore through red lights, causing other cars to honk their horns like a gaggle of angry geese. She turned, heading down towards the marina, then remembered at the last minute that Lynette had moved the boat. Swearing under her breath, she performed a U-turn in someone's driveway and skidded off towards the new mooring. The more secluded one Lynette had chosen, no doubt because no one would know her down there, had made it easier to cover her tracks.

It made so much sense now, in hindsight. Everybody would have known Abbie at the marina – they were a close-knit community. They would have stopped and talked to her, maybe even invited her for drinks and socials. Abbie had loved the social side, but it would have been a problem for Lynette. So she had avoided all that by moving the boat to a quieter spot, one where nobody knew her or Abbie.

What a shock it must have been for Lynette when she'd called out of the blue, to tell her she was coming home from Australia. Talk about putting her on the back foot. It was little wonder that she hadn't been there to meet her at the airport! She recalled how little Lynette had been around those first couple of days, up until Cyrus broke into the house, forcing her to pay her some attention.

She felt a flood of relief as she spotted Abbie's car in the car park. Lynette hadn't even attempted to park properly, and had left the car half in one space and half in the other. She'd even left the keys in the ignition.

Mel pocketed the keys and strode towards the steps that led down to the sea. The clouds billowed out like pufferfish. A fisherman was coming the other way, hauling heavy equipment on his back.

"You'd have to be mad to go out in that!" he warned, with a glance down at the stormy water. Mel ignored him and scanned the boats for Lynette. Adrenaline surged through her body when she spotted the *Catch 22*. The tarpaulin was off, and boxes of bottled water and other supplies sat on the deck, as if they'd been dumped there in a hurry. No doubt Lynette was prepping the boat to leave.

Mel hurried along the jetty, rattling her brains for a way to stall her until the police arrived. Did Peter even know where to send them? She wasn't sure if she'd told him where the new mooring was. She took a good look around, but it looked like all the other boats were empty. Most likely, the owners had heeded the bad weather warnings. She glanced back at the car park, but even the fisherman had left. There was no one else around to help her. If she was going to stop Lynette, she'd have to do it herself.

She watched the boat, moving carefully so as not to attract attention. Her heart thudded as Lynette heaved herself up the steps from the cabin. She appeared to be arguing with herself as she stomped about the deck, flinging her weight around, adjusting this and checking that. Preparing to take the boat out. Mel removed the Swiss army knife from her pocket and flicked it open, examining the blades. She thought of Peter and knew she wouldn't hesitate to use it.

The best way onto Abbie's boat was the swimming platform on the stern. She recalled seeing Lynette climb on and off it the day she'd taken her out. The problem was that she needed to get on board without making any sound, and there was quite a gap between the boat and the jetty. If she jumped, she might alert Lynette, but how else could she do it?

She eyed the next-door boat, a small sailing boat called *Solitude*. It wasn't very big, but it was moored close to the *Catch 22*. Perhaps she could use it as a stepping stone.

Quietly as she could, she crept towards *Solitude*. The boat wobbled precariously as she stepped on board. How did people make it look so easy? She got down low and crawled along the boat on her hands and knees, scared she might tip into the water. When she reached the end, she looked up at Abbie's boat. It looked steeper than she'd realised. She thought there had been a ladder, that day at the cove, but she couldn't see it now. She would just have to use some of the mooring rope to pull herself up.

She'd been no good at rope climbing at school, and she was no better now. The ropes burned her hands as she pulled herself up. Still, with a little effort, she was able to get high enough that she could reach the swimming platform, and from there, she hauled herself on board her sister's boat.

She glanced left to right, but she couldn't see Lynette. She hunted around for somewhere to hide. She wasn't sure exactly what she was going to do yet. She only knew that she couldn't let Lynette get away. There was a large box sitting in the middle of the deck. That would do for starters. She crawled towards it, keeping her eyes out for Lynette. She couldn't see her anywhere. Perhaps she was down in the cabin again.

She reached the box and hunched behind it for a moment, listening intently. She heard the crackle of a radio and what sounded like the shipping forecast. Lynette was swearing in response. Mel felt a slight glimmer of hope. If the weather was that bad, then Lynette would be delayed. This could work to her advantage. She glanced back at the car park. Hopefully, Peter had called the police by now. She just hoped they could pinpoint her location.

Peter.

That wound had looked pretty nasty. She felt a pang of regret at leaving him like that. He'd been in a bad way. What if he'd passed out or something? He could be bleeding to death on the kitchen floor. She got a flash of Cyrus's body but pushed the memory away. *Not now. I can't think about him now.*

Lynette climbed back up the steps, swigging from a bottle of what looked like water, but might have been something stronger. Mel held her breath, afraid Lynette would notice her, but she appeared lost in thought. As she watched, Lynette peered over the railings. The sea seemed as wild as she was, waves lapping at the side of the boat. Slowly, silently, Mel rose to her feet and took a couple of steps towards her. The noise of the waves blocked out her footsteps as she crept closer, the Swiss army knife poised in her hand. She was standing right behind her now, every muscle in her body primed for action.

One, two, three…

She tapped Lynette on the shoulder.

Lynette spun round and eyeballed her, a sadistic smile on her face.

"You just couldn't let it go, could you, Mel? You can't leave me the hell alone."

She should have been afraid. Hell, she *was* afraid, but she was also angry. Angrier than she'd ever been in her entire life. This wasn't Lynette's boat to take, it was Abbie's. She held the knife tight as she raised it to Lynette's throat.

"I want to know what you did to Abbie."

She expected Lynette to cower, or at least beg for her life, but she was the one who was shaking. She felt it in her arms, and she heard it in her voice. Lynette didn't even lose her cool.

"You can't hurt me. You don't have it in you."

"Don't I?"

Mel pressed the knife to her throat, forcing her backwards until there was nowhere left to go. She held as steady as her trembling arms would let her, not flinching as a trickle of blood ran down Lynette's neck.

"No!"

In one fluid motion, Lynette lifted her knee and kicked Mel hard in the stomach. Mel lost her grip on the knife as she went crashing down, and she lay there, wheezing for air. The knife flew across the deck, landing with a splash in the water.

"That was a good knife," Lynette complained. She stood over Mel and watched her for a moment, then kicked her hard in the chest. Mel gasped like a fish out of water, too stunned to move. Lynette grinned and sauntered over to the steering console. She turned the key in the ignition, and the motor started with a splutter. Mel rubbed her chest, and tears stung her eyes, but she couldn't catch her breath. She crawled on her hands and knees, desperate for release. She felt herself puffing up like an inflatable. Slowly, painfully, she managed a few small breaths that hurt her lungs.

She pulled herself up into a sitting position, and her breath gradually returned.

Lynette shot her a sneering look. "Last chance to get off."

Mel rose slowly to her feet. "I want to know...what you did to Abbie."

Lynette's face darkened, and her eyes flicked from left to right. She opened her mouth, and for a moment, Mel thought she was actually going to confess. Then she picked up a can of beer and lobbed it at her. The can hit her right on the forehead; then it rolled onto the deck, fizzing like crazy. Lynette was laughing, but the sound felt like it was coming from a long way away. Mel pressed a hand to her head and felt a lump. She heard humming in her ears, then a tingle in her neck and, finally, a flash of stars before she hit the deck.

31

Mel's first thought was that Otto was licking her face. She opened her eyes to see large grey clouds full to bursting. The wind howled in her ears, and salty waves broke over the boat. She was freezing cold, dazed and confused, sliding about as the sea vented its fury. Huge waves tossed the boat back and forth, but it wasn't the weather Mel feared the most.

She struggled to unscramble her thoughts, to decode the clues dancing around in her brain. *Where is she? Where is the assassin?*

A wave broke over the boat, dousing her in cold, salty water. She coughed and spluttered. She was freezing, but she was definitely awake now. She rubbed the lump on her forehead, and her eyes tracked Abbie. She had her back to Mel as she steered. The boat was listing slightly in the wind, and a fresh wave hit them, soaking her face, soaking Abbie. No, not Abbie, she realised with a jolt.

Lynette.

She hauled herself up into a sitting position, her

mind still trying to work it all out. Her eyes were playing tricks on her, the blurred lines making her see double. For a moment, it appeared as if there were two Lynettes or, in Mel's injured mind, Lynette *and* Abbie.

She rubbed her eyes and forced herself to focus until she was seeing one again. She was as quiet as she could be with her brain pounding in her skull. Her jaw ached, and there was still a slight ringing in her ears.

She looked out to sea. There was no land in sight and no lights on the horizon, which suggested she'd been unconscious for a while, though exactly how long, she had no idea. She forced her eyes to focus on Lynette, and with some kind of sixth sense, Lynette whirled round and stared at her.

"That was a nasty bump to the head, Mel. I hope you haven't got a brain injury?"

Mel looked around for a weapon, but she could barely focus, let alone make a grab for anything. She blinked, willing her body to cooperate.

"What are you staring at?" Lynette demanded, with a quick glance back at the wheel.

Mel thought it best to say nothing. Her stomach churned as another big wave surged towards them, and she fought for control of her body. She felt weak and lifeless, as if she were moving through soup.

She took a deep breath, knowing it might be her last.

"What did you do with my sister? I have a right to know."

Lynette let go of the wheel completely, causing it to spin madly, and the boat veered to the right.

"You really want to know?"

There was that creepy silent laugh of hers. Abbie never laughed like that.

"All right then," Lynette said, as if the notion

amused her. "I'll tell you what happened to your precious twin. Or, as it turns out, *my* precious twin."

Mel kept her face completely neutral, willing her to go on.

"I work in the freight business, transporting goods across the channel."

"People?" Mel said, holding tight to the side as the boat hopped about in the waves.

"Yes, amongst other things. I was doing good business up until four months ago when things went a bit sour. I took some business off some big fish, and they didn't take too kindly to it. I reckon they must have sabotaged my boat, because it took on water a few miles out to sea, and I lost some precious cargo."

Even now she appeared to be laughing, as if what had happened was just a big joke.

"Luckily for me, I had a small inflatable lifeboat, so I managed to get myself back to shore, but all those other poor buggers? Well, I told them I'd bring help, but there was no hope for them, really. Most of them couldn't even swim."

Mel swallowed hard. *Cyrus's family.*

"Anyway, I decided to let the bastards who sabotaged me think I was dead. They weren't the only gang I'd got on the wrong side of, so it suited me to disappear for a while. That's when it struck me that I could call on good old Abbie."

Mel shivered. "How did you even know about Abbie?"

Lynette flipped her hair back, out of her eyes. "I found out about her a few years ago. It was on the local news, babies switched at birth and all that. The nurse who did it even remembered our names. She told the police she thought you'd get a better life if she swapped us. She didn't give a shit that I got a worse one in return.

I told my mum I wanted to meet my real parents, and bless her heart, she went to a lot of trouble to track them down. But when she approached your parents, they didn't want to know. They said you had a perfectly happy life in Australia, and it wouldn't be fair to disrupt you."

Mel swallowed. She couldn't believe her parents had known all this and never told her. Never even hinted, but she could see that they'd been trying to protect her.

Lynette's face tightened. "They didn't even want to meet me. They said it was best to leave it, that we both had our own lives."

Mel bit her lip, wondering how her parents had managed to keep this from her. It must have been hard. Looking back, she could think of a few times when her dad had opened his mouth to say something and then seemed to forget what he was going to say. She'd thought it was a sign of aging, but now she knew differently.

"Anyway, I got to thinking. What could be a more perfect hiding place than at my identical twin's house? I could just slot into her life, and no one would ever know."

Mel shook her head, wishing she could will the words away.

"I already knew where to find her. I'd been following her on Facebook for a while. I couldn't help it, she was little Miss Perfect, you see. Lucky Abbie and her perfect little life. I was amused to learn that she was into boats, like me. We had so much in common, really, except that her life was great, whilst mine was a bag of shite."

"Our parents died," Mel pointed out gruffly.

Lynette acted as though she hadn't heard.

"So I came to Weymouth. I soon figured out where Abbie lived, and then I stowed away on her boat. I slept down in the cabin one night and waited for her. Luckily for me, she was on her own that day, just her and the open waves. She'd been planning to do a little diving, I think. She'd had all her equipment with her, the wetsuit and the gear. It was a sunny day, and she was humming to herself as she steered the boat. It was like looking at a Disney version of myself. I couldn't stop staring at her and wondering what my life could have been."

"And then?"

Lynette dropped her gaze.

"I revealed myself to her out at sea, in the middle of nowhere. She got one look at me and just started screaming. You should have seen the expression on her face! She thought I'd escaped from the mirror or something."

Mel felt acid working its way up from the pit of her stomach.

"Where is Abbie now?" she asked, her throat like cactus.

"Oh, I disposed of her." Lynette looked eerily over-board, and Mel followed her gaze, as if expecting to see her sister bobbing about in the water.

"How far out was this?" she asked faintly. "I mean, Abbie's a strong swimmer. She could swim for miles on a warm day. Maybe she found an island somewhere…"

"Not with a weight belt tied to her," Lynette said. "Honestly, I think she was already dead when I tossed her out. She didn't really stand a chance."

Mel should have been angry, but all she felt was numb. Even the waves thrashing against the side of the boat seemed to lose some of their power, as if the whole world had slowed down. There was no point now. Abbie was gone.

"I did up the house pretty nice after that and put it on the market." Lynette went on, as if she still cared. "I did a really good job of it. The estate agent was really impressed."

She poked Mel in the ribs to make sure she was still listening.

"Once the sale goes through, I'm going to take the money and run off to South Africa. I'm sick of this wet, drizzly weather. I want to live somewhere warm and sunny. It's nothing personal, Mel, but I'm afraid you're not invited."

And with that, she picked up the speargun and aimed it straight at Mel.

"Wait! Don't..."

Mel hurled herself to one side, screaming as the arrow grazed her shoulder and shot down into the water. The pain woke her up and sent a surge of adrenaline buzzing through her veins. She leapt to her feet and pounced on Lynette, catching her by surprise. The speargun fell from her hands as Mel clawed at her, biting and gnashing her teeth the way Otto had done. She only had a few seconds before she would lose her advantage. She noticed that the rope from the speargun was uncoiling into the water. She made a lunge for the gun and looped the rope around Lynette's neck.

"What the hell are you –"

The rope jerked, and Lynette grasped desperately at the air as she was dragged, arms and legs flailing, into the water.

"Help!" she gurgled.

Mel's heart beat frantically in her chest. Abbie's face flashed through her mind. She thought she heard her laughing, but it was probably just the sound of the gulls.

The last sound Lynette made was a loud, piercing scream, a wailing, haunting sound that seemed to echo through the waves that tossed her and thrashed her against the side of the boat.

Mel clung to the side, expecting to see her bob up to the surface, but she was nowhere to be seen. Where was she? Had she somehow freed herself and swum around the boat? She glanced nervously behind her. She felt raw and exposed, sitting there in her weakened state, not knowing which direction an attack might come from.

The water appeared darker, as if petrol were leaking from the engine. The boat creaked and shuddered, then there was movement in the water, and Mel spotted something oily and red. What was that? An arm? A leg? She looked again at the dark liquid. Was that...blood? She retched over the side of the boat as she realised what had happened. Lynette had got tangled up in the propeller.

She sprang into action. Ran on spaghetti legs towards the control panel. She stared at the controls for a moment, then threw the boat into neutral. The boat spun around, but it was too late for Lynette, just as it was too late for Abbie. Moments later, the body surfaced. It was horrendous: bloody and mangled. Mel leaned over the side and caught one last glimpse of her face. Her mouth was wide open, and her eyes had rolled back in her head. She didn't even look like a person anymore. More like a broken doll.

Pain throbbed in her head as the last few minutes played over and over in her mind. She felt shock at seeing Lynette's dismembered body, but more than that, grief at the loss of her twin. She tasted it in her nose, in her mouth and throat. She forced herself to breathe in and out, in and out, and the weight shifted downwards, settling in her heart.

32

The waves thrashed around her. Lynette was gone, but Mel was now stranded in the middle of the stormy sea. She'd never steered a boat in her life. She didn't even know where she was. She didn't have a clue how to get back. All she wanted to do was crumple in a heap and sob, but the waves continued to nudge the boat, making it spin and dip. Making her tremble and shudder.

She heard the purr of a helicopter overhead. She waved her arms manically, but it kept on flying, and she knew it must not have seen her. Only once it had gone did it occur to her that there must be a flare on board. Abbie would have had a flare, wouldn't she?

It didn't save her though, did it?

A bottle of vodka had rolled out of one of Lynette's boxes and smashed all over the deck. There were other things too, bottles of water, biscuits and tins of meat.

She looked up at the sky. Where was north? Where the hell was north? But even if she could figure that out, she didn't know which way she'd come from, or which way she needed to go. She was miles from home, maybe even further. The only indication of time was the dark brooding sky.

A ferocious wave rocked the boat, and she clung on for dear life. This wasn't good. Would she be safer below deck? The next wave flung gallons of water at her feet. No, she needed to stay up here. She needed to get help.

She fumbled for her phone, but she seemed to have lost it. Had Lynette nicked it from her pocket while she was unconscious? She cast her eyes around the boat, and her heart leapt as she spotted it lying under the seat. She grabbed it and held it up high, but she couldn't get a signal. Here came another wave. She stuffed the phone into her pocket and clung onto the side as it hit, drenching her with cold water. Her teeth chattered violently. She needed to turn the boat around and steer into the waves.

She crouched low and clung to the side as she made her way to the bow. She moved hand over hand until she reached the cockpit. She thought of Lynette's mangled body. Of Abbie's untimely death. The boat was tipping. She spotted a life jacket and pulled it on.

GULLS SHRIEKED OVERHEAD. She tried to remember watching Abbie at the helm. Watching Lynette. It always looked so easy; she'd never thought to pay close attention. She'd never thought she'd have to steer the boat herself.

The controls didn't look too complicated. She was looking at a steering wheel and what appeared to be a joystick. The keys were still in the ignition, and there were a few other buttons and a small monitor, which had to be GPS. Good, this was good. She already knew how to drive, didn't she? How hard could this be? She put the boat into gear and studied the GPS. Lynette must have charted a course for the journey. If so, perhaps she could just follow it back the way they'd come.

A big wave lashed the side, and she screamed. The boat felt as flimsy as a cup and saucer compared to those huge waves. She closed her eyes as the world tipped around her. She spun the wheel, tried to get a feel for which way the boat was moving, but it was hard to tell with the waves battering the sides.

She opened her eyes, first one then the other. Abbie had always plotted her route on a paper chart rather than just rely on the GPS, but there was none to be seen. She concentrated on the GPS and tried to understand the route, but it didn't make much sense to her. There were various little boxes on the screen in front of her, but she didn't know what they were. Were they points to aim for? Bits to avoid? She followed the little boat icon and tried to steer in a straight line, which just made the boat judder. The engine made a spluttering sound, probably due to the mangled body parts caught in the propeller, and now she was tilting precariously. She swallowed down her nausea and clutched the wheel, screaming as the boat dipped and rose. It was only then that she noticed the satellite phone fixed to the wall.

"Oh, my god, oh my god!"

She stared at it for a moment. How did the damn thing work? Did she just call 999? She tried it, but the call didn't go through. She turned it over, and on the back was a big white label.

'Emergency 112'.

Right. She glanced nervously at the big wave heading her way and sank down as low as she could. She dialled 112.

She could barely hear over the roar of the waves, but

there was someone there, she was sure of it, and then a voice came through loud and clear, a woman's voice saying:

"Emergency services. Which service do you require?"

"Hello?"

She had to shout to make herself heard. She sounded frantic, crazy, but she didn't care.

"My name is Mel Montgomery, and I'm stranded on a boat, the *Catch 22*, somewhere off the Weymouth coast."

She waited, but couldn't hear anyone on the other end. Dammit! How did this thing work? She kept talking anyway, just in case.

"This is Mel Montgomery on the *Catch 22*. I think there's some damage to the propeller…"

She glanced up and saw the biggest wave she'd ever seen. It was heading right for her, and it had to be at least thirty feet. She was sailing into the wind and into the waves. She needed to turn the boat around, but there wasn't time. There wasn't…

She grabbed the wheel and spun it as fast as she could. The wave was still coming. She wasn't fast enough. The wave was getting bigger. It looked like a monster towering over her, threatening to toss her little boat into the air. Then she was turning, spinning away. She was moving into the wave, but was it going to be enough?

"C'mon! C'mon!"

She clung to the boat, feeling as though she were going to take off. She hung on like she was on a roller coaster, riding it, rocking it. She didn't know how she managed to hang on, but it felt as though someone were helping her, hugging her tight to the boat.

The giant wave was receding now, and she turned

the boat around some more, hoping she'd got the position right now. She needed to get away from the waves, downwind.

After a moment's rest, she raised her head and saw the helicopter again. For all she knew, it was the same one she'd seen the first time. She waved her arms in the air, desperate to be seen. It hovered above her, and she hoped to god they'd seen her this time. She glanced around for a flare, but she didn't dare move. The helicopter disappeared again, and she screamed her frustration into the air. The waves rocked her this way and that, and tears ran freely down her face. She was going to die out here. It had all been for nothing.

Then an orange dot appeared on the horizon. She stared hard, not a dot, a boat! A bloody boat!

She could hear the engine now, humming over the water. She waved her arms and shouted as loud as her lungs would let her. She cried tears of relief. Abbie would want her to survive. If Abbie were here right now, she would be patting her on the back and hugging her and pouring her a Prosecco.

The boat was getting closer. Bright lights blinked at her, and she almost peed herself when she saw the figures in yellow coveralls. It was the RNLI! They'd sent a lifeboat.

"Here, over here!"

The lifeboat crew manoeuvred as close as possible. The yellow figures had white helmets on with clear visors that made them look like spacemen. One stood facing her, a coil of white rope in his hand. He indicated that he was going to throw her the rope. Shit, was she supposed to catch it?

Instinctively, she put her hands out, and the next thing she knew, it was right in her hands. *I caught it!*

"Tie it!"

She found a cleat to tie it to. She vaguely remembered learning to tie different kinds of knots in the Girl Guides, but the method escaped her, so she went for a regular double knot.

She looked across at the lifeboat just in time to see it being thrashed by the waves. It looked so precarious, the way it bounced around like that. They were trying to tow her now, but it didn't feel like it was working. Her boat listed dangerously from side to side, and she felt like any minute she would be pulled into the water. Then she was moving, rocketing over the waves, over the perilous sea. She cheered and gave the thumbs-up with one hand and held tight to the rail with the other. Less than ten minutes later, she could make out lights on the horizon. One of the yellow figures waved to her and pulled up his visor to mop his brow. They were going to make it. She was going to make it.

THEY PUT her in a side room at the hospital, which seemed like a bit of a luxury. Mel had rarely been in hospital, but when she had, they'd always placed her on a noisy ward with older, more sickly patients, people who groaned and coughed in the night and cried out for the nurses.

She was glad to have the dignity of a side room. She didn't want to have to explain herself to nosey roommates. This room had that same patented stench of cleaning fluids mixed with vomit, but she also had a window that faced the beach, and she could watch the birds picking at the gorse and heather.

"Well, it seems the doctors are pleased with you."

She looked up. It took her a moment to place him, the lanky man with the ginger hair. It was the detective she'd spoken to after she'd found Cyrus. What was his name? Dankworth. She clenched her jaw.

He hadn't believed her, had he? He'd looked at her like she was nuts. They all had.

"You should have listened to me," she told him now.

He pressed his lips together. He wasn't going to admit he'd been wrong. Course not. But he didn't deny it, either.

"How are you feeling?" he asked.

"I want to see Peter," she broke in. "I haven't seen him yet. Lynette stabbed him; he was bleeding badly…"

"Your husband was the one who called the police," he told her. "He had to have stitches, and they're keeping an eye on him. He's in pain, but he should make a full recovery."

"Thank god." She leaned back against the pillows.

He settled in the plastic chair beside her bed. "Do you mind if I ask you a few questions? I promise we won't be long."

"Go ahead."

She knew full well why he was here, and it wasn't to exchange pleasantries. She probably shouldn't even talk to him without a lawyer, but she was a victim in all this, even if she had ultimately caused Lynette's death. She wouldn't have done a thing to Lynette if her life hadn't been in danger. She'd have been happy for her to go to prison for the rest of her life. That would have been a fitting end for a murderer. She thought fleetingly of her parents and the fact that Lynette had been *their* child. She'd done what she'd had to. They would have understood.

In her place, she was sure that Abbie would have told the truth, but people had always believed Abbie. She'd had such a way with words. Abbie had always landed on her feet, until she hadn't.

"I never meant to cause Lynette's death," she said. "But if I hadn't, she would have killed me. Before she died, Lynette confessed to killing my sister and to abandoning a group of migrants on a sinking boat. She was a terrible person, and she was stronger and tougher than me. It's pure luck that I'm still here and she's not."

Dankworth's eyes were kind, but his body language was neutral. There would be a much longer interview, she knew, where they would have to get into all the gory details. And then he would have to discuss the matter with his superiors, maybe even with the Crown Prosecution Service to see if they had a case against her.

Well, she would take whatever was coming to her. The funny thing was, if she could have her time again, she wasn't sure she would handle it any differently. She'd had to go after Lynette. She'd had to get her answers. It would have eaten her alive if she hadn't.

She knew Abbie was gone, but she didn't really feel it yet. Perhaps that was down to the drugs they'd given her. The grief would hit her properly in time, and she would mourn for her as she had mourned her parents, but for now she was just grateful for the calm.

33

One Month Later

The airport buzzed with noise. Mel stood and waited as Peter pulled off his shoes and belt, ready for the customs screening.

"Well, I suppose this is goodbye," he said a little mournfully.

"It's not forever," she said. "I'll be just on the other end of the phone if you need me. Or on Zoom, now you've figured out how to work it."

He went for a smile, but there was no missing the sadness in his eyes.

"It's time for a fresh start," she reminded him. "For both of us."

"Are you sure you'll be all right, rattling around that big house on your own?"

"I've got Otto, haven't I?"

She was glad they were parting as friends, even if he still wanted more. That would fade, she told herself. He would come to accept it with time, and maybe, just maybe, they could actually be friends. She would like that.

"People are staring at us again," he said, stepping aside for an American couple with too much luggage.

"That'll die down too," she assured him.

There had been a lot about the case in the papers. Everyone was fascinated by the story of the twins switched at birth and the murders that had resulted.

The police had told her they would not be taking any further action against her with regard to Lynette's death, and Mel was in the process of getting Abbie legally declared dead so that she could sort out her affairs. The *Catch 22* was still undergoing repairs, and Mel expected it to take some time, but once the boat was fixed, she planned to donate it to a charity that rescued migrants who got into trouble coming over from France.

After her horrendous boat trip, Mel didn't think she'd have the stomach to go out on a boat again, at least for a while, and it seemed a shame to let Abbie's pride and joy go to waste. She hoped Abbie would have been happy with her choice, and she knew Cyrus would have liked it. He and his family had deserved so much better.

"Mel…"

Peter clutched her hand so hard she thought it would break. She squeezed her eyes tight, willing herself not to cry, but it was no use, her back was shaking, and she had to swallow a few times to pull herself together.

"You know it's not too late," he said. "You can still come with me."

Mel shook her head. Even if it was possible to buy a ticket just like that, it wasn't what she wanted. She would always have love for Peter, but that part of her life was over. She needed to step out from under his shadow and live her own life.

Slowly, she released his hand. "They're calling your gate. You need to go."

She let him slip away from her. He kissed her three times, once on the forehead and once on each cheek; then he reached for the handle of his new wheelie case, a gift she had thrust upon him in return for permission to dispose of his ugly brown duffel bag.

He might have felt dejected, but he hid it well, looking tall and confident as he merged into the crowd. She watched until he turned the corner, looking back at her briefly before disappearing out of view. Then she trudged back to the short-stay car park, where her shiny blue Mazda convertible was waiting. The bonus money hadn't come through yet, but she'd decided to go ahead and buy it anyway, despite the weather. The leaves were gone from the trees now, and there was a pale dusting of frost on the ground. The weatherman had said it might snow later this week, but they always got it wrong.

As she approached Weymouth, a new wave of sadness washed over her. Her emotions were like that these days, dipping and rising, just like the ocean. She drove carefully up the road and parked neatly in the driveway. Jiggling the keys, she opened the door, and Otto barked joyously as she walked inside. Her heart lifted a little at the sight of the excited dog.

The house still felt rather empty, Peter had a point about that. Otto trotted beside her as she removed her coat and boots, then headed into the living room. The silence was almost deafening now, and it all looked way too neat. She looked around, dissatisfied. She hadn't managed to track down her father's harp yet, but she was working on it. She poked a toe at the rug, deliberately scrabbling it up a little. She pulled off her hoodie and discarded it on the back of Abbie's chair. The room instantly looked more lived in. Then she went to the hearth and started a fire, the way her dad always used to do, using wood and newspaper to start the blaze.

After a few minutes, she had a nice roaring fire, and Otto lay in front of it, staring appreciatively into the flames. There was something primal about that look, as if it was in his blood.

Jumping to her feet, she went to the windowsill and picked up one of Lynette's wooden boats. It gave her an idea. She went from one room to the next, gathering up all the little boats. She almost forgot the one in the upstairs bathroom and had to go back to get it. She hurried downstairs with it and threw it on the floor with the rest. Otto pawed at them quizzically, as if asking what she was going to do with them all. She patted the dog affectionately.

"They'll make good firewood, don't you think?"

She picked one up and threw it on the fire. It ignited instantly. She watched the sail catch light, and the little mast glowed orange.

"Goodbye, Mum," she whispered.

It reminded her of a Norse funeral pyre. In Norse mythology, she seemed to recall, boats symbolised safe passage into the afterlife. She reached for another one, bright yellow, and tossed that on as well.

"Goodbye, Dad."

The blue one came next. The one that looked most like the *Catch 22*. She could barely get the words out.

"Goodbye, Abbie."

She watched it burn slowly, the hull catching first, then the flames spreading through the boat. It didn't smell so great, but that was probably down to the paint-work. She didn't care. She had started this, so she was going to finish. She said nothing as she threw on the fourth. Lynette didn't deserve a goodbye, but it was there regardless, smoking in her fireplace. This was a good thing, she told herself. A chance to exorcise herself of Lynette and remove her evil presence from the house.

She could hear the echoes of her family through the years. Felt their presence in the walls. This was home, yet it wasn't. Not without a family to call her own. She thought briefly of Peter. Her hand itched to reach for the phone. But no, it wasn't Peter she wanted. Not specifically. He was just a person, a body to lie beside her in bed at night. Life with him had been too much of a compromise. She wasn't going to make that mistake again.

The landline rang, making her jump. She walked over to it curiously. Occasionally, she would get a call from one of Abbie's many friends. Someone who'd been travelling and hadn't heard, or an old boyfriend wondering why he was being given the cold shoulder. Mel took a perverse pleasure in informing these people, who hadn't done enough to keep in touch with her sister, that they were too late. That Abbie was dead now. She didn't say as much, but she berated these absent friends as much as she berated herself.

You weren't there. You let her down. We all did.

The voice on the end was different this time. There was a strong northern accent, and the woman sounded too old to be one of Abbie's friends.

"Mel? Is that Mel?"

"Yes, who is this?"

"It's your mum, dear. Your real mum."

She dropped the phone as if she'd had an electric shock. Then she scrambled to pick it up again. The woman was still talking.

"Listen, these last few weeks have been awful for us all, but maybe we can salvage something from the wreckage. We're your family now, and we want to be there for you. What would you say if your father and I came down to visit you so that we could get to know each other a little?"

She didn't quite know how to react. It was still incredibly soon. She'd only just said goodbye to Abbie and sent Peter back to Sydney. She was still trying to get her head around all that had happened. It was hard to believe that two identical women could be so different. One so loving, the other filled with hate. Her birth parents must be grappling with this too, wondering where they had gone wrong, if there was anything they could have done. Feelings were bound to be running high, and it was almost certainly too soon to meet them, yet she felt so alone, so empty. Perhaps this was just what she needed.

34

I t boded well that they were on time. Perhaps she got that from their side, her propensity to be punctual, while the rest of the world kept her waiting.

She'd woken too early that morning, needlessly checked that the house looked tidy. She'd decided to shut Otto in the garden until she'd established whether or not Joy and Kev Parker were dog people. She watched him bounding up and down the lawn and trying to peer in at the window, tongue hanging out in anticipation, and she felt exactly the same.

She didn't want to get her hopes up, but a part of her was really pumped about this meeting. Something good had to come from all this, she kept telling herself. Maybe this was it. Peter had offered to fly back from Sydney so that he could be here with her.

"You're still fragile, Mel," he'd said. "Are you sure you're up to doing this on your own?"

She'd gritted her teeth and assured him she was. She wasn't going to call Peter every time she needed moral support. He needed to get on with his own life, and she needed to do this on her own.

Still, she felt a little jolt of electricity when the doorbell rang at exactly eleven. She cast her eyes around the
place one last time and hopped off the sofa.

She greeted them awkwardly on the doorstep. Joy
took the lead, stepping forward to embrace her in a big
bear hug. When she stepped back, Mel saw straight
away that Peter had been right. Mrs Parker did look
very much like her. More than she liked to admit. She
wore dark blue jeans and a blue and white striped T-
shirt, as if she were going sailing. She had a wider nose,
but the shape of her face was just like Mel's, and they
both had the same short legs, wide hips and freckles.

"Let's get a look at you!"

She turned her attention to Mr Parker, a large man,
with a rounded face and a wide toothy grin. He was
clutching a bunch of lilies. They looked impossibly
small and fragile in his meaty hands. She accepted them
with thanks and ushered them both inside.

"Please come in."

"Please call us Joy and Kev."

"Of course." She could hardly call them Mr and Mrs
Parker, could she? Nor could she call them Mum and
Dad. It didn't feel right.

She led them into the living room. The place had
seemed way too empty, so she'd laid out a cosy rug by
the hearth. She'd also added a bookcase in the corner,
but she only had a few books to fill it with, so it still
looked rather bare. She'd be putting some artwork on
the walls soon too, changing the lightshades for something a little brighter. Anything to add a little character
and make the place feel like hers again.

Joy took a tentative step into the room and nodded
her approval, taking it all in.

"Lovely place you've got here."

Mel cleared her throat, which had gone inexplicably

dry. "Thank you. I'll just find a vase for the flowers. Then we can have some tea."

She had the tea things ready by the kettle, a new packet of Hobnobs in the tin. As she set everything on the tray, she heard them talking and laughing in the living room and felt instantly more relaxed. She didn't know why she'd been so nervous. They were just ordinary people, after all. But it was hard to look at Joy and picture herself as a baby curled up inside her womb. And it was hard to imagine that she had been alone there, not a twin after all. Just a boring old singleton, like everyone else.

She carried out the tea things ever so slowly, the tray wobbling as she walked. She'd spill half the tea at this rate, but she just couldn't make her hands steady. She approached slowly and watched as Joy and Kev admired the bay windows and the fireplace. Kev muttered something about the age of the property, and then Joy said something she didn't quite catch, something like "I think this will do us just fine."

She quickened her pace, making the last few strides over to the coffee table, where she gratefully set down the tray. She'd dithered so long over it that the tea was probably steeped by now. She might as well pour it out.

"How do you take it?" she asked.

"Two sugars and not too milky," Kev said.

Mel smiled. "Just like me."

She handed him the mug with a steamboat on the front, one of Abbie's. For Joy, she used the cat mug. It had been her mum's. She felt a little treacherous handing it over, as if she were taking it right out of her mum's hand.

Joy held her cup in an awkward fashion, her pinkie finger sticking out a little. She looked so ridiculous that

Mel had to stifle a giggle. She was clearly trying to impress.

She settled into the chair across from them, and silence fell as they all hugged their tea.

She wanted to know more about these people, but it was impossible to ignore the elephant in the room. Lynette. She had been their daughter all these years. Much as Mel hated her for what she'd done to Abbie, Joy and Kev must be mourning her. Perhaps it would be wisest to avoid the subject altogether, but Mel felt like she had to address it. How could she hope to have a relationship with these people if she pretended Lynette had never existed? She licked her lips, choosing her words carefully, approaching the topic as delicately as she knew how.

"It must have been a shock for you," she said at last. "Losing Lynette like that?"

"It's been a roller coaster, as you can imagine." Joy produced a huge hanky and dabbed at the corner of her eye. Mel felt her heart open a little, like a flower reaching for the sun.

Joy closed her eyes for a moment, but when she opened them, she looked directly at Mel, as though she needed her to understand.

"Lynette was a difficult child, I can't say otherwise," she went on. "I always felt as though she was fighting us. I can't say if she would have been any different if she'd been with her real parents. It might just be in her nature, you know? I suppose we'll never know."

Mel wondered too. Despite some fascinating similarities, Lynette's personality had been nothing like Abbie's. Sure, they'd both had a fascination with boats, but then, they'd both been brought up in coastal towns. People had liked Abbie. She'd had a way about her. She had instinctively understood people. She'd known how to wrap them around her little finger, whilst Lynette had lacked that charm. She'd been sneaky and conniving and about as subtle as a sledgehammer.

"She was always getting into trouble," Joy said now. "I felt like people judged us, but I didn't know what to do with her. Even when she was just a little mite, she seemed to rub people up the wrong way. I always knew there was something off about her. I even took her to the doctors a couple of times, but they never listened to me. They thought the problem was with me, that I was a bad parent or else I was making it all up. By the age of fourteen, she'd dropped out of school, and she was hanging about with the wrong sorts. Lord knows we tried to help her, but she always threw it back in our faces. I didn't have any control over her, and if I'm honest, I was a bit scared of her. So she lived her life, and I lived mine. I didn't know how bad it had got. I could never have dreamt how bad."

Mel felt a pang of sympathy for the woman. How awful to have such a monster for a daughter.

Joy's lip trembled slightly. "I loved her, Mel, but she was a nightmare to live with. When she ran off, I should have been worried. I know this sounds terrible, but I wasn't worried. I was relieved."

Kev slung one of his huge arms around Joy's neck. There was something very natural about the way he did that, as if the two of them were a perfect fit.

"I can imagine," Mel said quietly.

Guilt engulfed her as she remembered those last terrifying moments on the boat. She didn't like to think about Lynette or the part she'd played in ending her life. She'd had to do it, she'd had no choice, but she couldn't change the fact that she was the one who'd killed her.

Joy broke through the silence. "I know what you're thinking."

"You...you do?"

"Listen to me, Mel. I want to say something."

"Okay." She hung her head low. She wasn't sure she wanted to hear this. The fact was, Lynette was never coming back, and Mel could never take back what she had done.

"Listen to me, I know you feel bad. You think I resent you for what happened. You think your father does, but believe me, Mel, we don't. You never asked to be put in that position. You didn't deserve any of it."

Slowly, Mel lifted her head. "I..."

"Just listen to me. You didn't kill Lynette, do you get that? You *are* Lynette. You're our daughter, and we want you to know we'll always be here for you."

When she put it that way, Mel couldn't really argue. She felt emotions bubbling up inside her. Couldn't stop the tears from pricking the corners of her eyes. She didn't want to be Lynette! The thought repulsed her. Why couldn't she just be Mel? She had had such a good life up until now. The best parents, the best family. She would give anything to turn back time.

She took a few gulps of air and struggled to control herself.

They all sat in silence for a few minutes. They were probably thinking of Lynette, Mel decided, and for her own part, she was thinking of the family she had lost, hoping that they would understand that this here was what she needed.

"You all right, love?" Joy asked.

Mel nodded.

The room seemed warmer now, and Joy unbuttoned her thick cable knit cardigan and slung it over the arm of the chair.

Instantly, Mel's eyes went to the distinctive emerald necklace that hung around her neck.

"Oh, I just noticed your lovely necklace," she said.

She gazed at it for a moment, trying to figure out where she'd seen such a necklace before. It had been in a picture, she realised. The one Cyrus had shown her, of his wife. She had been wearing an identical piece of jewellery around her neck.

She felt a tightening in her gut. Lynette must have taken it off the poor woman and given it to her mum as a gift. She felt a fresh wave of revulsion at Lynette, and she let out an involuntary shudder. She wouldn't say anything to Joy, of course. No one would want to know they were wearing a murdered woman's necklace.

Joy set down her mug, and her weathered hand caressed her throat.

"You like this? I got it in the January sales. Such a lovely colour, don't you think?"

Mel nearly choked on her tea. She stared into Joy's eyes and finally saw what she had missed: the evil that lurked within. This was not a poor, grieving mother. She knew exactly where the necklace had come from. Then she noted Kev's knowing grin. Joy raised her arms, positioning them comfortably behind her head as she slipped her feet neatly under Mel's table.

ABOUT THE AUTHOR

Lorna Dounaeva has a Masters in European Studies and used to work at the Home Office before turning to crime fiction. She lives in Godalming, Surrey with her husband, three children and a crafty cat.

Did you enjoy *The Wrong Twin*? Please consider leaving a review on Amazon to help other readers discover the book.

Published by Inkubator Books
www.inkubatorbooks.com

Printed in Great Britain
by Amazon